STILL LIFE

Books by Dani Pettrey

ALASKAN COURAGE

CHESAPEAKE VALOR

CHESAPEAKE VALOR

BOOK TWO

STILL LIFE

DANI PETTREY

BETHANYHOUSE

a division of Baker Publishing Group
Minneapolis, Minnesota

© 2017 by Dani Pettrey

Published by Bethany House Publishers
11400 Hampshire Avenue South
Bloomington, Minnesota 55438
www.bethanyhouse.com

Bethany House Publishers is a division of
Baker Publishing Group, Grand Rapids, Michigan

Printed in the United States of America

Library of Congress Cataloging-in-Publication Data
Names: Pettrey, Dani, author.
Title: Still life / Dani Pettrey.
Description: Minneapolis, Minnesota : Bethany House, a division of Baker
    Publishing Group, [2017] | Series: Chesapeake valor ; Book 2
Identifiers: LCCN 2016035448| ISBN 9780764230073 (cloth) | ISBN 9780764212956
    (trade paper)
Subjects: | GSAFD: Suspense fiction.
Classification: LCC PS3616.E89 S75 2017 | DDC 813/.6—dc23
LC record available at https://lccn.loc.gov/2016035448

Cover design and photography by Kirk DouPonce, DogEared Design

Author is represented by Books & Such Literary Agency.

17 18 19 20 21 22 23   7 6 5 4 3 2 1

To Brenn Matthew:
Nannie loves you and can't wait for all
the adventures we'll have.
Just don't tell your momma. ;)

PROLOGUE

He glanced around what had become a dumping ground by the river's edge. Dark, silent . . . deserted. *Perfect.*

Popping the trunk of his car, he hefted the heavy garment bag out and trudged through the mud, the foul odor of rotting garbage and brackish water pungent on the wind lashing his face. A thunderstorm was brewing, churning the humid air. Lightning pierced the murky sky.

He found a fitting spot and tossed her away like the trash she was.

1

Inhaling a steadying breath of the steamy August Baltimore air, Avery Tate paused a moment, clutching the metal door handle. This was it. Her first return to the Baltimore art scene since she'd been ostracized over a year ago.

Her grip tightened.

One more breath of the thick, sticky air and she yanked the cherrywood-and-beveled-glass door open. The cool of the gallery's AC rushed over her, rippling up her bare arms, her red satin dress thankfully not clinging to her after the muggy ten-minute walk from the parking spot she'd been lucky enough to find. An event like this made parking insane in Fell's Point.

The frenzy of conversation and lilting music buzzed as she stepped farther inside Christopher Fuller's gallery.

Her right heel wobbled, every nerve ending alive and dancing beneath her skin, whether from the cool of the building or from the circumstances she didn't know, but she fortified her gait and took another step forward.

She could fake walking in heels. How hard could it be?

One step at a time. You can do this. Hold your head high.

She'd overcome so much more than this petty group encircling her. The only reason the ostracism had hit so hard was because photography was where her heart lived . . . or had. Now it lived for Parker—a man of such depth, such sincerity albeit mixed with a playful spirit she adored and . . .

And why was she thinking about Parker Mitchell *again*? It'd been six months since they'd worked together as crime-scene investigator and crime-scene photographer. Nine months since she'd fully realized the depth of her feelings for him, but . . . She swallowed, the motion painful. Parker could never be hers, at least not fully.

Part of his heart, a huge part, would always belong to Jenna McCray. She understood. Jenna was Parker's first love, and her devastating murder seven years ago, when Jenna was just shy of her eighteenth birthday, had been horrific, but Avery couldn't spend the rest of her life with a man who loved someone else so deeply, a man who loved another woman more than her.

Forcing her attention back where it belonged, at least for tonight, she squared her shoulders and assessed her surroundings, as Parker had taught her to do.

Man, he lived in her head—her thoughts always drifting to him and their time together. Oh, she still saw him through mutual friends, but she could no longer handle working side by side. Unless she could permanently be at his side, she couldn't continue long hours, late nights, and close proximity in his lab. She missed him something terrible.

"Avery Tate, is that *you*?"

She needn't bother turning to find it was Marjorie Thrasher. Her effervescent voice—the unmistakable combo of shrill pitch and Yonkers accent—readily identified the elderly yet vivacious woman. Of all the people to run into first, Marjorie was a great one.

Avery turned—well, *teetered*—around, praying her heels held firm on the recently buffed hardwood floor.

Marjorie's copper-painted lips puckered. "Oh, darling. I knew it was you. Whatever are *you* doing here?" Her faux lashes fluttered as she looked Avery up and down. "Don't tell me you're back in the crowd?"

"No." *Most definitely not.* "Just here to support a friend." Maybe if she kept reminding herself of that, along with the pivotal fact she was supporting Skylar *here* and not where they'd grown up . . . *Here* wasn't much more comfortable and, in all fairness, was probably just as toxic, but at least it wasn't *physically* hostile. Verbally hostile—absolutely—but fear of what others might say no longer paralyzed her. As her momma said, she had a fighter's heart.

The fact her mom had said those words the day she'd abandoned Avery imprinted the description on Avery's young mind, but it was true. She *was* a fighter and she loved that fact. Skylar Pierce was a fighter too, just on a very dangerous path, which Avery kept trying to yank her from.

Marjorie's thoroughly plucked brows, or rather what little remained of them, attempted to arch, but it was difficult when they were practically fastened in place due to Marjorie's addiction to Botox injections. Her smile, whether genuine or not, was permanent, her lips double the plump. "You aren't referring to Gerry, are you?"

Avery smothered her upchuck reflex. "No."

"I don't understand." Marjorie took a sip of her chocolate martini, the brown syrup swirling around the glass in fanciful patterns. Marjorie loved her martinis.

"A friend of mine modeled for him," she said. She and Skylar had been friends since birth. Or at least their mothers had been. Both young, pregnant, and living in the same trailer park, they had naturally gravitated toward each other, and in turn Avery and Skylar had grown up together. That's what made their current relationship so difficult. She loved Sky like a sister but felt utterly helpless to do anything to prevent her self-inflicted destruction.

"Oooh. Which one?" Marjorie's bony fingers grasped Avery's arm, tugging her from her thoughts and through the milling crowd huddled at the center wall's morbid display.

Leave it to Gerard "Gerry" Vaughn to present a distasteful Black Dahlia–inspired showing.

Five portraits—each of a woman appearing to be captured post-mortem—hung perfectly aligned on the white surface, the lighting deftly illuminating each image. The women, dressed in fanciful gowns and striking makeup, appeared frozen in time— nearly lifeless. *Nearly*, except Skylar's. Something about hers stood out. Something was different. But what?

Skylar's pale skin, which must have been enhanced—no one's skin color was that even and flawless, even with makeup— formed a striking contrast to her red lipstick and the matching bloodred dahlia cradled in her open palm. Gerard had paid impressive attention to detail—the gleaming black nail polish, the silky texture of the scarf wrapped like a choker around her neck, and her dark hair pulled back, accentuating her dark eyes and pale face. Despite the grotesque subject matter, the portrait was artistically brilliant. But something was tugging at Avery. Something about Skylar's eyes. They were so dark, her pupils larger than usual, void of life—wells of emptiness.

The arresting image reminded Avery of the Brothers Grimm's description of Snow White—*"Soon afterward she had a little daughter who was as white as snow, as red as blood, and as black as ebony."*

"Come, dear," Marjorie said, pulling Avery to the next image before she was fully finished studying Skylar's. "This one is to die for. Oops." Marjorie giggled, tipping her martini glass and nearly spilling its swirly brown contents onto Avery's favorite and only dressy dress.

"No pun intended." Marjorie broke into another round of giggles as several lackeys in the surrounding crowd chuckled along with her, or more likely, at her. Marjorie was hardly a conformist, and most people weren't sure how to take her. While Avery admired her individualism among a crowd of clones, there wasn't a whole lot else to admire. She'd just ended marriage number three, and rumor was she'd already begun a dalliance with one of Gerry's understudies.

"What do you think?" Marjorie poked her finger into Avery's exposed right shoulder.

The image Marjorie gestured at was stunning composition-ally, but again highly grotesque in content. The woman—dressed in a mustard-yellow satin ball gown and posed upon a fluffy white comforter covering a pitch-black four-poster bed—was bent backward, her torso hanging over the edge of the bed. Her blond hair, hanging long and free, flowed from her pale face. Her lips were a deep shade of burgundy, her eyes vivid blue with charcoal shadow. The entire image was a striking juxtaposition of colors: light and dark, life and apparent death. Even her expression was impressive—nearly devoid of life.

As Marjorie tugged her to the next piece in the showcase, Avery searched the crowd for Skylar. She wanted to congratu-late her friend on landing the "gig of the century," as Sky put it, and head out before Gerry appeared. He *adored* making a grand, fashionably late entrance, even if he was already in the building, just waiting somewhere in the shadows for his moment. While she was thankful he hadn't appeared yet, she really wished Skylar would.

The portrait now before her was vastly different from the first two—a woman, dressed in a simple eyelet dress, falling into the depths of a body of water. Her arms and legs limp and lifeless, round rings circling up to the surface from whence she came. It looked eerily real. Though pompous and vapid, Gerry was extremely talented.

"Of course *you* show up. The wrong piece of trailer trash doesn't help me any," Gerard said mere inches behind Avery, his breath hot on her neck and reeking of gin, as usual.

Balling her hands into fists, she turned to face him. Man, how she'd like to get him into the kickboxing ring just once. "Excuse me?"

"You're not interchangeable, you know," he said.

"What are you talking about?"

"You show up for Skylar's showing, but she does not."

"What?" Skylar was a flake when it came to timeliness, but she'd gone on and on about how important tonight was. Was she seriously late for her own showing?

"She's not here," Gerard said, turning to face Skylar's portrait. And a string of expletive-laden sentiments followed. "What. Is. That?"

"Skylar's portrait," Avery said. Exactly how inebriated was he?

"It's magnificent," Marjorie gushed.

"It's trash. Just like the girl in it." Gerard pushed past them, nearly knocking Avery over, and hollered, "*Who* did this? You think this is some kind of joke?"

A woman scurried over, moving as fast as her tight pencil skirt and three-inch heels would permit. "What's wrong?"

"Who. Did. This?" He shoved her toward the portrait, enunciating each word with disdain.

She took a brief moment to study it. "I don't understand."

"Well, that makes two of us, Nadine. Did you oversee the hanging of the showcase or did you not?"

"I . . . I did."

"And?"

"Your original portrait of Skylar was hung."

"Then how did *this* get in its place, and where is my masterpiece?"

Christopher Fuller, the gallery owner, rushed over, concern and a tad of horror mixed on his handsome face.

Patrons were staring, murmuring. This was not good for business. And with Gerard being one of the highest-paid photographers in the country, an egomaniac worth millions with zero tolerance for incompetence, if something had happened to Gerry's photograph, Christopher was looking at serious financial damage.

"What happened?" Christopher asked, glancing at Avery with disdain, but rapidly shifting his focus to the distraught and fuming Gerard Vaughn instead.

"*This*," Gerard said, "is an outrage."

Christopher swallowed. "I don't understand." Even he was scared of the man. It was ridiculous. He loosened his collar, his gaze darting to the crowd. "Every piece was hung and lit to your exact specifications. Nadine oversaw the entire process."

"That," Gerard hissed, pointing at the portrait of Skylar that Nadine had lifted off the wall and now held in trembling hands, "is hardly my work."

A mixture of confusion and concern danced through Avery's gut. "If you didn't take that photograph, then who did?"

"That is the pertinent question, is it not?" Gerard's plump cheeks were nearly as red as his drinker's nose. For an artist of his standing in the photography world, he certainly didn't act like a professional.

"I checked everything fifteen minutes before the doors opened," Nadine said in a flustered flurry. "Someone would have had to change it very quickly while we were all in Christopher's office."

So Christopher still held his preshow pep talk for the artists and staff before opening the gallery doors.

"Did they think I wouldn't notice? They stole my masterpiece and replaced it with *this* . . . ?" Gerard gestured to the portrait. "Outrage, I tell you. Outrage!" he roared at Christopher. "I'm calling the authorities."

"FBI handles art theft," Avery said. "You'll want to contact them."

Gerald let out a burst of air. "At least you're good for something."

Avery forced herself to remain silent as Gerard stomped off. He wasn't worth it. Instead she retrieved her phone and dialed Skylar. What had she done?

2

Skylar's phone went straight to voicemail. *Again.*

Avery left a message, praying she'd turn to see her friend walking through the door, but her unease heightened with every passing minute—her stomach tightening in sync with each tick of the enormous, ornate clock hanging high on the wall next to Christopher's lofted office. According to him, it had once hung in Grand Central Station. It was beautiful, but its tick was a constant reminder of the time passing without Skylar's arrival.

Nadine nibbled her nails while they waited on the gallery floor for a federal agent to arrive.

Avery tried to wrap her head around it all. Someone hadn't just stolen Gerard's image—they'd replaced it. But why?

"Who would do such a thing?" Marjorie shook her head. "I understand why someone would steal your work. It's brilliant and worth five figures, but why replace it with *that*?" Precisely echoing Avery's sentiments, she indicated the portrait now leaning against the wall. It made no sense.

"Perhaps they thought you wouldn't notice," Nadine offered.

"Wouldn't notice my own work gone? Please." Gerry scoffed. "No, someone did this to insert their work into my showing. Some pathetic attempt to try to garner a name for themselves."

"Sebastian," Nadine snapped.

Gerard's face pinched. "Of course. That little weasel."

"Who's Sebastian?" Avery asked.

"A photo hack," Gerard said. "Hangs around the scene. Always trying to pick up my crumbs."

"Gerry graciously allowed Sebastian to shadow him for a shooting now and again over the past month," Nadine explained.

Gracious. Ha! Avery nearly laughed. It wasn't out of Gerard's graciousness. It was out of his ego, needing an underling praising his every move to make him feel like a man. *Pathetic.*

"I allowed him to walk in the footsteps of greatness, and this is how he repays me?" Gerard thumped his chest. "Trying to destroy my reputation by replacing one of *my* pieces with that pathetic attempt at art."

"What's Sebastian's last name?" Avery asked, biting her tongue against voicing her opinion that the imposter's photograph was the best of the lot. Infuriating Gerard wouldn't get her any answers.

Gerry's bleary eyes narrowed. "Why?"

"Because maybe he knows where Skylar is. I haven't been able to reach her all night."

"Who cares where she is." He snorted. "I gave her the opportunity of her pitiful life and this is how she repays me? It's a good thing she *didn't* show."

Avery stood firm. "Or what?"

Gerard scanned the crowd around him and apparently thought better of responding. "I'm going to wait in

Christopher's office until the Feds arrive. I'm tired of looking at that piece of drivel." He shuffled past Skylar's portrait without another glance.

Nadine turned to scurry after her boss. "Shall I throw the portrait away?"

"What do you think?" he growled.

"You can't throw it away," Avery said.

Gerard turned to face her with an immense scowl, his face pinched like a bulldog's. "It's *my* show. *My* wall. I can do whatever I want with it, and it is going in the trash."

"It's part of a crime scene."

"No. The *crime* was the theft of my masterpiece. *That* belongs in the trash." He turned and proceeded upstairs.

Avery waited until he was out of sight and lightly tugged Nadine's arm as she tried to whiz by. "Don't do it."

Nadine pulled her lips in her mouth, looked up toward Christopher's office, and sighed. "I have to. If he comes back down and sees it still here . . ."

"Okay, let me take it," Avery said. She'd take it and preserve the portrait's integrity until whoever ended up in charge of the case could process it properly. If she left it on site, it'd end up in the trash.

Nadine pushed her glasses up her nose. "Why?"

"It's important." She glanced at Gerard's shadow pacing behind the office door's frosted glass. "Please."

"Fine, but you'd better hurry."

Avery pulled a pair of latex gloves from her clutch—a habit from her time working with Parker that she hadn't been able to kick—and carefully lifted the portrait. Fortunately, she'd left a box of trash bags and plastic wrap in her trunk after stopping at the store earlier. They would have to serve as an evidence bag.

As Avery gave the portrait a once-over, Nadine paced

nervously. "*Please* leave before he sees you." She gestured toward the office door Gerard had entered.

Avery considered putting the portrait in her car and returning to wait for the FBI agent, but she was becoming increasingly concerned about Skylar. "I'm going to try to find Skylar. Give the agent my contact information." Holding the portrait one-handed, Avery ungracefully tugged a business card from her clutch and gave it to Nadine. "Tell him or her that I have the replacement portrait and I'm keeping it safe."

Nadine nodded, and Avery jetted for the door, careful to hold the portrait at arm's length, praying she'd be able to keep it from bumping against anyone in the thick and milling Friday-night crowd.

She stepped out into the warm night air with a load of questions and an unnerving feeling in her gut.

Where are you, Skylar?

3

Avery pulled down the narrow dirt road leading past the memories that often haunted her at night.

Skylar's photograph rested on her backseat, sealed as best as the trash bag and Saran Wrap would allow.

She exhaled. Gerard wasn't the only one curious about the portrait's origins.

Seriously. Why had Skylar bothered calling her, begging her to come to the event, if she was going to pull a stunt like that and not even show?

Granted, Skylar was flakey and unreliable at times, but her call, her plea for Avery to come to the showing, the enthusiasm in her voice, the pride of what she'd accomplished, made it sound as if Skylar was *finally* turning her life around.

Avery had tried to help for so long, but Skylar only tried to bring *her* back down. Not in a mean or spiteful way, but she wanted the "fun Avery" back—and that girl was long gone. She'd never go back to the person she was before coming to Christ. She'd prayed so hard for Skylar. Prayed she'd reach out

for Jesus, but it was all some joke to her friend. But tonight
. . . Avery had believed Skylar might actually be taking a step
in the right direction. What had gone wrong?

A lean tabby cat skittered across Avery's path, forcing her
to pump her brakes. In her rearview mirror, the red taillights
illuminated the run-down playground she'd used as a child.
Though, to be fair, it'd been equally run-down then.

She glanced at the swings, remembering how she and Skylar would always try to fly higher than each other, and then
in their teens they'd done the same, only trying to fly with
something far more dangerous. She swallowed as she turned
the corner, the mere thought of drugs leaving a bitter taste
in her soul. God had literally picked her up out of the muck
and the mire. She'd prayed the same for her friend—over and
over—desperate pleas.

Skylar's trailer came into view, Avery's headlights bouncing
off the smudged windowpanes as a light bounced inside the
otherwise dark trailer. *Odd?*

She cut her engine and lights, peering at the small light moving through the trailer. A flashlight?

As quietly as she could manage, she exited her car. It was
probably nothing more than Skylar having not paid her electric
bill again, but on the off chance . . .

She sighed at the change Parker had effected in her. She paid
far greater attention to her surroundings, always on alert for
any possible threat of danger.

The temperature had probably dropped five degrees in the
last hour, but eighty-five at night wasn't much relief, especially
for those without AC. She'd hated growing up in the metal oven
across the road, which she purposely didn't glance in the direction of. Instead she focused on the rickety metal steps leading
up to Skylar's pale yellow trailer.

The sun-faded wooden door sat slightly ajar, and she nudged it open. "Sky?"

The interior light source clicked off, and a mass of darkness raced at her.

Declan Grey approached the Christopher Fuller Gallery in Fell's Point. On a Friday night, traffic getting into Fell's was heavy—on a showing night, it was flat-out ridiculous. Instead of fighting it, he'd walked, living only a dozen blocks away in Little Italy. His close proximity was the reason he was here. Dave Moore, a friend and agent in the Bureau's art theft department, had called in a favor. Knowing Declan lived so close, and being in Solomons Island for his daughter's wedding festivities for the weekend, Dave had called to make the request. Declan agreed to take the initial report and cover the investigation until Dave returned to the office Monday morning.

Gerard Vaughn was big, but they weren't talking Michelangelo. Declan covering the case for a few days was just fine, so there was no need to bring his relatively new partner, Alexis Kadyrov, into it on their weekend off. If he arrived and the situation necessitated, he'd call her. He was becoming accustomed to Lexi, as she preferred to be called, but he'd never worked with someone like her before. She was tough, a great agent, but quirky as all get-out. He hadn't gotten a full handle on her yet, and it sometimes made him uncomfortable. He liked categorizing people, and Lexi didn't fit into one he'd encountered before—for that matter, neither did Tanner.

Tanner.

Why did his thoughts keep returning to her?

Glancing up and down Thames Street, he shook his head at the groups participating in the pub crawl, then entered the gallery.

It was humming but with a weird vibe. All over a stolen photograph? He supposed it was worth well into five figures, but an underlying current of unease accompanied the typical panic seen with a theft.

"Can I help you?" an agitated man asked.

Declan flipped open his badge and ID. "I'm here to speak with Gerard Vaughn."

The man swallowed. "We close in an hour. Is there any way this can wait until then?"

"Sorry."

The man inhaled and exhaled slowly. "Very well. You can use my office." He extended his hand. "Christopher Fuller."

"Special Agent Declan Grey."

The front door opened, and Christopher's neck nearly snapped on the double take as he ogled the person who entered.

Curious, Declan turned, and surprise filled him at the sight of Tanner Shaw. *What is she doing here?*

Tanner looked stunning in a knee-length cocktail dress with spaghetti straps and silver strappy heels crisscrossing several inches up her shapely calves.

Her long brown hair was pulled up into a loose knot with tendrils framing her face. She wore makeup, which was unusual for her, but while the makeup accented her features in a stunning way, her skin still held that fresh appearance he found incredibly attractive.

He stepped toward her. "Tanner?"

"Declan?" Confusion marred her beautiful brow.

"What are you doing here?" they both asked at the same time.

"You first," Declan said.

"Avery invited me, but I'm really late. There was a crisis at work."

Tanner flocked to help in any and every crisis situation. It was admirable and not surprising that she'd stay late to help at work, considering she worked as a crisis counselor helping refugees, but work was her life, though his wasn't a whole lot better.

He raked a hand through his hair. "Avery's here?" he asked, trying to divert his attention from how amazing Tanner looked. He turned, scanning the crowd.

"Her friend is one of the models and—"

"She never showed," Christopher said, interrupting.

Tanner frowned. "Avery?"

"No. Skylar."

"Avery's friend?" Tanner asked.

"Yes." Christopher wrung his hands. "Her not appearing was nearly as scandalous as the theft of Gerard's photograph and, of course, the replacement being hung in its spot."

Declan arched a brow. "Why would her not showing cause such a stir, and what do you mean *replacement?*"

"When the main model of the showing doesn't come to represent her artist, it's a massive insult," Christopher explained. "And to answer your second question, someone put another photograph in place of the one that was stolen."

"I imagine Skylar not showing was disappointing to Avery since she came to support her," Tanner said more to herself than to either of them.

"Can you point me in the direction of—"

"Gerard," Christopher said before Declan could finish. He was going to say in the direction of the crime scene, as protecting that was of first importance, but he let the man finish.

"He's the one fuming over there." Christopher indicated the middle-aged man with crystal tumbler in hand, pacing in front of the most morbid display of art Declan had ever seen.

"I didn't realize you and Avery socialized," he said as Tanner followed him over to the featured display and crime scene.

"Yeah, I hang out with all of the gang." She slipped a tendril dangling in front of her face behind her ear. "Except you, of course."

"Of course." Was that meant as a simple fact or an insult? It was no secret they didn't see eye to eye. He found her passion for the hurting people of the world impressive and moving, but her lack of concern for her own personal safety was reckless. And he'd let her know it repeatedly. Over the nine months since her sudden arrival in the middle of an intense investigation, he'd only become more concerned with her safety, which had only increased her frustration with his efforts to keep her "under his thumb." Her words, not his.

"So . . ." she said, making polite conversation, as she was not a fan of silence. "You're here about stolen art? How exciting." A smile lit her face, revealing her dimples.

He arched his brows. "Exciting?" Of course she'd find theft exciting. She was the most curious of women. He didn't understand women in general, but Tanner was certainly unique. She both annoyed and intrigued him, lingering in his thoughts.

"You know what I mean," she said.

He slipped his hands into his trouser pockets. "I'm not sure I do."

She shook her head and rolled her brown eyes. "Sometimes I think we're from different planets."

His sentiment exactly, but that was part of the attraction. An attraction that befuddled him. Not because Tanner wasn't wonderful, but because she drove him mad half the time. He'd been pondering how she didn't fit in a box, and while that intrigued him greatly, it also kept him on his toes. He just couldn't decide if that was a good or dangerous thing. He'd made a mistake falling for Kate—his best friend's girl—but thankfully those feelings had passed. He just wanted to be cautious, careful with his affections. Wanted to play it smart, basing his choices on logic rather than emotion. Emotion never ended well for him.

"Excuse me," he said, his fingers skimming her lower back as he stepped past her to the man in front of them, trying to ignore the shock that ricocheted up his arm at the feel of his fingertips dancing across her soft skin. "Mr. Vaughn?" he said, trying to refocus.

The man turned. His eyes were bloodshot, his nose red as Rudolph's. *Great*. He was drunk. That would help the situation.

"Yes?" the man sputtered.

"I'm Special Agent Grey. You called to report a theft."

Gerard exhaled dramatically. "It's about time."

Declan glanced at his watch. He'd arrived within a half hour of Dave's call. He pulled his pad and pen from his pocket, still preferring to do things the "old-school way," as Lexi described it. "I need to secure the crime scene, and then I'll need you to walk me through what happened."

"Very well," Gerard began. He then paused, a smile forming on his cracked lips. "Well, hello, dear. I don't believe I've had the pleasure." He stepped past Declan and took Tanner's hand in his. "Gerard Vaughn."

"Tanner Shaw," she said politely.

Knowing Tanner, her interest in crime, and her steadfast persistence, it came as no surprise she was still standing there. He just prayed she didn't become a distraction. He had a job to do.

"Enchanting." Gerard lowered his head and placed a kiss on Tanner's hand.

"Thank you." She yanked her hand back. "Please don't let me interrupt."

"Too late," Declan said under his breath, already distracted.

"Not at all," Gerard said.

"I've worked with Agent Grey in the past," she began. "If you wouldn't mind I would love to stay and hear what happened."

"Of course."

Gerard had responded before Declan could protest. He wouldn't have described what they'd done as *working* together. More like she'd shown up in the middle of a case that had nearly gotten them all killed. The trafficker she'd crossed was a suspect in another murder they'd been investigating last fall.

Christopher Fuller came up behind him and whispered, "Why don't we all step into my office? It's just upstairs." He pointed at the loft.

"That would be great," Declan said. Fewer staring eyes and listening ears. "But first I need to secure the crime scene." He'd brought a roll of crime-scene tape in his jacket pocket. Time to rope off the area.

"Of course." Christopher moved his arm in a genteel, sweeping motion, giving him the go-ahead he hadn't asked for.

Declan withheld comment as he worked, difficult as it was given the disturbing images in front of him. What kind of man was Gerard Vaughn, and who would bother stealing one of the distasteful, if not disgusting, images?

"Which of these is the replacement image you mentioned, Mr. Fuller?"

"It's no longer here."

"Excuse me?"

Gerard stepped forward. "I had my assistant, Nadine, throw it away."

Declan lowered his head, eyes pinned on Gerard in disbelief. "You did *what*?"

"Oh, don't tell me you're going to give me the same spiel Avery Tate did."

Good for Avery.

A slight woman with curly red hair and librarian-fashioned glasses sidled up to Declan. He looked at her, waiting for her to speak.

She looked at Gerard, swallowed, and then handed a business card to Declan.

He glanced at Avery's business card in confusion. "What's this?"

Nadine cleared her throat. "She took the photograph."

"She did *what*?" Declan and Gerard said in unison, both of their tones heated and displeased.

"I told you to throw it away." Gerard's skin shifted to an unpleasant shade bordering on purple, the veins along his temples visibly throbbing.

"It's evidence," Declan said, aghast the man had suggested throwing it in the trash. Didn't he realize the contamination that would have caused? He wasn't pleased Avery had removed it from the scene, but he supposed she knew how to treat evidence—and anything was better than the trash. Still, they'd be having a talk.

Christopher looked around anxiously at everyone's gaping. "Now that the scene is secured, can we please take this to my office?" He looked around. "Nadine, please join us, in case you can provide additional information."

Declan nodded, and they climbed the stairs, Gerard leering at Tanner with each step up. Declan balled his hands into fists, ready to knock that leer right off the vile man's smug face.

Entering the office, Declan pulled Tanner to his side. "Since we're *working* together, you should probably stay close."

Clearly glad to be at least a little farther away from Gerard and his none-too-subtle advances, she didn't argue for once.

Declan allowed Gerard to run through the entire set of events before asking any questions. "Do you have any idea who may have stolen your portrait and replaced it with theirs?"

"I told Avery and Christopher it had to be Sebastian."

"Sebastian?" Declan asked.

"An upstart who I was kind enough to take under my wing, and this is how he repays me."

"Any idea why he'd do what he did?"

"I assume to try and weasel his way into the show."

"And why take your art?" Declan asked. "It would be too hot to sell."

"I have no idea. Probably stole it to try to replicate my genius."

Tanner managed to put on a smile. While clearly forced, at least she was trying to placate Gerard. Declan, on the other hand, was trying his hardest not to throttle the man. What an egomaniac. "Any idea where Avery might have taken the replacement photo?"

"I hardly keep tabs on people like her."

He was referring to Declan's friend in a very unflattering manner, but while Declan longed to put Gerard in his place, getting the necessary case information needed to come first. Instead, he turned to Tanner. "We need to find out where Avery went."

Nadine stepped forward from the corner she had settled into. "She said she was going to locate Skylar."

Declan nodded. "Thank you."

Gerard jiggled his crystal tumbler, the ice clinking against the glass. "Perhaps Avery can get some answers out of her—like how she could take my offer to make her a star and throw it all away to pose for some hack."

"She seemed quite concerned about Skylar not being at the show," Nadine said.

"Simply because she didn't show, or was there more to it?" Declan asked.

Nadine shrugged.

"Do you know where Avery went to look for Skylar?"

She shrugged again. "Her house?"

Declan leaned over to Tanner and lowered his voice. "Why don't you give Avery a call and make sure everything's all right?"

Tanner nodded. "Good idea. Gentlemen . . . " she said as she moved for the door, "if you'll excuse me."

Declan turned his attention to the gallery owner. "Mr. Fuller, I'm going to need a list of your employees and their contact information. Unless they are all present tonight."

"Most of them are working tonight."

"I'd like to speak with them."

"I'll send them up one by one."

"Thank you. I appreciate it." He turned to Gerard. "Before you go I'd like to ask you about Skylar."

"What about her?"

"How did she come to pose for you?"

"She was a model. Approached me at a gallery opening. I saw something there. The angles of her face . . . I thought she'd make a good addition to my showcase lineup."

"When was this?"

"About a month or two back."

"How was she to work with?"

"Compliant. Flirtatious. I can see now it was all a game to her."

"Why's that?"

"Because she posed for someone else." He crossed his arms. "My contracts include a noncompete for a three-month period around the showing. I can't believe she had the nerve to pose for someone else and to let the pictures be swapped."

"Why do you assume she was involved with the swap?"

"She posed for the photograph. She had to know it would be used."

"Any idea who she might have worked with?"

He looked at Declan, his jaw tight with irritation. "As I've already explained to everyone, it had to be Sebastian. The piece reeks of his work."

"Let me guess . . . You don't recall his last name?"

"I don't trifle with details that don't concern me. He was a young kid. Trying to work his way up the ranks. Anxious. Eager. Reminded me of myself when I was younger. Probably why I tolerated his presence."

"He worked for you?"

"No."

"Was an understudy?"

"Heavens no, not in the official sense. I gave him feedback on a few pieces of his work. Out of the goodness of my heart. Let him watch a shooting once or twice, but that was the extent of it. The very idea he'd return my favor by pulling something like this will get him blacklisted in the community."

Just as Avery had been, Declan thought. One would think that Avery's photographs proving a state senator had attempted to rape a woman in the back room at a gallery showing would have made Avery a hero, but instead it had cost her the business she'd worked so hard to build—not to mention the disdain of the art scene.

"When was the last time you saw Sebastian?"

"Last week."

"He wasn't here tonight?"

"Not that I saw, but it was a full crowd, and I was otherwise occupied."

"Then how do you propose he made the switch if no one saw him or Skylar tonight?"

"That, my dear fellow, is for you to discover."

"Thank you for your time. You can wait downstairs, or if

you'd like me to call you a cab, you can head home. I've gotten all I need from you tonight."

"So you're *dismissing* me?"

"I doubt he'd do anything of the sort," Tanner said, reentering. "Agent Grey simply knows what a trying night this must be for you and is offering you the opportunity to leave and rest. He'll contact you as soon as he knows anything."

Gerard looked to Declan.

"We'll be in touch," Declan said.

Gerard nodded and reached to kiss Tanner's hand, but she quickly skipped to Declan's side. "It was a pleasure," she said. "But I see our next interviewee is here." She looked past him at the young lady standing in the doorway.

"*Our* next interviewee?" Declan said through gritted teeth.

"Would you rather I go back downstairs with Gerard?" she whispered.

"Please come in and have a seat," he said to the woman, as Gerard brushed past her.

Tanner sat at his side with a grin that half made him want to laugh and half made him want to throttle her.

4

As Finley cleared the dishes after their supper with Kate Maxwell, Griffin stared at the blurry photograph Kate laid out on his kitchen table. It had once been a clear image, but of a large crowd somewhere in Malaysia. When they'd zoomed in on the person in question, the image became too pixelated, but they could still see the man they'd attempted to focus on was about six-one and lean. He was wearing a blue baseball hat, a blue long-sleeve shirt, sunglasses, and cargo pants. What little was visible of his face was covered by a beard, the sunglasses, and the hat's brim.

He supposed it was better than the news footage she believed she'd spotted Luke in last fall. She'd come in Thanksgiving Day ecstatic that she finally had proof Luke was alive, but when they'd gone to the news site the next day to view the video, where she claimed she'd spotted Luke in the background of a riot in Thailand, the video was nowhere to be found. She'd contacted the news site but, despite several attempts, was unable to get any information about the missing footage. Unwilling to let the lead go, Kate had hired an investigator, but she had received no leads from him . . . until now. A very questionable lead.

"It's him," Kate said, helping Finley clear the last of their dishes from the meal—his spicy Italian lasagna, at Finley's request. The oregano, peppers, and tomato flavors still danced on his taste buds.

"You really think this is Luke?" he asked, knowing he was treading on thin ice. Kate had been tracking her missing boyfriend, his missing friend, for almost seven years, and since Thanksgiving and the questionable video, she was convinced she finally had proof of life.

Kate hadn't grown up with the gang, rather joined them when she met and started dating Luke their freshman year at University of Maryland, College Park. All the guys had gone there, and Kate was quickly assimilated into the group.

She turned to him, the nearly empty basket of garlic bread still in her hand. "How can you not see it's him?" Frustration drenched her tone.

He exhaled, looking to Finley for support, but before Kate arrived she had told him that, since she had never met Luke, she was reluctant to weigh in. "Because I can barely see him." He knew his answer was disappointing to her. He seriously wasn't trying to dash her hopes. He prayed it *was* Luke Gallagher, but he had to be honest. Lying to make Kate feel better wouldn't be helpful in the long run.

She tossed the basket on the counter and strode back to the table, his dog, Winston, padding after her. "You can see his entire torso and face." She pointed at the eight-by-ten image. "Look at his jawline, his shoulders, his build." She gripped the photograph's edge.

Griffin studied it. Really studied it. "He's bigger than Luke."

She shook her head in frustration. "It's been seven years.

Instead of a twenty-one-year-old college kid, he's twenty-eight, going on twenty-nine. Of course he's filled out." Her voice heightened with each response.

"Fine. If it is him, what's he doing in Malaysia? And how'd you get this photograph again?" The source sounded sketchy at best.

"I *told* you. I hired an overseas investigator. One of his contacts sent me this."

"And how much did you pay him for it?"

She grunted, clearly knowing exactly where he was going with his questions. They'd worked together enough, been friends far longer. She knew how he approached an investigation—steady and skeptical. The complete opposite of her impulsive, going-in-arms-swinging approach—at least when it came to Luke. "That's not the point," she said in a flustered rush.

"It *is* the point. He could be taking advantage of your—"

"My?" She cut him off, cocking her head. Never a good sign with Kate. It signaled an impending brawl.

"Your . . ." He was going to say *desperation*, but that wasn't the word she needed to hear. "Your persistence to produce evidence."

She jabbed the photograph. "It's him."

***

Avery's eyes flickered open. Searing pain radiated through her skull, along her jaw.

Save for the misty moon overhead, darkness enveloped her. The surface beneath her was cool—rough in parts, smushy in others.

Lifting her head to assess, she saw she lay at the bottom of Skylar's steps, her beautiful dress splayed out in the mud, every bone in her body feeling as though she'd been bulldozed.

Reaching for her phone, she dialed 911.

The police took their sweet time responding, no doubt anticipating a domestic call in the trailer park as was typical, but this was nothing of the sort. Skylar was nowhere to be seen and someone had been in her home.

Officer Kim Fuller was the first to arrive on the scene. Avery liked Kim. She had worked with her several times as Parker's crime-scene photographer . . . and she and Kim also shared a history.

"Avery, you sure I can't have a paramedic look at you?" Kim asked as Avery tried to explain what had happened.

"Nah." Avery cricked her neck to the side and it popped, releasing some of the tension. "I'll be fine." She wanted the focus to be on Skylar's disappearance and not her neck.

"Okay, if you're sure." Kim looked back to her notebook. "You were saying Skylar was supposed to meet you at Christopher Fuller's gallery in Fell's Point?"

"Yes. Skylar was the featured model of the photography showcase."

"Oh yeah?"

"Yeah. She told me she was making some positive changes in her life."

"I'm glad to hear that."

Kim had come from a similar neighborhood and upbringing. While their high schools had been rivals, the three girls had always managed to click—at least until Kim joined the force and Sky remained in her ways. Skylar had her run-ins with the law, though Avery held the majority of the blame for that.

"But she never showed," Avery continued.

"And you came here to look for her?" Kim asked.

"Yes." Avery rubbed her temples.

"All right. And then what happened when you got here? Walk me through it."

"As I pulled up, I saw what looked to be a flashlight moving around on the inside of the trailer. I climbed the steps and found the door ajar. I called her name and someone ran at me, bowling me over and knocking me out. I woke up and called 9-1-1."

"Can you describe the person who knocked you down?"

"No, but I'm sure it was a man."

"Why a man?"

Because she could hold her own with any female. "Because of his size and the strength. I'm telling you, it had to be a man."

"We've both seen our share of larger women."

"True, but it definitely wasn't Skylar." She was one-twenty soaking wet.

Kim flipped to a fresh page in her notebook. "Anything else you remember about this person?"

"No. Sorry. It was too dark and it happened so fast."

"All right." Kim flipped her notebook shut. "We'll file a report for the assault, but without much more to go on . . ."

She got it. "What about Skylar?" she asked.

Kim arched her brows. "What about her?"

"I'm worried something's happened to her." Unease had fixed in her gut.

"Based on?"

"Her not showing up at the event, someone breaking into her place . . ." *The emptiness of her eyes in the portrait.*

"There were no signs of breaking and entering," Kim's partner said. "Maybe whoever was inside had a key."

"Then why use a flashlight?"

Kim shook her head. "Can't say, but no one *broke into* the trailer, and nothing of value appears to have been taken. The place looks about as messy as the last time I saw it, but it hasn't been tossed."

As Kim's partner, who hadn't had much to say, other than commenting on the lack of a break-in, climbed into the passenger seat of their patrol car, Kim tucked her notebook in her pocket. "Look, I'm sorry, Av. I truly am. I know you're worried about Skylar, but we both know it's not uncommon for her to pull stunts or to take off for days or even weeks at a time. Her car is gone, as is her purse."

"Her car got repossessed last month."

"I'm sorry to hear that. But she's probably just on public transportation somewhere. Have you talked to Gary?"

Last thing in the world she wanted to do was talk to Skylar's on-again, off-again boyfriend. "No." She glanced at his place, not far from Sky's. "Not yet. His trailer's been dark since I got here."

"Knowing Gar, he's probably over at McDougal's Pub. It's Friday night."

"Yeah." Gary usually closed down the place. At least he used to, but she doubted he'd changed much. He was a carbon copy of his father.

"I wouldn't worry, Avery," Kim said. "Sky'll turn up. She always does."

"What about a missing persons report?"

"Typically we need a family member or someone she lives or works with to report her missing."

"You know she doesn't have any family." Other than Avery. "She lives alone." Though Gary stayed over a lot. "What if Gary hasn't seen her either?"

"Okay," Kim relented. "Talk to Gary when you see him. If he fears Skylar's missing too, I'll file the report. He's as much a live-in as she's got."

"Thanks, Kim."

Now just to convince Gary.

She watched the patrol car disappear from the park, the unease in her stomach only gnawing harder. Something was wrong. She could feel it, and she wasn't willing to go in search of Gary at the bar until Skylar's place was properly checked out. Pulling out her cell, she opened her favorites—still unable to remove his name—and rang Parker, knowing he was the person she needed for tonight, but *only for tonight*. Afterward she'd track down the last person or next-to-last person she ever wanted to see—Gary Boyd.

5

Parker was going to see Avery for the first time in months. Well, technically, he'd seen her at Griffin and Finley's summer cookout, but she had avoided him all night—or at least it had seemed that way. But from the details Avery had just shared over the phone, they were going to be partnered up like old times, if only for the night, and he'd gladly take whatever he could get. He hadn't realized how strongly, how deeply, he cared for her until she was no longer at his side daily—working together in close quarters, in adrenaline-fueled situations, into the long, late hours of the night.

He loved Avery, but he still loved Jenna. Jenna was his first and, until now, only love. He'd been planning to propose at an appropriate time, like when he'd graduated from college and could have provided a solid future for them. He'd never shared that with anyone, given the circumstances—she was his best friend Griffin's little sister, and only Jenna's mom and Declan had known about the relationship. He'd wanted to tell Griffin from the start, but Jenna begged him not to. She'd insisted he'd interfere, that he wouldn't approve of the four-year age difference. But everything imploded, including his ability to love fully, with Jenna's brutal murder just days shy of her eighteenth birthday.

Then, after years of his suffering a torturous abyss, Avery Tate walked through his door and something sparked back to life. He hadn't thought it possible, but little by little he'd come alive again—or as close to it as he ever believed he could. But it wasn't fair to promise anything to Avery while he still loved Jenna. While her memory still danced through his mind and she still held a piece of his heart.

He pulled into the trailer park Avery had grown up in. She'd never told him about living here, but due to the sensitive nature of their work, he'd run a full background check when hiring her. She knew about the check but never commented on it or asked about what he'd uncovered.

He spotted Avery's car parked in front of the trailer on the left, wondering which trailer had been hers, wondering what had occurred during her formative years to make her so formidable in the kickboxing ring. It was the only time he'd glimpsed the emotional turmoil beneath her strong veneer—when she laid it all on the table and fought the demons that clearly haunted her past. Her strength ran deep, but so did raw wounds—he just didn't fully know from what.

Stepping from his Land Rover, he grabbed his equipment out of the rear. How would he act once he was in the same room with her? His hand was ridiculously clammy on his kit handle—though that he could blame on the hot, humid Maryland summer. He dropped his kit, swiped his hand across his pants, picked up his kit again, and headed for the door.

Avery opened it, and the air choked from his lungs at the sight of her in that dress. She gave him a half smile. "Hi."

"Hi," he managed to squeak out before she turned to lead him inside—the back of her dress consisting of a single satin ribbon running up the center of her graceful back to meet with two ribbons at her neckline, the three tying into some intricate knot to secure the satin sheath gown.

A delicate tattoo marked the hollow of her left shoulder blade. He couldn't believe he'd never seen it before—a black feather that morphed partway up into colorful birds soaring free. It was delicate yet conveyed a powerful message. He longed to trail his finger along the curve of the feather.

"Thanks for coming, especially on such short notice." Her sandy-blond hair was pulled up into a twisty knot, a loose strand grazing her bare shoulder. She slipped it behind her ear. "I hope I didn't pull you from anything."

Was she fishing for details about how he'd been spending his evening? *Nah.* He was being foolish—reading more into it than there was. Hoping for more. *Hope.* He hadn't experienced any in a long time until Avery entered his life. "No problem at all," he said, "especially if you suspect your friend is missing. You know the sooner the search starts, the higher the chances of locating her."

She dipped her head. "Thank you."

He smiled. "I haven't done anything yet."

She looked him in the eye, and his heart momentarily stopped. "You believed me," she said, her green eyes mesmerizing.

His brow furrowed. "The police didn't?"

She shook her head. "No. It didn't help that the officer in charge knows Skylar."

"Oh?"

"It was Kim Fuller. I didn't mention it the times we worked with her, but the three of us hung out as teens. She knows Skylar hasn't changed. I'd hoped . . ." She shook her head again. "It doesn't matter. The point is, Skylar is flakey and takes off from time to time. Kim believes that's the situation here."

It was good Avery wasn't trying to sugarcoat the situation or deny who Skylar was. But that wasn't Avery's style, and he adored her for it.

"Why do you believe differently?" he asked.

"Because she was so excited about tonight. This was a big opportunity, to have worked with a significant photographer."

Maybe he was off base, but it seemed like Avery might have been excited about tonight too—like there was more involved than the show itself.

"And yet she posed for someone else?" No reason to dance around that fact. Skylar had to know that would stir an enormous commotion. Perhaps that's what she wanted—how she thought she'd make a name for herself, but if so, she'd only shot herself in the foot.

"True," Avery conceded, "but she's not answering her cell, and when I came to check on her an intruder bowled me over."

She cricked her neck to the side again; it was obviously still bothering her. "As you can see the place is a mess," she continued. "But this"—she pointed to the clothes flung willy-nilly over furniture and in a mound on the eighties-style pile carpet—"is sadly Skylar's norm. The cops said the place hasn't been tossed, and after looking around, I agree."

He tried to rein in his thoughts and gain some composure. "You also mentioned they found no sign of a break-in?" He set his kit down on the only open space on the otherwise magazine-and-mail-filled table. An empty pizza box sat discarded on the floor beside it, a handful of empty beer and soda cans on the shelf beneath the coffee table.

"No."

"Okay. Did they file a missing persons report?"

"No, but they said if her boyfriend—who occasionally lives with her for all intents and purposes when they are 'on'—reports her missing as well, then Kim said she'd file the report."

"Did the police track Skylar's cell?"

"Yes. Kim tracked it as a favor to me."

"And?"

"It's not showing up. Not tracking."

"Did she have an iPhone or Android?"

"It's an iPhone. She just messaged me a couple days ago all excited about the showing, which is why this makes no sense." Her eyes narrowed. "Why does it make a difference which type of phone Skylar has?"

"Because an iPhone will still emit a signal even if it's turned off, and since you can't pull the battery out . . . if it's not tracking, then it means it has been destroyed."

She swallowed.

"Third," he said, this question being most important to him, "did the police file a report about the assault on you?"

"Yes, on the assault report. No, on the break-in since . . ."

"There were no signs of a break-in, despite someone being inside. Any chance Skylar knew the intruder? Perhaps he had a key?"

"Then why the flashlight?"

Parker glanced at the tiki lamp beside them. The lights were clearly working.

"Don't worry. I wore my gloves when I turned them on," she said.

"You still carry them with you?" She now worked photographing vitamins and supplements for a major pharmaceutical company out of Baltimore. Gloves not required.

She shrugged with a sheepish smile. "Old habits . . ."

He smiled, glad to hear that, because the habit of working

with her at his side wasn't dying for him at all. The loss of her in his daily life still stung deep. He'd wondered if she felt the same, and the gloves were the first sign that might be the case. He glanced around before his hopes got too high. It could just be habit, like she said. "Any idea what the intruder was after?"

"Not a clue, but that's why I called you. I thought we could run the place as if she's a missing person. Find some clue to the circumstances under which she left, when she did so, and I pray some clarity as to where she was headed. Not to mention what the intruder was after. Also, I have the secondary photograph I told you about in my car. Wrapped as securely as I could manage with what I had on hand."

"You removed evidence from the crime scene?"

"You sound just like Declan."

"Declan?" He frowned.

"Crazy enough. Turns out he is the federal officer who responded to Gerard's call about the art theft."

"Art theft is not Declan's area."

"He's doing a favor for a friend."

"I see, but why did you remove evidence? I can only imagine how Declan flipped out."

"I had a call waiting from Tanner when I came to. When I called her back, I got Declan. That was fun. But as I explained to him, Gerard was going to throw the portrait in the trash. I did what I had to do to keep it protected. It's in my car. Declan wants you to process it when we get to your lab."

"Okay. We'll finish here and then head for the lab, but one thing first."

"Of course."

"You didn't allow the paramedics to check you out, did you?"

"I'm—"

"Fine." He cocked his head. "You said he knocked you down and out."

"Yes."

"So you hit your head?"

She bit her bottom lip.

"I'll take that as a yes." He wiggled two fingers in her direction. "Come here, lass. Let me check you out."

6

Nice try." She smirked, holding her ground. "You've been trying to *check me out* since we met." It was hard enough being in the same room as Parker, but his hands on her . . .

Heat rushed into her cheeks.

"See . . ." He smirked. "This is precisely why I miss working together. My new photographer has no sense of witty banter, but he's a *him*, so on second thought, I'm rather thankful we don't have the same chemistry."

"You hired someone new?" Of course he had, but she hadn't anticipated it stinging quite so sharply, and it was easier to respond to that than the chemistry comment.

"Trust me, I didn't want to, but since you insisted on leaving . . ."

She swallowed. She'd had no choice. Well, that wasn't entirely true. The choice was to stay and get her heart pummeled or to leave and have it break anyway.

Despite her greatest resistance, he tugged her to sit in front of him, her head angled so the light illuminated her hair. His fingers wove through it, the tips of them moving tenderly across her scalp, feeling for bumps.

She gnawed her bottom lip, trying to ignore how good his simple touch felt. *This is a terrible idea.*

"Cold, love?" he asked, his Irish lilt resonating deep inside her.

He skimmed his fingers along the length of her forearm. "Gooseflesh," he whispered.

Mortified. She was absolutely mortified. He was checking her head for injury, and his touch had rippled goose bumps along her skin. "I'm fine," she eked out. *More like, I'm a mess.* A thoroughly ridiculous mess.

She wasn't some simpering female, going weak in the knees at the sight of a handsome man. She was a strong, independent woman, but Parker . . . He'd reached her on an up-to-then-unknown level. His gorgeous looks aside, he was captivating—intelligent, innately curious, loving, protective, and loyal. Loyal to his friends, his family, and his first love. She swallowed. She admired him for it, but at the same time the latter sheared her heart.

"You've got a decent wallop," he said, the spot his fingers hovered over tender even to his soft touch. "Stay awake for a while, and I'll keep my eye on you. You should be fine."

"Thanks." She swooped to her feet, away from his touch, and smoothed out her dress. "It'll take us quite a while to run the trailer, and then the photo, so no problems there."

He nodded, a soulful longing lingering in his eyes. Had he felt the current coursing through him too? Did she intrigue him as he did her? Admire her? That would be funny given her past, which, unfortunately, he was standing smack in the middle of.

Hours passed, and Parker reveled in the comfort and peace Avery's presence always brought him. It'd been so long since he'd felt peace. It was addictive. She was addictive. But she was off tonight.

Naturally, she was concerned about her friend, but something else lingered there. Unease. Tension. Restlessness.

Was being in Skylar's place, back in her old neighborhood, the cause?

He longed to ask, but now was not the right time. Instead, he focused on the task at hand, running the next set of fingerprints, which he'd found on the nightstand, and within a moment he got a hit.

"Connor Davis," he said, showing Avery the DUI mug shot of the twenty-one-year-old on his scanner's screen. "Recognize him?"

She shook her head. "Nuh-uh. Not familiar."

"Skylar date younger guys?" Close to eight years.

"Skylar 'dated' whomever she felt like, despite the fact she had a boyfriend."

"That couldn't have gone over well with her boyfriend."

"It didn't."

"Any chance her boyfriend could have played a role in her disappearance? We found his fingerprints all over the place."

"What exactly are you accusing me of?"

Parker turned to find a broad-shouldered, brawny man looming in the doorframe, a metal bat poised to swing in his thick-fingered grip.

His angry gaze pinned on Avery. "What are *you* doing here? And who's this guy?"

7

Avery's heart plunged at the dangerous bite in Gary's voice. He wasn't going to make this easy. Then again, he never did.

He cocked his head, and an obnoxious grin spread across his face. "Knew it wouldn't be long before you came back." He slithered to her side and leaned in, his breath thick on her neck. "Playing a part only lasts so long, darling."

Every inch of her skin crawled.

Parker stepped toward them, intensity flaring in his green eyes. "Why don't you take a step back, mate?"

"Mate?" Gary chuckled and looked at Avery. "Who is this guy? Don't tell me you two . . . ?"

Please let this all go away.

"Let me guess," Gary said. "You haven't told him about us, have you, kitten?" He cupped her neck, running his fingers along her hairline.

Parker lunged forward, but before he could reach her, she

took Gary's hand, twisted, and dropped him to his knees, holding his fingers tenuously at the breaking point.

Gary hollered an expletive and moved to swing the bat with his free hand.

Parker kicked it out of his hold and tugged Avery into his arms. "Nice move," he whispered.

"Thanks." Kickboxing and self-defense had paid off, and yet she still felt that horrible sickness in the pit of her belly. That pet name slipping from Gary's lips . . . the life she'd been part of . . . so many painful memories mingled here, taunting her.

She glanced over to see Gary shaking out his hand and bending over to pick up his bat.

Parker pulled his Wilson .45. "I don't think so."

"You brought a cop with you?" Gary roared as he straightened without the bat.

No sense clarifying his misperception. Parker was a crime-scene investigator—one of the best in the country—who contracted with the local police departments and federal agencies on a regular basis, but letting Gary think he was a sworn officer worked fine.

Gary pointed at Avery, his entire body taut like a cord about to snap. "You're lucky you got backup with you."

Parker cocked his head, his gun aimed at Gary's center mass. "Was that a threat?"

Gary's gaze bored into her.

Just like old times. Trying to intimidate her. Only back then it worked. Now, not a chance.

"Yeah, it was a threat, so you better watch your back, Av."

"No worries," Parker said with a salty smile. "I've got her back."

"And you don't intimidate me anymore," she said. Gary was nothing but a bully, and she no longer played those stupid games.

"Keep telling yourself that, sweetheart." He winked.

"I think it's time you left," Parker said, his finger caressing the trigger.

"Wait." Avery rested her hand on Parker's tattooed forearm. "I need to ask him a few questions."

Gary chuckled. "You *seriously* think I'm going to help you in any way after this little stunt?"

"I'm trying to find Skylar."

"Yeah, aren't we all."

"*We?*"

"You, me, a couple chicks, couple dudes." He swiped his finger under his nose. "Suddenly Sky's quite popular."

"You know who they were? What they wanted?"

"I can guess what the dudes wanted."

Avery shook that off. "When was the last time you saw Skylar?"

He shrugged. "The other night."

"Which night?"

"Thursday."

"So last night? What time?"

"I dunno. Maybe nine or ten. I was headed for McDougal's."

"She say where she was going?"

"No, and you know Sky. She never said. I never asked."

That wasn't true. At least not in Avery's case. Gary had been like a warden when they were together. Keeping tabs on everywhere she went. She'd never allow herself to be in a position of vulnerability like that again. Hence why she left the one-sided relationship with Parker. One-sided in the sense Parker could never give as fully as she.

"She have luggage with her?" she asked.

Gary swiped his nose again. "You mean that ratty duffel she always carried around?"

"Yeah."

"Not that I saw."

"Why are *you* looking for her now?" He'd never chased after Skylar before. Just let her do her thing and hooked back up with her when she returned. Sadly, she always returned.

"Why do you think?" A gross, leering smile curled on Gary's lips.

Fearing she might hurl, Avery quickly let that thread of conversation drop. "The other people you mentioned . . . Anything you can tell me about them?"

"I dunno. The one dude was talking with Sky at her door a few days ago, but she didn't let him in."

"Any idea what they were talking about?"

"Nah. Like I said she didn't let him in. Just talked to him through the screen door."

"Can you describe him?"

"Average height, lightweight, brown hair. Never really got a good look at his face."

"You said there were a couple girls?" That was odd. Sky didn't play well with other women. Only reason she and Sky were friends was because their moms were besties until Avery's took off.

"Yeah. Saw the one chick banging on Sky's door once, but Sky wasn't home that day."

"What day?"

"I don't know. Last weekend, maybe."

"Can you describe her?"

"Yeah. She was hot."

"We're looking for a bit more than that."

"I don't know. Little thing. Blond ponytail. Would've introduced myself but she left pretty quick."

Lovely. Gary hit on anything that walked.

"And the other lady?"

"Came sometime last week. Saw her also banging on the door as I was heading out to McDougal's."

His nightly ritual.

"So around nine or ten?"

"Probably."

"What'd she look like?"

"It was dark, and I was driving past. Really couldn't say."

"Was Sky home?"

He shrugged. "Saw the porch light flick on in my rearview mirror."

"Did you see Skylar answer?"

"I was already out on the main road by then." He frowned. "What's this all about?"

Avery quickly explained everything that had occurred at the gallery and about the intruder.

"Some dude broke into Sky's place? He's lucky I wasn't here. I would have taken care of 'im."

She didn't need Gary going all vigilante on anyone, but she did need his help. "Will you call the police and file a missing persons report?"

Gary frowned. "What?"

"I think something's happened to Skylar, but with her rep for taking off and no family to report her missing, the officer said since you lived off and on with Skylar, she'd file a report if you also said she was missing."

"You know I'm not a fan of talking to the cops."

"But aren't you worried about Skylar?"

He laughed. "She'll turn back up. Always does."

Avery exhaled her frustration and handed Gary her business card. "It's got my cell on it. Call me if you see Sky, change your mind about filing a report, or think of anything else that might be helpful."

"Whatever." Gary tucked the card in his pocket.

She prayed he didn't use it for any other reason than what she'd stated. Gary was the last person she wanted to hear from unless it was regarding Skylar.

Parker waited until Gary cleared out before speaking.

Great. He was going to ask her about Gary—the biggest regret of her life. Well, the second.

"Any chance Gary's the one who broke into Sky's place?" he asked.

She frowned, uber thankful he hadn't asked about her past relationship with Gary, but the question rocked her. She hadn't considered . . . "Why would he break into his own girlfriend's place?" Although he did have a key, and the police said there'd been no signs of a break-in, which she and Parker confirmed after running the place.

"Maybe she had something he wanted and she's nowhere to be found," Parker suggested.

"But why all stealth, using a flashlight? Why sneak around?"

"Not something he'd do?" Parker asked.

She tossed it around. "If he had a motive, I suppose I wouldn't put anything past him."

"I think I'll go continue the conversation with Gary," Parker said, moving for the door.

"I really doubt he's going to answer any more questions." Not from him. Maybe from her, but not from Parker. To Gary he was an outsider, and you didn't talk to outsiders, especially outsiders with guns.

"He may not give me information verbally," Parker said. "But everyone has tells."

And Parker was certainly gifted at seeing them, and that's what terrified her. Could he read her heart? Did he know how she felt about him? She shifted the topic back to Gary before she freaked out over the thought. "Why the interest in Gary?" Because he'd threatened her? He was most likely just talking smack, and if he wasn't, he didn't frighten her the way he used to.

"Because we found his fingerprints all over this place," Parker said.

"I told you—he and Sky were *together*. Of course his prints are going be present," Avery said.

"Yeah, but one place was odd even for a couple. At least I find it odd, especially after meeting him," Parker said.

Avery frowned. "Where?"

"Her Chinese puzzle jewelry box."

8

W hy didn't you say something before he left?" Avery asked, striding for the door.

"Because, as you said, they were a couple, and I wanted to run it past you, but he's probably more likely to answer without you present. Guy to guy."

She exhaled. That was probably true. Except Parker was an outsider, and he just wanted Gary out of her presence. Wanted her safe. It was endearing, really, but she could hold her own with Gary now.

"Any idea what she kept in her jewelry box?" Parker asked.

"*Kept?* As in it wasn't in there?"

"*It?*" Parker arched a brow.

"A three-carat diamond ring."

"Three carats?" Parker's jaw slackened.

"It was an engagement ring offered to her mom by a really old dude. She said she refused to be a gold digger—which wasn't entirely true, except in that case—but he said because she was honest and in need she could keep it. She gave it to Sky before she died, said she wanted Sky to have a better future."

"So why didn't Sky sell it?" Parker asked.

"Because it was a gift from her mom. One of a very few, and the last one. No way Sky would get rid of it. She never even wore it for fear of losing it. Are you positive it's not in there? There's more than one compartment."

"I found three—all empty," Parker said.

"Then you found them all." She strode into the room, got Parker's okay to lift the box now that he was already done with fingerprints, and checked for herself. How had nitwit Gary gotten the box open? "That's it. I'm going to confront him with you." That ring was all Skylar had.

"You better do it fast," Parker said, staring out the window. "I'm pretty sure he's leaving."

"What?" She grabbed her keys and flew down the front steps to her car, climbing in as Gary's truck whizzed past.

Parker hopped in the passenger seat next to her.

"What are you doing?" she asked, shifting into Reverse.

"You're crazy if you think I'm not coming with."

She could argue, but what was the point?

Besides, now that Parker was actually back in her company, she didn't want their time together to end.

"Fine." She eased back on the gas. "I don't think he saw us. No sense letting him know we're following. We'll stay a ways back and confront him when he arrives at wherever his destination is."

"Good plan. We can start working the list afterward."

"List?" She frowned.

"Of fingerprints."

"You identified more than Gary and that preppy twenty-one-year-old? Who do we have?" Maybe she'd recognize some of the names. The trailer park wasn't large.

His masterpiece was now in the hands of a nosy friend of his

model. He couldn't risk claiming it at the show. It was too risky.
The woman had questioned Skylar's whereabouts all evening.
It limited his maneuverability and altered *his* showing, but he'd
had to leave his masterpiece behind.

He wanted, no, *needed* it back. It was his. *She* was his.

Now to track down the woman who'd taken what belonged
to him.

Parker pulled the list of fingerprint hits from his jacket pocket
and held it up to the dash light, not wanting to turn on the
overhead lights and alert Gary to their tailing presence. "Well,
there is, of course, Connor Davis and Gary Boyd," he began,
"and next is a Crystal Lewis. She and Gary are in the database
for a range of offenses—DUI and shoplifting for Crystal, assault and trespassing for Gary."

"Crystal was at Skylar's?"

He half glanced over at her, still keeping his focus partially
on Gary's taillights a quarter of a mile ahead. "I take it you
know Crystal Lewis?"

"She lives in the park. I didn't realize she and Sky were still
friends."

"Okay." He moved on to the next name on the list when
she didn't elaborate, not wanting to push her about her past.
"Megan Kent is the next name. Do you know Megan?"

Avery shook her head. "Doesn't sound familiar. I'm guessing
she has a record too?"

"No. Looks like a background check was run for her job.
She's a nurse at St. Agnes. What about Sebastian Chadwyck?"
he asked. "His fingerprints were also on file for a background
check. He also works at St. Agnes but as an orderly. I didn't
even know they still had orderlies."

"Sebastian?" Her voice hitched up an octave.

"I take it you know Sebastian?"

"No, but Gerard blamed a guy named Sebastian for the portrait switch." She indicated the portrait in the backseat with a tilt of her beautiful head.

Parker glanced back, examining her wrap job as best he could in the headlight beams shining through the back windshield from the car behind them. From what he could see in the dim light, she'd done a decent job. He shifted back around. "But why would an orderly swap portraits?"

"Gerard said he was an up-and-comer in the art scene. Gerard *mentored* him," she said, using air quotes on *mentored*. "Probably works as an orderly to pay the bills while he pursues his dream."

"Since both work at St. Agnes and both have been at Skylar's place, odds are Megan and Sebastian know each other."

"Maybe Megan was one of the women Gary saw at Skylar's," she said.

"And Sebastian one of the dudes?" he asked.

"Possibly." She tapped the wheel. "After we get Gary to talk, I think we should visit Sebastian next."

"First thing in the morning," Parker agreed.

She glanced at the clock, and he followed her gaze.

It was nearly three thirty and dark as could be.

"Who else?" she asked. "Any more names?"

"One more name and a good number of unknowns."

"Who's the last name?"

"Lennie Wilcox."

"I don't know him."

"Unfortunately I do." He gripped the paper tighter.

She glanced sideways at him. "Why don't I like the sound of that?"

"Because Lennie works for Max Stallings."

"And he is?"

"One bad dude. I'll have Declan and Lexi talk to him."

"Why?"

"Let's just say they have a history with Max Stallings."

"Speaking of Declan," Avery said, cricking her neck to the side, "I'm curious to find out what he learned."

"That makes two of us." Parker raised his brows, his innate curiosity clearly flaring.

She'd never met anyone more curious, and it was so captivating—like watching a little kid spot a butterfly for the first time. She loved that about him.

"So Tanner and Declan ended up together tonight. . . ." Parker's lips twitched into a smile.

"Yeah. What's with the smile?"

He rested his hand on his knee. "I just find the interchange between the two interesting."

She smiled. "That's one word for it." She missed this. Missed *them*, but *them* was clearly defined differently by both.

Parker was flirtatious and clearly wouldn't mind some sort of relationship, but she wasn't into casual. She wanted to be in for the long haul with a man who could give his whole heart, and unfortunately, that would never be Parker. His heart, or a great part of it, still belonged to his first love—Griffin's younger sister, Jenna.

Ever since Jenna's murder at seventeen, Parker—who'd been twenty-one at the time—had never been the same. He played it light when it came to dating, and rumors swirled about the stunningly handsome Irish American. His Irish brogue alone jellied her knees, but there was so much more. He was brilliant—creatively and intellectually—and possessed a depth few men did. He saw stars where others saw faint dots. He danced across her mind with an intensity that elated and terrified her. But she needed something he couldn't give.

So rather than focus on how severely that stung, she let herself be soothed by the scent of his cedar aftershave—the woodsy scent triggering happy memories of her trip to Deep Creek Lake a couple summers ago, the feeling of the sun's warmth on her face, its rays reflecting off the rippling water, and the fresh, crisp fragrance of evergreens. It was calming, and yet the cedar scent on Parker was highly intoxicating too. She was easing back into the comfort of his presence far too easily.

They followed Gary in silence until he turned east onto 404. "Any idea where he's going?" They'd been following him for nearly an hour.

"I'm guessing his brother's place. He lives on the eastern shore. Whenever Gary's in trouble he runs to his big brother." She shook her head. "Some things never change." But thankfully other things did.

<hr />

Parker glanced back at the portrait, squinting in the dark interior, anxious to start examining it. Then his gaze shifted to the car behind them. *Still* behind them. "Hmm."

"Hmm, what?" she asked in that inquisitive tone he found so adorable.

"We've had the same car behind us since shortly after we left the trailer park."

"Really?" Avery glanced in the rearview mirror. "You think they're following us or Gary?"

He looked back again. "My guess would be Gary."

The car lengthened the distance between them.

Avery glanced in the mirror again. "I think they know we've made them."

"Ease off the gas. Try to close the gap just enough for me to get the license plate with my flashlight. It'll scare them off, but I just need a few seconds to get the plate number." He put his arm out the window, peering at the vehicle's front plate and clicking on his flashlight, but the plate was smeared with something black, covering the numbers and letters beyond the point of recognition.

They approached a cop turnaround, and the car, a Fiat convertible, made a hard left. Parker lifted the flashlight's beam at the driver, glimpsing what looked like the swish of a long blond ponytail as the driver made an illegal U-turn and headed in the opposite direction.

"Get the plates?" Avery asked as he settled back in his seat.

"No. They were smudged out."

"Old trick," she said. "Sky used to do that when she was trespassing or . . ." she exhaled, ". . . when we were trespassing." She said it as if it were new information, but he'd seen her rap sheet when he'd run her background check. Normally that kind of background would negate his hiring said person, but with more than a handful of clean years, it was clear the woman beside him had changed and made a fresh start.

"It typically keeps the cops from pulling you over because the plates aren't *technically* missing, but they are harder to read if you get caught and are fleeing," she continued, yanking him back to the situation at hand. "But Sky and I were smart enough, or stupid enough in hindsight, to dirty up the rest of her car, so it actually looked plausible. That Fiat looked pristine."

"It was." *Interesting.* A Fiat wasn't the type of vehicle he'd picture Lennie or any of Max's thugs driving. But it stood to reason, if Lennie was in Skylar's place, she owed him something. Maybe Gary did too. Maybe that's why he'd broken into Skylar's jewelry box. Maybe that's why he was fleeing.

An hour and a half later they watched Gary pull off at what Avery said was his brother's place.

Two and a half hours in the car and he felt like he knew Avery better than ever. This was the first time she'd talked openly about her past. Clearly being back in the setting was stirring memories. And while she may not like the memories, he finally felt like he was seeing the fullness of who Avery was—scars and all. And he appreciated her resilience and fighter's heart all the more. She was a remarkably strong woman.

He watched Gary step from his car and head for the house. He couldn't believe the guy hadn't figured out he was being followed. Granted, they'd kept their distance, but still . . . though Gary was hardly the sharpest tool in the shed.

Avery pulled to a stop at the end of the drive. "How do you want to handle this?"

"Is Gary ever armed with more than a bat?"

"A knife sometimes. No gun, at least not that I've ever seen, but it's been years."

"What about his brother?" Parker gazed across the eastern shore property. He spotted a two-story farmhouse, barn, silo, and a fair amount of acreage as the first wisps of dawn broke the still of night.

"Billy's into hunting, so my bet is he at least has a rifle."

"Do me a favor. Wait in the car. I'll go in and see if I can't have a chat."

"I'm not sitting this one out."

"He's obviously hostile toward you. Give me a shot." He prayed she'd listen. Just once. She was too precious to lose. It'd kill him.

After a moment's pondering, she sighed. "Fine, but be careful. If you aren't out in ten, I'm coming in."

"No. If I'm not out in ten, you call the cops."

9

Avery sat in her car, staring at Billy Boyd's farmhouse as the sun broke the horizon. She worried what Gary and Billy might be telling Parker about her past a whole lot more than what Billy may or may not be packing. The porch and front room lights were on, the silhouette of people pacing back and forth through the sheer-curtained windowpanes.

Still dressed in her evening gown, she raked a hand through her hair. What a night.

Moving her hand over her head, she winced at the lump that had formed just above the base of her skull. Maybe she should have allowed Kim to have the paramedics look her over after all, but there was no time for that now. As soon as they finished with Gary, they were headed for Sebastian Chadwyck's.

Headlights approached, and Avery slid down in the seat and watched as Crystal Lewis's refurbished Trans Am drove past.

What on earth was Crystal doing at Billy's, especially so early in the morning? What was going on in there?

Crystal exited the car and strode quickly into the house, not even bothering to knock on the front door.

Avery took a deep breath and climbed out of her car. This turn of events was just too curious to ignore, even if she hadn't waited Parker's required ten minutes. And she wasn't calling the cops. Not yet. Not until she assessed the situation.

She, unlike Crystal, knocked on the door, and her breath caught in her throat when Billy's wife, Carol, answered.

"Avery Tate, is that you? Ha!" Wearing red silk PJs and a tattered white terry-cloth robe, she rested her hand on her hip, her strawberry-blond hair still tousled with slumber. "I cannot believe you have the nerve to show up at *my* door and in that choice of attire. Just wrapping up another night of partying, are we?"

She ignored the comment. Her history with Carol certainly couldn't be described as amicable. There was no need wasting breath explaining she was no longer the party girl Carol used to know.

"Avery?" Parker said, ducking around the doorframe. "Is everything okay?"

"Yeah. Sorry." *For not listening to you.* "I saw Crystal arrive and—"

"You just had to stick your nose in other people's business." Carol shook her head.

"What is *she* doing here?" Crystal's voice emanated from the room to Avery's right.

Carol stared at Avery, her bathrobe double knotted, her expression grim. And then, to Avery's shock, she stepped back, allowing Avery entrance. "Make it quick. I don't want my boys woken up or witnessing any kind of scene, if you understand me."

Her boys—the twins from Hades, as everyone in the trailer

park referred to them—were hardly going to be fazed by a conversation between her and Crystal. And that's all it would be—a conversation. She'd moved beyond girl fights.

"What are you doing here?" Crystal asked as she stepped into the hallway. She was curvy and wearing skintight leggings that showed every angle, slope, and well, *everything*. Her white short-sleeved blouse, way tighter than the designer intended, was tied above her waist. Black boots with crisscross straps completed the ensemble.

"Hello?" Crystal said, clearly annoyed she hadn't received an answer yet.

Avery took a deep, steadying breath, refusing to get pulled into Crystal's drama. "I suppose I could ask you the same thing. What are *you* doing here?"

Crystal did a sassy neck swish with her head, her blond curls bouncing with the rapid movement. "For your information, this is my boyfriend's brother's place. I have every reason to be here." She glanced over at Parker standing in the doorway, and Avery didn't miss the momentary flash of admiration in Crystal's brown eyes. "Who is he?"

"Parker Mitchell." He extended his hand.

"Oh." Crystal giggled as she shook his hand. "Nice accent."

"Thanks." Parker winked. "Had it all my life."

Of course he would use the situation to be friendly with Crystal. It was a strategic investigative move, but why did it bug *her* so? She knew exactly why. "Wait." She mentally backtracked. "Did you just say you are Gary's *girlfriend*?"

Gary walked up from behind Parker, and Crystal slid her arm around his thick waist, her neon orange nail polish a stark contrast against his black T-shirt. "That's right."

Avery looked at Gary, confused. "But I thought you and Sky . . . ?"

Crystal stiffened. "That's over." She patted Gary's midsection. "Tell them, Gar Bear."

He cleared his throat. "Sky and I are over."

That's not what he'd implied back at the trailer.

"So if you and Skylar are over . . ." *Please.* Those two had the most dysfunctional relationship ever. One Avery sadly doubted would ever be fully "over." "Why were you in her place? In her jewelry box?"

Crystal didn't look the least surprised. If she was dating Gary and believed that things were over between him and Skylar, why didn't she protest about his presence in his supposed ex-girlfriend's place? *Because she knew he'd been in there, and so had she.*

"And if you and Gary are a thing, why were *you* in Skylar's place?" Avery asked.

Pink flushed Crystal's round cheeks. "What?"

"Your fingerprints were in Skylar's living room and kitchen," Parker said.

Crystal's eyes narrowed. "Who are you? Magnum, P.I.?"

"I'm a crime-scene investigator."

Crystal frowned. "Crime scene? *What* crime?"

Gary squeezed Crystal's shoulder. "They think Skylar's missing."

"What? Why would you think that?"

Parker explained enough of the pertinent details to catch Crystal up to speed.

When he finished, Crystal plopped down on the sofa. "That's ridiculous. Come on, Av . . . You know how Skylar likes to take off. It's probably just some stunt to get my Gar Bear's attention because he's with me now."

Just like Crystal was probably being used by Gary to make Skylar jealous.

"I'm not so sure that's the case. She's not answering her phone. It can't even be traced."

"Traced?" Crystal's eyes widened. "You guys really are serious?"

"I'm afraid so," Avery said with a release of air. Reentering the art scene was uncomfortable enough, but being forced back into her past . . .

She looked at Gary. A past that really made her skin crawl.

"Okay," Crystal said. "Suppose you're right—what does any of this have to do with us?"

Parker linked his arms across his broad chest. "You tell us."

"I told you," Gary grunted. "I didn't do nothing."

"Then where's Sky's mother's ring?" Avery asked.

"I don't know." Gary shrugged. "Wasn't in her box when I looked."

"Humph," Carol huffed, making the first peep since they'd somehow worked their way into her living room. Billy had yet to say anything—just sat in his Barcalounger with a cup of coffee in his hand, taking it all in, or simply not caring. Avery suspected the latter. She focused her attention back on Gary. "Why were you in her jewelry box to begin with?"

"Because . . ." He shifted his stance, broadening his shoulders. "I . . . I . . . gave her a ring a while ago, and I wanted it back."

"A ring?" Crystal said, hopping up and staring at him with pinched lips. "You didn't say nothing about having given *her* a ring."

"It was a while back. Anyway, I went to get it so I could hawk it, then get the cash and buy you one now that we're together."

"Oooh. Gar Bear, that's so sweet." She planted a kiss on his scruffy cheek.

"Where's the ring?" Avery asked.

"What?" Gary paled slightly.

"Where's the ring you bought Crystal?"

"I haven't got it yet." He tugged Crystal tighter into his embrace. "She deserves the perfect one, and I haven't found it yet."

Avery shook her head. Crystal, bleary-eyed in love, actually believed the guy.

"Fine. Where'd you hawk the ring?"

"W . . . what?" Gary sputtered.

"Where'd you hawk the ring you bought Skylar?"

"Oh. Uh. Modell's, I think."

"You *think*?"

"It was a busy day. I went shopping for the new ring at a lot of places. I can't remember where I started. Besides, what does it matter?"

It mattered because she was absolutely going to follow up on his supposed claim. She turned to Crystal. "When was the last time you saw Skylar?"

She shrugged. "I don't know. Maybe a week ago."

"Where at?"

"Her place."

Yeah, right. Crystal and Skylar both dating Gary and actually being chummy. She highly doubted it. "For what?"

"We hung out, drank beer, watched a movie. Same stuff we all used to do."

Memories Avery preferred to forget.

"Which one?" Parker asked.

"Which one, what?" Crystal said, frowning.

"Which movie did you watch?" Parker asked.

Avery smiled. The devil was in the details, and Parker was impeccable at his job.

"Oh." Crystal twirled a blond curl around her finger. "*The Other Woman*."

"That's ironic," Avery said. "I mean wasn't that awkward considering you were sleeping with her boyfriend?"

"*Ex*-boyfriend." Crystal glared at her. "I didn't do anything wrong. Gar Bear and her were done."

Avery looked at Parker. Neither of them was buying it.

"Any idea why someone would be following you?" Parker asked Gary, switching tactics.

"Me?" Gary tucked his chin in. "What are you talking about?"

"While we were following you here, someone else was tailing you."

Gary swallowed, a shadow of fear filling his dark brown eyes. "Are you sure?"

"Positive."

"Maybe they were following you," Crystal suggested.

"We haven't done anything," Avery said.

"Neither have we," Crystal protested.

"Other than breaking and entering and stealing a ring." Avery pinned her gaze on Gary.

"I didn't break in. I have a key and, like I said, that ring belonged to me. And, like Crystal said, Sky and I were no longer together."

He still has a key. Maybe he was last night's intruder. He was the right height and build, and using the key would prevent any signs of a break-in. Maybe he and Sky really had split yet again and taking her mother's ring was Gary's way of getting back at her. If he took a ring, it was Skylar's mom's. Avery knew him too well. No way Gary had ponied up money to buy Sky a ring. Even if, on the outlandish chance he actually had bought her one, no way would Sky care enough about it to keep it in her puzzle box. Taking a deep breath, she linked her arms across her chest, feeling silly she was still in her evening gown. "Where were you before you showed up at the trailer?" she asked.

"McDougal's. Like I already said."

"What time did you head over there?"

"I don't know." He shrugged. "Eight thirty."

Her eyes narrowed. "Come on, Gary. You never hit the bars until close to ten."

"What can I say?" He took a seat in a burgundy La-Z-Boy separated from Billy's lounger by a small table still lined with empty beer cans. Gary tugged Crystal down in his lap. "I felt like starting early."

"Uh-huh." They'd be verifying that information too. She looked at Parker and he nodded. They'd gotten enough to go on. Time to let Gary and Crystal sit and stew about who was after them. A little panic and they might just make a move that exposed what was really going on. There was more to it than some supposed ring.

"I'll call Kate and ask her to send a sitter over to keep an eye on Gary and Crystal," Parker said as they exited the house and climbed into Avery's car.

Clementine rays of sunshine flooded through the windshield. It wouldn't be long before the sun was high in the sky and the temperatures soaring up with it.

"So," she said, starting the engine. "They're both full of it."

"Ya think?" He slipped off his black CSI windbreaker, his cobalt blue T-shirt accentuating his toned physique.

She quickly shifted her gaze to the window.

"You okay?"

Always so darned perceptive.

"Yep. Just thinking." About exactly what she shouldn't be. "So what now?"

"We head to Modell's and confirm Gary's story or we track down Sebastian Chadwyck." He paused. "Actually, I think the most pressing need is for me to take that portrait back to the office and examine it. Then we can coordinate with the whole gang so we can divide and conquer."

"Sounds good. Let's head in."

The long drive to Charm City Investigations—the private investigation firm that Kate Maxwell owned—provided Avery with plenty of time to ponder exactly what Gary may have said to Parker before she'd entered Billy's house.

"So . . ." She drummed her fingers on the steering wheel. "What went down with Gary before I came in? Did you get anything out of him?"

"Just asked him to give it to me straight. Man to man."

Greeaaat. "And?"

"He played the bravado card. Said he'd moved on from Skylar."

"But you think he was lying?" She could hear it in his voice.

"I think *she* moved on from him."

"So he decided to take what mattered most to her, her mother's ring, and hawk it? I bet *that*'s what he hawked, not some ring he supposedly bought Sky. Gary is *not* the jewelry-buying type. His idea of a gift is a new pair of tires."

"So a practical fellow." Parker smiled, still not asking about her and Gary's past.

The suspense was gnawing at her. When *would* he ask? Or would he really just let it go?

Could *she* just let it go? It felt like a secret burning a hole in her heart, something she had to release before it burst.

The past was in the past—at least that's what she kept telling herself, and she'd actually believed it right up until today.

Now she was smack back in the middle of it, and the one man she had hoped would never gain an inkling about her past was right in the thick of it with her.

While she loved having him at her side—far more than she

should—her past was the last place she wanted him. Talk about a nightmare sprung to life.

She wasn't that person anymore, but that life, *her* past life, would always be a part of her—even if she didn't allow it to control her anymore. It was a buried memory that had just busted through the surface, and the man she loved was going to learn about it no matter what she did. He was too good, and this time, it was to her detriment.

She shook her head.

"What?" He arched a brow.

"Nothing. Just thinking."

All this time she'd always thought it was his past that was going to keep them apart. Now she wasn't so sure.

10

After dropping Parker at his car back at the trailer park and making a quick stop at home to shower and change her clothes, Avery felt more prepared for whatever the day would bring. The coffee and espresso she held in her hands from Pitango Bakery, two blocks over on the water next to Urban Pirates, only added to her optimism.

Parker held the glass door of Charm City Investigations open for Avery, while also holding the pastries they'd picked up at Pitango as well. Griffin, Finley, and Kate were already present, thanks to Parker's call, as was Tanner.

Tanner?

She had been staying with Kate for the last nine months while she adjusted to life back in the States and was no doubt intrigued by the case she'd gotten a glimpse of at Declan's side last night.

Tanner and Declan.

Avery saw something there, and apparently Parker did as well. It was nice to finally see Declan over Kate. The shift had begun around Kate's announcement of Luke's proof of life on

Thanksgiving and with the entrance of Tanner into their lives, but regardless of the core cause, Declan was finally over Kate.

Ready to move on with Tanner? She wasn't sure.

Parker said he'd probed a little last week while he and Declan were hiking, but that Declan maintained his typical cone of silence. Though, Parker did say the flicker in Declan's jaw upon hearing Tanner's name and the possibility of the two pursuing a relationship indicated there was something lingering there. Question was, how long until it surfaced?

"Hey, Tanner. I'm sorry," she said, refocusing on everyone in the room and feeling horrible for not bringing Tanner something. "No one told me you'd be here. You can have my drink."

"No worries." Tanner shook her head and lifted her ceramic brewing cup she was never without. "I've got tea."

"Intrigued by the case?" Avery asked. Tanner was always curious, and Avery appreciated that about her.

Tanner blew a loose strand of brown hair from her lightly freckled face and smiled. "From what little Declan shared with me."

Parker smiled widely as Declan entered. "So how was your evening with Declan?" he asked Tanner, but kept his gaze fixed on Declan, who stopped short at Parker's grin, his eyes narrowing.

"What?" Declan asked, hesitation in his eyes.

"Tanner was just telling us about your time together last night." Parker's grin widened.

Declan's cheeks flushed.

Avery chuckled. Declan was too easily riled, but his reaction was yet more evidence that he at least felt *something* for Tanner.

"She was at that gallery for Avery," he responded, a little too abruptly.

Defensive. This is getting interesting.

"I was helping a friend out by taking the initial report, what little the inebriated Gerard Vaughn was able to tell me," he continued, his tone leveling as he shifted gears to focus on the case. Work mode was his comfort zone.

"You'd think Gerard would have at least tried to sober up some before the authorities arrived," Avery said, shaking her head. "He is such a drama queen."

"I also talked with the staff on hand," Declan said. "No one seemed to know anything overly helpful, but at least *they* were sober." Declan took off his black blazer, revealing a white button-down shirt with black trousers and patent leather shoes. Clearly he was not trying to hide his profession, even on a Saturday, even in August's heat.

Declan was most certainly the boy scout of the gang, and yet Avery sensed something underneath—something lurking, longing to be set free, something separate from his feelings for Tanner, whatever they were. He was wrestling with something, but the question was, what? He possessed far more depth than he showed, a lot more humor—she'd gotten the occasional glimpse—and a hunger for the outdoors, but he was always so set on being straightlaced. That's what would have to change before he and Tanner, or any relationship, could work for him. Declan had to relax into himself.

He tossed his blazer over the silver rack by the door, and Avery handed him his coffee.

"Thanks." He rolled up his sleeves. "But I'm still annoyed that you removed a key piece of evidence from a crime scene. You know better."

"I didn't have a choice. They were going to put it in the trash bin. That would have compromised its integrity far more than me carrying it with gloved hands and wrapping it up."

"Where is it now?"

"Right here," Parker said, carrying it in and heading for his lab. "I'll place it in my office and be right back." On the drive back that morning, Parker had explained that, needing greater flexibility, he'd moved his office from the ME's office downtown to Charm City Investigations a month ago.

Declan exhaled. "Thanks for protecting it the best you could."

"No problem," she said, and then proceeded to hand out the rest of the drinks she and Parker had picked up.

"I love you," Finley said as Avery handed her the steaming marrochino. Same drink she'd gotten. Espresso and dark sipping chocolate, which basically equaled perfection.

Griffin had ordered a triple espresso and Kate a vanilla latte. Declan, of course, was the only plain coffee drinker—medium, dark roast, black. Not surprising for the Fed. Simple and straightforward in everything he did. Another reason why his dating life never lasted past the third date. He was too precise, too focused on his job, too withdrawn to really give a partner what she needed. And yet, something deep inside told Avery it would just take the right lady to change all that, to push him past his boundaries. Once the right person walked into your life . . .

Her gaze shifted to Parker, returned from his lab and now setting out the pastries. The man had turned her world upside down. Shaking off her giddiness at simply being in his presence again, which was ridiculous because she of all people didn't do giddy, she forced herself to focus her attention on the pastries.

The buttery, flakey croissant had her name written all over it. Grabbing it, she took a swallow of her marrochino and sank into the chair next to Parker, ready to lay this case open and get the entire team on board—each having their areas of expertise.

They were all highly respected in their professions and, together, practically unstoppable. But most importantly, they

were on her side. She couldn't feel more blessed . . . or anxious.
She sighed.

*Forgive me, Lord, for being so antsy. For worrying. I know
it adds nothing to my life or any help to the situation at hand,
but it's my friend's disappearance that we're investigating, and
I don't know where to start. I don't want to choose the wrong
lead. Please direct our investigation and help me to bring Skylar
home. I'm the reason she is the way she is. Please don't let it
be too late.*

A hollowness gnawing in the pit of her stomach said it already was.

*"Are you sure we should be doing this?" Skylar, only six
months younger than Avery, asked as they crept past the NO
TRESPASSING sign.*

*Avery knew exactly what she was doing, had done it plenty
of times before, but usually with Gary at her side. Tonight
she'd brought Sky instead. Now she just had to nudge a little.
"What, are you chicken?" she asked.*

*Skylar's quivering chin tightened, her slender arms stiffening,
her hands balling into dirty fists. "No."*

*"Then, come on." Using the wire cutters she'd stolen from her
stepfather's toolbox, Avery made an opening just big enough
for their preteen bodies to wriggle through and led her best
friend to the other side—introducing Skylar to her first taste of
crime, hoping she too would experience the rush. For Avery, it
had become addictive. The only way to feel . . . something . . .
something other than pain.*

Tears bit Avery's eyes. Mercifully, things had changed when
she came to know Jesus, but Skylar . . .

"You okay?" Parker asked.

She sniffed back the pain and straightened her shoulders. "I'm—"

"Fine." He finished for her. "Av . . . ?" He touched her knee. Tears threatened, but fortunately Declan stepped to the white-board, dry-erase marker in hand, as he always did when they began a case, providing her with an out on that discussion, at least for the moment.

"One person we need to check out is Kenneth James," Declan said. "He runs the warehouse at Fuller's gallery, but he was already gone by the time I arrived last night. James, according to Nadine and Fuller, is the one responsible for receiving the artwork as it comes in and helping hang it."

Avery shifted, and Parker moved his hand, resting it on his knee instead. She wanted his hand back, wanted the innate sense of protection and intimacy it provided, but it was safer this way. He also shifted his focus to Declan and the case at hand.

Thank you, Lord. I'm not ready to have that discussion. Not ready to admit. Remembering is horrific enough.

"Then we'll definitely want to talk with him," Parker said.

"It would probably be best for you two to take him." Declan gestured between her and Parker. "Avery's connections to the art scene might encourage him to talk a little more readily."

Avery nodded, only half sure of what she'd just agreed to.

Declan lifted his chin at Parker. "What's next?"

"Well," Parker responded, likely having no clue about the demons she was battling as they sat there mere inches apart, his thigh occasionally brushing hers. "We've identified six sets of prints from Skylar's trailer, along with at least a dozen or so unknowns, but at least we have a starting point."

He ran through the names, and Avery swallowed, trying to still her mind—to make it focus on the case and not her past shredding through her memory.

"Lennie Wilcox," Declan repeated as Parker shared the last name. "Well, that's not good."

"No." Parker shook his head. "I was hoping you'd take him."

"Not a problem. I'll drop by Max's first. See if he can give me a lead, which, of course, I doubt, but it's worth a shot. If not, I'll head down to his housing projects. Lennie loves to hang out in the diner there, hassling the poor folks Max has under his thumb."

"How'd you get this case anyway?" Griffin asked Declan. "Art theft isn't your usual area."

"Dave had his daughter's wedding this weekend, so I said I'd cover the case until he returns from Solomons Island Monday morning."

"That was nice of you," Kate said before taking a sip of her drink. "Did Alexis join you?"

The whisper of a smile crossed Avery's lips at Kate's inquiry, finally tugging her out of her past. Kate definitely had set her sights on pairing up Declan and Lexi—always working to get the two together outside of work, hoping to spark Declan's interest in his beautiful partner, but those two didn't fit in Avery's mind. He and Tanner made much more sense, even if neither of them fully realized it yet.

"The projects," Tanner said, having waited longer to jump on Declan's comment about visiting the housing projects than Avery had anticipated. Whenever there was someone in need, Tanner pounced.

"Sorry," Declan said, nipping Tanner's idea in the bud—they all knew where her question was headed. She wanted to go along. "I'll be on official business. I'm gonna grab Lexi on the way over to see Stallings."

Tanner shifted to sit cross-legged in her chair. "I'm not talking about going with *you*. I'm thinking it's an area I need to pay more attention to. See how I can help. Go down and check it out."

"The area Max runs is one of the roughest neighborhoods in the city. Please at least wait until someone can go with you."

"Fine." She lightly grunted. "I suppose it'd be helpful to have someone who knows the area show me around."

Declan was extremely protective of Tanner, unfortunately to the point of treating her like a child. He wasn't that way with the rest of the gang, so why all the concern for Tanner's wellbeing? Especially given her background working overseas with the Global Justice Mission combatting sex traffickers. She could hold her own.

Avery had questioned Parker about it once, and he'd said that Declan only acted that way when he really cared deeply for a woman, but if that were the case, it was a terrible way to show he cared. He needed to treat Tanner like the competent adult she was, not some helpless damsel in distress. Tanner was anything but. And yet, it was another clue to his feelings for Tanner. Avery smiled. The two of them would certainly be entertaining—two strong, stubborn personalities. That was one show she'd enjoy watching.

"Avery and I will examine the portrait, visit Kenneth James, and then pay Sebastian Chadwyck a visit," Parker said.

Avery's temporary diversion ended and she prayed earnestly, with all her heart, that they'd find answers today. Prayed even harder Skylar would reappear and it would all have been some stupid stunt on her part. But Sky'd learned from the best— a truth that weighed on Avery's conscience. The lead weight sinking to the bottom of Avery's stomach landed with a thud. How was she going to make it through this without losing it? Her past and present were connected by a thin thread she feared would snap at any moment, fully combining the two. She'd worked so hard to keep them separate. What if all that work had been in vain? What if Parker discovered the full truth of her past? Would he look at her differently? He'd have to. She certainly did.

"You two have already interviewed Gary Boyd and Crystal Lewis, correct?" Griffin asked, saving her from Parker's appraising gaze.

"Correct." Parker nodded, his gaze darting between her and Griffin.

"All right." Griffin stretched out, wrapping his arm around Finley's shoulders in the chair next to his. "How about Finley and I take Connor Davis since I'm on my leave days. Having a beautiful woman along might make Connor talk easier."

After working Marley Trent's case last fall, Griffin, who had been working as a park ranger at Gettysburg, returned to police work, joining up with Baltimore County rather than city since it was closer to his home. He served his time as a patrol officer until he was able to apply for an opening in homicide. With Griffin's experience on Marley's case, along with several murders he'd worked with a detective, homicide had swooped him up. He'd officially been homicide for two months now and was loving it. Avery was so thankful he had some time off and could help with investigating Skylar's disappearance.

"Sorry, honey," Finley said. "I'm teaching two archaeology workshops at the campus symposium this weekend."

"Right. No worries." He turned to Kate. "You have info on Connor?"

Kate nodded, pulling up Connor Davis on her laptop. "He's a senior at Loyola. Home address is Roland Park, but we've got a rental house in his and a . . . Kyle Eason's name not far from campus."

"Great," he said. "So since Finley is busy . . ."

"I'll do? Is that what you're saying?" Kate stuck her tongue out. Seven years later, despite Luke's disappearance right before their graduation, she was as tight as ever with them, so much a part of the guys' bond it was funny.

"You said it, not me," Griffin replied with a chuckle. "We got both the home and rental addresses?"

"Yep." Kate nodded. "Let's hope we find Connor at one of them."

"I don't understand." Avery paced while Parker set up his supplies to process the portrait after expressing his distaste for the portrait's subject matter.

All Skylar could talk about for weeks was modeling for Gerard, and then this . . . ? Maybe this really was just one of her stunts. Maybe she was somewhere safe—as safe as Skylar ever was. And maybe, just maybe, Avery still had time to finally convince Skylar of her desperate need for Jesus.

Parker arched a brow. "Don't understand what, love?"

"That." She pointed at the portrait. "Why would she trash a great opportunity by posing for someone else?" *Or . . .* Her heart dropped as what she feared rose up her throat. "Or . . . what if she didn't *pose*?"

He looked up from his supplies. "What do you mean *didn't pose*?"

"Look at the emptiness in her eyes, the unnatural skin tone. It appears too perfect, but now, under your examination light, there's an iridescent blue that shows through."

Concern edged his voice. "Her skin color was . . . altered?"

Avery nodded.

"To what purpose?" he asked.

She exhaled her fear. "What if Sky was photographed after she was . . . ?"

"Dead."

Avery wrapped her arms around her trembling stomach and nodded.

"So that's what's got you all knotted up. You fear she's already dead." He took a step to her and pulled her into his hold.

He smelled like the outdoors—cedar, fresh air, and cascading streams. Considering they'd been up all night investigating, she wasn't sure how that was possible, but it made her want to burrow even deeper.

For once she *refused* to stiffen. Instead, she actually allowed herself to mold into his embrace, to let him comfort her. She was terrified for Skylar, and it felt incredible to be held in the arms of the man she loved. Even if he didn't know or reciprocate the depth of her feelings, he *did* care about her. That much she knew. If Skylar was dead, it would destroy her. It would mean she was too late—that she'd led Skylar to hell . . . and hadn't been able to pull her back.

"We'll find her one way or another," he said, softly brushing a kiss to the top of her head.

She swallowed, knowing that if she remained in his embrace much longer, allowed her guard to stay down, she'd start bawling, so instead she forced herself to step back. "Thanks." She sniffed. "But we best get to it."

"Right." He cleared his throat and straightened, his gaze still locked on her.

Please look away. She couldn't let him see the devastation in her eyes. She needed to get in the gym. To kick and punch her frustration and fears out on a bag before they ate her alive. Even five minutes would allow her to work off the worry and fear.

After a moment, Parker turned and grabbed his work gloves.

Slipping them on, he angled his work lamp to better illuminate the portrait, then spent a few minutes really studying it. "The most apparent clue is her eyes," he began.

"Lifeless, right?" she said. She *knew* it. As much as she'd tried to convince herself otherwise . . .

"Yes, literally, I'm afraid." His Irish brogue dipped lower than usual. "Look at her pupils. They're dilated. Based on scale I'd estimate seven millimeters."

"And that's significant because . . . ?" She was afraid to ask, but she forced herself. She needed the facts.

"It's significant because people's eyes dilate upon death. It doesn't prove Skylar's dead, of course, other things cause dilation, but it's in line with the possibility."

"And the scarf positioned like a choker around her neck." Avery exhaled the tension knotted in her belly. "To me, while the texture is a good addition, it looks compositionally out of place."

He sat back, bracing his arm on his bent knee. "It could be covering her cause of death."

She swallowed again, her throat squeezing tighter, narrowing her airway, her chest compressing . . . The weight was so heavy, and she deserved for it to be.

Parker's gaze softened, and he reached for her, clasping her hand, his fingers intertwining with hers. "I'm sorry, love. But remember, it's just a theory at this point."

She nodded, knowing, *feeling* in her gut their theory was true, but she'd keep fighting, keep praying, forcing herself to hope that Skylar was still alive until they found her body. Until they had definitive proof.

Gently pulling her hand back, she leaned against the desk and linked her arms over her chest. There was something more. She could read it in his eyes. "What else?"

He raked a hand through his hair and then looked back at the portrait.

"Might this all be Gerard? Maybe a crime . . . but might it all be a publicity stunt? I mean, he did choose the Black Dahlia-esque theme."

She mulled that over. "Could be, but now that I have looked at it more closely, this portrait is far more visually stunning—grotesque subject matter aside—than any of Gerard's work."

"You said both Gerard and his assistant blamed Sebastian?"

"Yes, they said he was a young upstart, trying to break into the art scene."

"But why make such a bold move? You said Gerard was allowing him to shadow him on shoots. Sounds like he was making headway. Though . . ." Parker turned his attention back to the portrait. "You're the expert, but to me it seems the depth of his feelings for his subject comes across in spades."

"You think the photographer, whoever he was, had a thing for Skylar?"

Parker scooted his chair back. "I'd say more than a thing. This is the work of a man in love, or more precisely, a man obsessed."

Now they were touching his portrait, putting powder on it, examining it as if it were something to be taken apart. It was a work of art. An act of creation. How dare they treat it like one of their science projects. It was *his*, and he was getting it back, no matter the cost.

11

Parker yearned to reach his arms out and wrap them around Avery. He ached to comfort her. This was wearing hard on her. She clearly felt a deep connection to Skylar. He didn't know the particulars of their relationship, other than the fact that they'd grown up together and ran away together when Avery was sixteen to live on their own for a couple years. Everything else was locked away in Avery.

He had so much he longed to ask, but if she wanted to share about her past, she would. He would respect that boundary, but it wouldn't be easy. There was much he wanted to under-stand about the woman he'd fallen for, but it wasn't fair to delve any deeper when there was a fixed blockade in place. *Jenna.*

He exhaled. Was it possible to stay faithful to Jenna and her memory and yet love Avery? Jenna deserved better from him, and so did Avery. He'd let them both down, and yet he couldn't walk away. Not when Avery needed his help. He just prayed he had the strength to do so when the case was over. Her leaving his employ six months ago had been excruciating. Separating again when this case was finished would break him.

"You okay?" she asked, also intuitive. When it came to working cases, they were unstoppable, but on the personal side, their heightened intuition could prove dangerous.

He cleared his throat and gave the same answer she usually gave. "Fine."

After Parker finished processing the photograph, they decided to see if they could catch up with Kenneth James at Fuller's gallery. The day was warm as they stepped outside and into his Land Rover. The temperature display above his rearview mirror read ninety-one. Typical August in Baltimore, though he never minded the heat. It reminded him of growing up by the water's edge, running around barefoot, getting burned across the bridge of his nose. The laughter and antics he and the guys would get into. Their poor mams.

Parking his vehicle in a slot along the cobblestone road, they climbed from the SUV and approached the rear entrance of Christopher Fuller's gallery via the back alleyway, the brick road worn and dusty. He held the warehouse—aka basement—door open for Avery.

Fell's Point was a prime spot for art galleries as the entire neighborhood was an artsy community in numerous forms—portraits, paintings, pottery, gourmet food, and the list went on and on. Not to mention, it was an extremely vibrant community. But being historic and boxed in by the encroaching neighborhoods, it had its set boundaries, and there were no modern warehouses in the area. Hence the basement functioning as the Fuller warehouse.

They followed the narrow blue stairs down to the chilly brick-walled room where they found a man in his early twenties sitting on an overturned crate with his profile to them.

"Kenneth James?" Parker asked.

The man looked up, his gaze fixing on Avery. "Yeah?"

"Parker Mitchell," he said, internally chuckling at the gape of the man's mouth as he noticed Avery. "This is Avery Tate," he said.

"*Avery Tate*?" Kenneth swung his legs around, fully shifting to face them. "*The* Avery Tate? You have quite the rep in the art community."

"Yeah." She exhaled. "Well, we're not really here about me."

"Hey, I didn't mean no disrespect," he said, standing and slinking flirtatiously toward her. "I think what you did is awesome. How you busted that perv." He punched out his arm and shook his head. "Mmm, now that's a strong woman."

"Thanks." Surprise tickled her tone.

"So . . ." Kenneth smiled, his gaze tracking her up and down. "What can I help *you* with, darling?"

Irritation pinched Avery's brow, but she withheld a retort. "We're looking into what happened with the swap of Skylar Pierce's portraits."

Kenneth's smile vanished. "Yeah, that was some crazy stunt. I'm sure Gerard went nuts."

"Any idea how it happened?"

"No clue." He shrugged. "Everything was kosher on my end."

"You helped hang the portraits?" Parker asked as Kenneth moved for his workbench.

"Yeah." He grabbed one of the clipboards off a peg.

"Did you hang Skylar's?"

He flipped through what appeared to be shipping invoices. "The original, yeah," he said, not bothering to glance up.

"And then . . . ?" Parker pressed.

"Then *nothing*. I finished my job and left."

"Did you see anyone unusual hanging around before the opening, anyone who stood out?"

"I didn't know all the artists, but no one seemed out of place, if that's what you're asking."

"How long between your hanging Skylar's portrait and the unveiling, would you say?"

Kenneth shrugged. "I don't know. After all the pieces are hung and the center showcase veiled, Mr. Fuller likes to hold a powwow in his office for all the artists and staff working that night. That's my cue my job is done and I'm outta there. My guess is they're probably up there fifteen minutes or so. Mr. Fuller likes to talk. As to when it was unveiled, that depends on the artist's ego. With Gerard Vaughn, I'm guessing he wanted a big reveal—maybe twenty, thirty minutes after the guests began arriving."

Exactly what Nadine had said to Avery.

"So . . ." Avery leaned against the worktable. "How do you suppose someone carried another portrait into the studio, swapped them out, and walked away without anyone noticing?"

"No clue."

"Seems to me the only way a person could appear unnoticeable is either if they snuck in during the short time everyone was in Fuller's office, or if it was their job to be unnoticeable—to fade into the background as the event began. Someone who was supposed to be hanging portraits, perhaps."

"Whoa!" He flung the clipboard onto the countertop. "I resent what you're implying."

Avery tilted her head. "What am I implying?"

Parker smiled. He loved her directness.

"That I had something to do with what went down."

"Christopher, his staff on site that night, Gerard, and his

assistant—not one of them reported noticing anyone present who wasn't supposed to be. The only person they saw hanging portraits that night was you."

"I did my job and left. Like you said, someone could have snuck in and swapped portraits."

"But how would they know Christopher was going to have the preshow meeting, and how would they know the precise timing? Seems to me it had to have been someone on the inside."

"In addition," Parker said, "Mr. Fuller reiterated to the federal officer called in after the theft that the gallery's front door is always kept locked until the event begins." Declan's investigation had proved extremely helpful to theirs.

"Yeah?" Kenneth crossed his arms.

"So that means the only way in is through the warehouse."

"So maybe I forgot to lock up. What's the big deal? I'm sure Gerard had his photograph insured."

"We're not here about the portrait. Not directly."

Kenneth's brow bunched. "Then why are you here?"

"About the model, Skylar Pierce. She's missing."

"Missing?" His brown eyes widened, genuine concern flashing across his face. "Oh man." He swiped a hand over his shaved head. "He didn't say nothing about a missing woman."

"Who didn't?"

Kenneth swallowed, his thick Adam's apple bobbing in his stout throat. "Sebastian."

"Sebastian?" Avery's eyes narrowed, fixing in on her target. "Are you two friends?"

"In a way," Kenneth said with an exhale. "Look, Sebastian just wanted a shot, and guys like Gerard and Fuller, they prevent young artists from getting a chance unless they grovel at their feet and dance to their demands. Sebastian ain't that kind of guy."

"What kind of guy is he?" Avery asked.

"A hardworking guy just looking for a break."

"Sounds like you can relate?"

"I was told I needed to work my way up before I could show. It's been six months and nada. I'm stuck in this warehouse. You know what I'm saying?"

"So *you* made the switch for Sebastian while everyone was in Fuller's office?"

Kenneth shrugged, but his shoulders were tensing, his movements growing taut, rigid. "Dude deserved a shot. His piece was stellar. Gave me a couple hundred bucks and I made the switch."

"And Gerard's portrait?"

"Sebastian took it."

"What for?"

"I don't know. Probably to trash it. Wasn't my business. Besides, by him taking the original portrait it looked more like a theft than just a switch since it wasn't found."

"Yeah, well, Skylar hasn't been found either. You know anything about that?"

"Nah, I swear. Sebastian photographed her the night before the show. She's probably just laying low because she knows Gerard's ticked, and you don't want to cross Gerard."

"Then why'd she do it?" Parker asked. "Why risk ticking off Gerard when she could have been his star?"

According to Avery, it had been all she'd talked about for weeks. Her shining moment.

"Dude. The chick's a rebel. Always skating the edge. Sebastian's portrait was ten times better than Gerard's. If she wanted to be noticed, going with Sebastian was the way to do it."

12

Griffin glanced over at Kate as they approached the two-story brick townhome mere blocks from Loyola's campus. "Nice house for a couple of college kids."

"Rich parents," Kate said. Her Internet search had revealed Connor's parents were both lawyers and lived in a gigantic home in the heart of Roland Park—the most expensive and luxurious neighborhood in Baltimore—and Connor's townhouse reflected that same wealth. Griffin hoped he wouldn't be too difficult to deal with.

"Here goes nothing." He rang the bell.

It took a moment, but the black door finally swung open.

A young man—twenty-one according to his driver's license—answered. He was five-ten, a hundred and seventy-ish pounds, with brown wavy hair cut relatively clean, and brown eyes. He seemed like an average college guy. "Connor Davis?"

Connor rested his right arm along the doorframe, leaning toward Kate and ignoring him. So he was *that* type of guy.

Griffin stepped forward. "We'd like to ask you a few questions."

"And you are?"

"Detective McCray." Griffin showed his badge. "And my associate, Kate Maxwell."

Connor's eyes narrowed. "You're a cop too?"

She shook her head. "I'm a PI."

"Seriously?" He laughed. "No way. A gorgeous number like you."

She ignored the "compliment," likely not counting it as such. "Can we come in?"

Connor stiffened, glanced back at Griffin's badge, and then turned his attention back to Kate. "What's this all about?"

"Skylar Pierce."

"Who?"

"Oh, come on, Connor." Kate pulled out Skylar's picture and showed it to him. "You know exactly who I'm talking about. Your fingerprints were in her trailer, on her headboard. . . ."

"Oh, right. Her. What about her?"

Griffin decided it was time to take this conversation off the front stoop. "Can we come in?"

Connor looked into the house and then back at them. "Fine, but make it quick. I have a test in an hour."

"No problem," Griffin said, taking in the nicely furnished home. A mommy job if ever he'd seen one. Paintings on the walls, a grand flower display on the hall table, and elegant lighting. The place was immaculate. *Hmm*. Perhaps a girlfriend's upkeep as well, unless Mommy made regular visits.

Connor led them into the den. A fifty-five-inch flat screen was mounted on the wall over the fireplace. A leather sectional arched around a coffee table in front of it. Open textbooks covered the glass table along with cans of Red Bull and a bowl of Doritos.

"Summer classes?" Kate asked. Griffin could tell she was

working to keep her tone friendly. They wanted Connor on their side. He decided to play it cool and let her run the show.

"Yeah. Anatomy and Physiology."

Kate's eyes widened. "Oooh. Tough course. You studying to be a doctor?" A bit over the top in Griffin's opinion, but Connor didn't seem to notice.

"Nah. Going to vet school, but my dad wanted me to keep my options open, so he has me picking up some pre-med classes."

"Sounds like a rough workload."

"It's crazy, man."

"I bet." Kate took a seat when he offered, but Griffin continued standing. "I also bet you need some stress relief now and again."

Connor smiled. "You interested?"

"I'm flattered, but let's talk about Skylar. Is that what she was?"

"Yeah. We hooked up."

"Often?"

His smile faded. "Once."

"How come only once?"

He shrugged, but his shoulders tensed and his gaze flashed to a picture on the bookshelf. "Just the way it was," he said.

"Where'd you meet?" Kate asked as Griffin shifted closer to the photograph. It was Connor, his roommate, Kyle Eason, according to his MVA records—they'd looked him up when his name appeared on the lease with Connor's—and a slender blonde between them.

"At a bar," Connor said, growing twitchy.

"Which one?" Griffin said, stepping from the photograph.

"Why does it matter?" His jaw stiffened. He was about done playing along. "She's not saying I raped her or anything crazy? I've heard that happens. Girls trying to get money from guys."

"No. Nothing like that. Skylar's missing."

"What do you mean *missing*?"

"As in hasn't been seen," Griffin said. "So tell us more about you and Skylar."

"Whoa!" He jumped up from the couch. "You think I had something to do with some chick's disappearance. You are way off track."

"We're not suggesting anything of the sort."

His eyes narrowed. "Then why are you here, asking questions?"

"We're here because your fingerprints were in her place, and we're talking to everyone whose prints were there."

"That must be a long list," he scoffed.

"Meaning?" Kate pressed.

"Not like it's a secret what kind of girl she is."

Griffin linked his arms across his chest, looking at the photograph Connor had looked straight at when they asked why he'd only slept with Skylar once. "Any chance your roommate slept with her?"

Connor's jaw tensed.

"Slept with who?"

Griffin turned to find the blonde from the photograph standing in the entryway.

"Hey, Mandy," Connor said.

"What's going on?" She eyed Kate and Griffin skeptically.

"They're here about some missing girl."

"Why here?"

"Because I hooked up with her."

"And?"

"And as I was explaining to Connor"—Kate stood and stepped toward the girl—"we're following up with everyone who saw or interacted with Skylar before she went missing." She put out her hand. "And you are?"

The blonde ignored Kate's hand and looked from Kate to him. "Amanda."

"Amanda . . . ?"

"King. I'm a friend of Connor's." She looked at Connor, her gaze communicating something. What was she attempting to hide?

"Did you know Skylar?" Griffin asked.

"How would I know one of Connor's conquests?"

"Conquest?" Kate said. "Interesting choice of words."

"Would you prefer *hookup* or *skank*?" There was venom in Amanda's tone.

"Are you sure you didn't know Skylar Pierce?" Griffin asked, taking Skylar's photo from Kate to show Amanda.

She barely glanced at it. "No."

She was clearly lying. The question was why.

Kate followed Griffin outside when their questioning was done. "Nice car," she said, gesturing at the convertible Fiat parked in the drive that hadn't been parked there upon their arrival. "Must belong to Amanda. *Hmm* . . . Might have to be my next vehicle."

"Please, you're already a nightmare on the roads with your Mini Cooper, driving around like the world's a racetrack."

Kate climbed into Griffin's truck with a smile. "Is there any other way?" As she buckled her seatbelt, she lifted her chin, indicating the front window of the townhouse.

He looked up to find Amanda King standing there, staring at them.

13

"Agents Grey and Kadyrov." Max Stallings reclined in his office chair, steepling his fingers. "What brings you to my establishment?"

The establishment to which he referred was a sports bar on the ground level of his three-story building on the Canton waterfront. The second story housed his office and the third a luxury apartment, where he occasionally stayed with lady friends while his wife, Ramona, maintained their sprawling six-thousand-square-foot home in Hunt Valley. Maintained with the help of a maid, housekeeper, and full-time nanny, of course.

"We're looking for Lennie," Declan said, getting straight to the point as his partner, Alexis "Lexi" Kadyrov, stood beside him. Now that they were dealing with a man they often investigated, it was only appropriate for Declan to pull his partner in, even if this case was only theirs until Monday.

Max frowned, though it was hard to distinguish from the almost permanent scowl he normally brandished on his full jowls. "What do you two want with Lennie?"

"We need to speak with Lennie in reference to his fingerprints being found at a missing woman's home."

"I'm sorry to hear that. This missing woman have a name?"

"Skylar Pierce," Lexi said.

"Skylar's missing?" He sat forward, something akin to concern skittering across his furrowed brows. "Since when?"

"You know Skylar Pierce?" That didn't bode well for her.

Max exhaled and reclined again. "We have an . . . arrangement."

So Max had nothing to do with Skylar's disappearance or he'd never have admitted the arrangement in the first place.

"What kind of arrangement?" Lexi asked.

"That's between me and my client."

"We're not here for you," Declan said. "We're just looking for Skylar, who if I'm guessing right owes you money, so it's to your advantage to help us out."

"Off the record?" he asked.

Declan looked at Lexi, got the head tilt, and then nodded an affirmation at Max. An entire task force had been assigned to Max Stallings for the last two years, and the most they made stick was racketeering, which resulted in nothing more than time served and two years' probation. Basically a slap on the man's thick wrist. Declan had no interest in getting sucked into another exercise in futility.

"Skylar needed some funding," Max said.

"For?"

"Gambling debt. She and her pals got in over their heads at a bachelorette party. Skylar dug herself the biggest hole and needed help crawling out. She assured me she had a way to pay me back."

"Which was?" Lexi took a seat in one of the swivel chairs opposite Max's desk, crossing her legs.

"She didn't say, but she hawked an item of value to give me a sign of good faith."

Lexi's green eyes narrowed and her throaty voice conveyed her suspicion. "Hawked what?"

"Some item of jewelry. Something her mom gave her, I think. I told her to go to Modell's. He gives the best rates, but I heard from Vinnie that she held out on me."

"Meaning?"

"She held back some of the cash."

Declan exhaled a sigh. "That couldn't have gone over well." Not with a man like Max Stallings.

"I called her in, asked her about it."

"And . . . ?" Declan feared the worst, but it's not like Max Stallings would admit to anything.

"She said she needed the money for a safe deposit box. It was part of the score she was working on to pay me back my money."

Declan leaned against the tall black metal filing cabinet, crossing his arms over his chest. "When was the balance due?"

"Tomorrow."

Maybe Skylar didn't come up with the funds and had to take off. If Skylar had taken off and not even bothered to give Avery a heads-up, that was just cold.

"So it really is in your best interest to help us find Skylar," he said.

Max smiled, the creases in his forehead smushing together. "So it would seem."

Lexi lifted her chin. "Where's Lennie?"

"Downtown."

Which meant collecting in the projects Max owned. He really was a piece of work.

Avery and Parker were headed for Sebastian Chadwyck's home in northwest Baltimore when Declan called.

"Hey, Declan, you're on speaker with me and Avery," Parker said.

Me and Avery. She loved the sound of that.

"Same with me and Lexi."

"Hey, Lexi," Parker said. "How was the game last night?"

"Machado hit it outta the park in the bottom of the ninth for the win. It was awesome. Thanks again for the tickets."

"My pleasure. So how'd it go with Max? Did he tell you where Lennie is?"

"Shockingly, yes. Said Lennie's down in that diner he likes by Patterson Park."

"I'm shocked he told you where to find him—not that it's any big surprise. That's Lennie's 'office.'"

"Yeah, it turns out it's in Max's best interest to help us find Skylar," Declan said.

Avery looked at Parker, not liking where this was going.

"Why's that?" he asked.

"Because according to Max, Skylar owes him a hefty sum from a gambling debt."

"What?" Avery's pulse increased. "I know Sky likes to play a game of poker now and again, but she's a lightweight."

"Max said she was at his club with a bachelorette party and got in deep."

Oh, Sky.

"Did he say how much she owes?"

"No, only that she hawked a piece of her mom's jewelry to give him a show of faith. A down payment, of sorts."

So that's where Sky's ring went. If a three-carat diamond was just a down payment, she hated to imagine how deep Sky was in to Max.

"Unfortunately, she went to Modell's," Declan continued, "and when Max talked to Modell, he learned the good faith money she gave him was not the full amount."

"What?" Panic surged through Avery's chest, Modell's name bringing back a flood of unpleasant memories. Did Vinnie Modell work for Max Stallings?

"That couldn't have gone over well with Max," Parker said.

"It didn't."

Dear God. Had Max killed Skylar? Or *had* Skylar killed?

"He had her brought in," Declan said.

"And . . . ?" Parker asked before she could form the word, her heart lodged in her throat.

"She said she'd kept a small amount from the money Modell gave her because she needed to purchase a few items for a scheme to pay Max back."

Parker brows furrowed. "What kind of items?"

"What kind of scheme?" Avery asked.

"I don't know anything, except he said she'd gotten a safe deposit box."

"A safe deposit box?" Avery frowned. "For what? I mean, she'd hawked the only thing she had of any worth."

"Max just said it was part of her plan to get him the money she owed."

"So she was working a con?" Parker asked.

"Sounds like it," Declan said.

"Do me a favor," Parker said. "Give Kate a call and see if, when they're done interviewing Connor Davis, she and Griff can track down which bank the box is at. Avery and I are on our way over to Sebastian Chadwyck's now."

"You got it. We're heading down to Patterson Park."

"Good luck."

"Same to you."

Parker disconnected and looked at Avery. "Want to run by Modell's first?"

He really could read her mind—well, part of it. She prayed he couldn't read the other part that was nearly sick at the thought of returning to Modell's, but she had no choice. "Yeah," she said, with little enthusiasm.

Parker turned the car around without hesitation.

She couldn't let the one thing that meant the most to her friend be sold off.

They pulled up to Modell's, and her stomach lurched as images of the items she'd hawked over the years played like a bad movie through her mind.

"You all right?" Parker asked. "You just turned green."

"Fine." Maybe Vinnie wouldn't be in. It'd been years. Maybe his staffers wouldn't know her. Maybe Parker wouldn't find out how desperate she'd been for cash when she and Sky ran away and were living on their own.

Entering, she spotted Vinnie at the cash register and her stomach flipped. She was so thankful Parker was with her for support, but she hated he was about to learn of this side of her past.

Taking a deep, fortifying breath and saying a quick, desperate prayer, she strode to the counter.

Vinnie glanced up and then did a double take. "Avery Tate." He laughed. "Didn't think I'd see you again. What's it been . . . ?"

"Eight years."

"Back in the neighborhood, are we?"

"Just helping out a friend."

"Ah, you're here about Skylar's ring."

So it was true. Skylar must be in deep to hawk the one thing that meant so much to her.

"Is it still here?" she said, twitching her leg back and forth, her anxiety sky-high.

"Yeah. She said she'd be back for it yesterday, but she never showed, so it's up for sale." He lifted his chin at the front counter.

There it sat, on crushed red velvet—cheap as the fabric could possibly come. No doubt, Vinnie Modell's idea of an elegant display.

"I'll take it," she said, her heart humming.

"It won't be cheap."

"With you it never is. How much, Vinnie?"

A dash of shock momentarily danced across Parker's handsome face, but he quickly reined it in. Now he knew—at least part of it. Shame engulfed her.

"Two grand."

"I haven't got two grand."

"Then I'd say you're out of luck, sweetheart."

"Don't call me that."

"You never minded back in the day."

"Times change. I've changed."

"You know the saying—a tiger never changes his stripes."

"Well then, good thing for me I'm not a tiger. Now let's talk price."

Vinnie smiled. "Still feisty. I love that."

"Then give me a price break."

He looked to Parker, who was impeccably and expensively dressed.

Vinnie rubbed his chin. "I'm thinking, no."

Parker pulled out his wallet. "We'll take it."

"No credit here. Only cash."

"Of course." Parker looked around. Was he really going to—

"There's an ATM out front or a Western Union on the corner."

Parker looked to Avery. "I'll be right back. You'll be okay?"

She nodded. "I'll be fine, but are you sure? It's a lot of money."

Parker smiled. "I'm positive."

"I'll pay you back."

"I know you will, even if I tried to dissuade you from doing so." He winked and exited the building.

"He your new beau?" Vinnie asked.

"None of your business."

He lifted his hands. "Just trying to make pleasant conversation."

"Let's not."

"Suit yourself."

What was she doing? Sky knew Vinnie well. Maybe she'd shared what she needed the money for—all of it. "Did Sky tell you what she was going to do with the cash?"

"Oh." Vinnie linked his arms across his chest with a smug grin. "So now you wanna talk?"

"Cut it, Vin. Just give me the deets."

"What's in it for me?"

"I don't kick your rear."

"Seriously?"

"Sky's missing. Really missing."

He didn't budge.

"Please."

"There's the magic word." He rested his forearms on the glass countertop, leaning in toward her. "Sky said she owed a gambling debt."

"And the rest?"

Vinnie laughed. "Max said someone would be along asking questions. Just didn't realize it'd be you."

"So?"

"So she said she had a gig lined up to pay Max back."

"Like the old days?"

"Old days?" Vinnie laughed. "I don't know what Sky's been telling you, but there ain't no old days. She never stopped pulling gigs."

Avery didn't even have time to react to the disturbing news before Parker strode back in and laid the cash on the counter, and Vinnie wrapped up the ring.

As they turned to leave, Avery thought to ask him about Gary. "So, Vinnie, has Gary Boyd been in here to pawn anything recently?"

"Gary, huh." He gave her a smarmy grin. "Are you still hanging around with that lowlife?"

"No, but he told me he pawned a ring recently. If he hasn't been in here, do you know where he might have gone? Could you make some calls for me?"

"Sure, doll." He leaned over the counter, and Avery could barely resist lurching back. "How do you plan on thanking me?"

Avery sensed Parker stepping forward behind her and prayed he wouldn't say or do anything. "How about you consider it a favor for an old friend, Vinnie?"

He straightened and crossed his arms. "I suppose I can do that. I'll call you if I learn anything. You still at the same number?"

"Yes, and thanks."

"Sure." He lifted his chin a notch. "And I hope you find Sky."

Avery's eyes narrowed.

"What?" He shrugged. "I can't be concerned?"

"About someone other than yourself? That'd be a first."

Max's "neighborhood" consisted of housing projects and a strip of businesses ranging from overpriced grocery stores, laundromats, and beauty salons to less savory establishments—all of which were owned by Max Stallings. All of which he ran via his thug Lennie Wilcox.

Max would send Lennie to find the downtrodden, the homeless, the evicted and promise them a better life. He arranged work for them that paid practically nothing, then loaned them money to purchase their necessities at a huge markup. In the end he basically owned them. It was a horrific cycle that was nearly impossible to break out of.

Max knew how to work the system. He wasn't *technically* doing anything illegal—that they could catch him on—and he had the top defense lawyers just sitting on his payroll. The appalling and complete perversion of justice made Declan sick, and he knew it would affect Tanner too when she made it down here. Now that she knew about this place, nothing would keep her away, but at least she'd promised him she would bring someone with her.

He was just trying to protect her. He wanted her to help others—really, he did—but seeing her nearly die mere days after they'd met . . . He knew he was too heavy-handed at times, but he was simply trying to keep her safe—though he was doing an awful job at it and completely alienating her in the process.

Declan held the door to LuAnn's Diner open for Lexi and lifted his chin at Lennie sitting at his usual table in the rear.

The scent of tuna fish and burnt coffee wafted around them as they moved toward the lanky man seated at the back table.

"Grey and Kadyrov." Lennie smiled like this was all some sort of a game. "Always a pleasure."

Declan indicated the empty seats. "May we?"

"Be my guest." He looked at the woman behind the counter, her hair pulled back in a ponytail, wisps of brunette strands slipping loose across her brow. "LuAnn, some coffee."

She nodded. "Be right there."

Declan pulled one of the empty chairs back, the metal legs scraping across the tile floor. Lexi took the chair beside him.

LuAnn brought their coffee over.

"Thanks," Declan said as she sat his cup in front of him on the table.

"Thanks," Lexi added.

Lennie looked at LuAnn impatiently, and she quickly retreated to the counter.

"So," Lennie said, dumping sugar packet after sugar packet into his cup, "what brings you two down here? Not that I ever mind seeing you, hon." He fixed his gaze on Lexi.

"Sorry to say I don't share the sentiment," she retorted.

He grabbed his chest. "Ouch."

"We're here about Skylar Pierce," Declan said, getting straight to the point.

"Skylar." Lennie smiled. "She's quite the looker too. What about her?"

Lennie was a lech. And that was exactly why he didn't want Tanner down here. Lexi was an agent. She had to put up with this stuff—it was part of the job—but Tanner . . . He wanted her nowhere near a man like Lennie Wilcox.

Despite what Tanner did for a living—which he admired the heck out of—and despite the horror she'd battled, he saw purity and innocence when he looked at her. And something deep inside him yearned to protect that. Making her feel belittled or incompetent was never his intention. But she never worried about herself, never looked before she leapt. He half loved that about her, but it also terrified him.

"You were in her place," Lexi said, pulling Declan back to the conversation. "Why?"

"We had a business transaction to discuss." Lennie took a sip of his coffee as his focus moved to a man entering the diner.

"Max told us," Declan said. "Did he send you to bring her in when he heard she was holding out?" Max had said she was brought in, but not by whom. If Lennie had seen her, maybe he knew more.

"Now, you know better than that." Lennie set his cup down. "Max has said all he's going to say. Now, if you'll excuse me, I've got another meeting." He signaled to the waiting man, who was shuffling his feet anxiously back and forth.

"What do you think?" Lexi pulled her hair back into a pony-tail as they stepped outside. Another scorcher at ninety-five degrees and 100 percent humidity.

"I think that's exactly why Lennie went to Skylar's—to bring Skylar in to Max. Max wouldn't trust anyone else. Question is, what did Lennie do with her afterward?"

14

As Parker pulled away from Modell's, Avery shifted in her seat, trying to get comfortable. Like that was possible with the conversation she was about to have. "I'm sorry you had to see that," she whispered.

Parker arched a brow. "See what? The pawnshop?" He chuckled, clearly trying to ease the tension he read in her stiff posture. "I assure you it wasn't my first time."

It was time she just laid it all out because it was bound to come up at some point. She'd rather just take it on the chin. "I mean the glimpses into my past." She slunk down in her seat, wanting to hide under it. "It's ugly."

"Your past is . . . in your past, for one. For two, it's what made you who you are."

That's what she feared.

He pulled over into the Chick-fil-A parking lot and shifted the car into Park.

She braced herself for how deep this conversation might go.

He unbuckled, shifted to face her, and tenderly cupped her cheek in his hand. "You are the most amazing woman I've ever had the pleasure of meeting. You're strong and tender, intelligent, and far too witty for me to keep up with. Not to mention beautiful inside and out. Don't be ashamed of your past. You're a new creation in Christ. Focus on that."

That was true. *Truth.* That's what she needed to focus on—who God said she was as a child of His—rather than the ugly memories tugging at her mind. She knew where those were coming from, and it wasn't God. But how could she ignore the influence she'd had on Skylar? She'd put her best friend on the road to destruction. If anything happened to Skylar before Avery could reach her for Jesus, she had no idea how she'd live with herself.

"Truth be told," he said, caressing her cheek, grounding her in the moment, "I'm glad I got to see a bit more of your life. If you haven't noticed, you aren't exactly a sharer."

She smiled. "Pot. Kettle."

He laughed. "See, there's that wit I adore. Fair enough. You let me see into your past. Tonight, when we're back at your place, I'll share more of mine." He moved fully back into his seat and buckled up.

"My place?"

He put the car in gear and drove toward the drive-thru. "I'm starving. How about you?"

"Yes, but how about you explain about the 'your place' comment."

Parker inched closer to the ordering booth, the line wrapped around the building. "You can't seriously think I'm going to let you stay on your own after Gary threatened you."

"Gary's just talk." *Well, mostly. Well, occasionally.* "I—"

"I know," he said, quickly cutting her off. "You can take care of yourself. I realize that, but how about—just once—letting someone stand by your side? You don't always have to go it alone, you know."

It sounded like a wonderful, terrifying way to go, but after living as she had, keeping her distance, relying on herself and only herself, could she really trust others enough to change? Was it worth the risk to experience the joy that no doubt came with living in community with those she loved?

They placed their order, and she focused on eating rather than responding, her thoughts jumbled, fearful she'd tear up if she thought too much about the possibility.

Parker was at her side and she wanted him permanently there, but when it came down to it, could he really, solidly be there when he still loved another woman?

A half hour later, they pulled to a stop in the working-class neighborhood along the northwest edge of Baltimore's city-suburban line. Sebastian's address led them to a well-kept brick row home. All the homes and yards showed pride of ownership. It was a beautiful neighborhood. They climbed the steps and knocked on Sebastian Chadwyck's door.

No answer.

Parker knocked harder.

Avery glanced in the bay window. "Looks empty."

"He's not there," a man on the neighboring porch said, lifting his trash can. "Moved out a few weeks ago."

"Any idea where to?"

"With his girlfriend." The man hefted the can down the steps and along the short concrete walk to the curb.

"Any chance you know the girlfriend's name?" Avery asked with a smile.

"Nah. Never paid that much attention."

"Could you describe her?" Parker asked.

The man's brown eyes narrowed. "What's this about?"

Avery explained they were looking for her missing friend, and that Sebastian might know where she was.

The man mulled it over and then said, "Girlfriend was shorter than Sebastian. Five-three or four, at most. Shoulder-length brown hair. Seemed nice enough."

"Any idea where she lives?"

"May have said something about Glen Burnie once, but I could be wrong. I'm not really the sort who keeps tabs on people. For that you'd want Miss Edith."

"Miss Edith?" Avery asked.

He gestured toward the house across the street, and the front curtain quickly fell back in place.

Parker nodded. "Thanks."

"Take it easy." The man waved and headed back up his front steps.

"Oh, wait," Avery said, rushing toward him and pulling Skylar's picture from her pocket. "Any chance you saw her around Sebastian's?"

"Nope."

"That was a quick response."

"Trust me, I'd remember seeing her. Is she the one missing?"

Avery nodded.

"I'm sorry to hear that. Hope you find her."

"Thanks. Appreciate your time."

She joined Parker in walking across the street, dodging the kids riding their bikes in the street. They walked past the mature dogwood in the front yard and climbed the steps of the row home, the brick painted red, the shutters white.

Avery rang the bell, and a dog started yapping. A moment

later, the little dog, a Jack Russell from the looks of it, poked his nose through the lace curtains and jumped up into the bay window seat.

The door opened and a petite red-haired woman with misty blue eyes stared up at them. "So you wanna know about the photographer."

Hope sprung in Avery's chest. "Yes."

Edith turned and slunk back into her house, leaving the door open for them to follow. "There ain't much to tell."

"Anything you can offer might be helpful."

She turned, narrowing her eyes, wrinkles sagging at the corners. "What's this about?"

The dog jumped down, following Edith closely.

"We think he may be able to help us find my friend." Avery handed her Skylar's picture.

"Pretty girl."

"And missing."

Edith handed the picture back. "Sorry to hear that."

"Did you ever see her around here?"

"Nope."

"Do you know where Sebastian moved to?"

"In with that girlfriend of his."

"This girlfriend have a name?"

"Megan Kent."

A match to another set of the fingerprints found in Skylar Pierce's apartment.

⌒⌒⌒

Avery's heart thumped like a whale plummeting back into the depths of the ocean as they drove toward Glen Burnie and Megan Kent's home—at least going by her last known address. The couple, according to Edith, had been together awhile, but

Sebastian liked his privacy and space, apparently only starting to bring Megan around recently.

As private as he was, it was a surprise to Edith when he actually agreed to move in with somebody else.

Money trouble was Edith's theory. But all that mattered to Avery was that they were about to question two of the people who'd been in Skylar's home, and most likely the photographer who'd taken her picture.

Other than the prints of Nadine, who had taken the photo off the gallery wall, the frame and picture had been fingerprint free, suggesting whoever had handled the image had worn gloves, which indicated either a meticulous clean freak—which Edith said Sebastian was not—or someone who didn't want the portrait traced back to him. Was that because it would enrage Gerard or because something more sinister was at play? She swallowed, Parker's earlier words coming back to haunt her. *"Eyes dilate upon death."*

Please, Father, don't let Sky be dead.

15

After leaving Lennie, Declan and Lexi had walked the neighborhood, checked in with a few business owners, and then grabbed a couple dogs from G&A. Declan's cell rang as they climbed into his Suburban, Lexi slipping her sunglasses on and her blazer off.

"Grey," Declan said, answering the call while also shrugging out of his blazer.

"Agent Grey, it's Bob Matthews."

Bob Matthews was head of Maryland Port Authority. An odd person to get a call from.

"Hey, Bob. What can I do for you?"

"We've got a situation down here at MPA Terminal Six. We could use your help."

"No offense, but isn't the harbor yours and the Coast Guard's area?"

"I called your director. He told me to call you and your partner. I'll call Agent Kadyrov next."

"No need. She's right here with me."

Lexi looked over with arched brow.

"How can we help you, Bob?" FBI didn't typically have jurisdiction at the docks.

Bob? Lexi mouthed.

Matthews, Declan mouthed back.

"We've got smuggled refugees, a dead first mate, and a dead federal agent."

Shock surged through Declan, and he swallowed hard. "We'll be there in twenty."

"What's up?" Lexi asked.

Declan explained the situation as they headed for the port.

Twenty minutes later they arrived to a mirage of swirling red patrol lights dancing through the parking lot as MPA police cordoned off the area.

Parker and Avery approached Megan Kent's home. The exterior was a combination of brick and tan siding. A carport stood at the end of the short drive, lining up with the house's side door.

For some reason it wasn't what Parker had anticipated, but he wasn't sure why exactly. It looked too domestic, he supposed, like a home a family shared. And from what he knew of Sebastian, based almost solely on Skylar's portrait, he did not seem a settled or happy man.

Parker knocked on the storm door while Avery stood beside him, scoping out the neighborhood. It was quiet. No kids playing. The only other person he spotted was an elderly man mowing his lawn.

A young lady opened the door. She was about five-three, as Sebastian's neighbor had described. Slender. Mousy brown hair and light brown eyes—the color of amber. "Hi, we're looking for Sebastian Chadwyck."

She rolled her eyes. "Aren't we all."

"Excuse me?" Parker asked.

"I haven't seen Sebastian."

"Since . . . ?" Avery asked.

"Last night."

"Are you Megan?"

"Yeah." She looked directly at Avery. "Who are *you*?"

"Avery Tate, and this is Parker Mitchell. Can we ask you a few questions about Sebastian?"

"What's this about?"

Parker explained they were looking into the disappearance of a young woman Sebastian had recently photographed.

Megan frowned, her eyes narrowing. "Who?"

"Skylar Pierce."

Anger burned in her eyes. "He *photographed* her?"

"Yes. Apparently shortly before she disappeared."

"You're certain?"

"That's what we've been told, but we need to talk to Sebastian to be positive."

"Where's the photograph?" she asked, irritation streaked across her freckled face.

"We have it," Avery said.

"Before we talk anymore, I want to see it."

"It's evidence in a criminal investigation. We can't just bring it."

Megan linked her arms across her chest. "Then I'm not talking."

"What if we took a picture on my cell of it?" Avery asked, praying it would suffice.

Her jaw shifted. "Fine. Bring me the picture of it, and then I'll talk." Megan slammed the door.

16

"Agent Grey, Agent Kadyrov." Maryland Port Authority director Bob Matthews strode toward them wearing a navy blue suit, navy-and-white pinstripe shirt, and yellow tie. Very professional but still personable—the image the director had been trying to portray as he worked to make Baltimore America's number one transit port. "Thank you for coming. Let me introduce you to the key personnel."

He escorted them aboard the *Hiram*, a merchant ship flying the Malaysian flag.

Coast Guard, MPA, and Customs were all present. The refugees were huddled with extremely itchy-looking gray blankets draped across their trembling shoulders. Declan's heart went out to them. He couldn't believe what he was about to suggest, or rather *who*, but it was clear no one was helping the refugees, just guarding them. "I know a wonderful crisis counselor with the Intercultural Resource Center. I could call her if it would be of help with the refugees."

"Excellent idea. We've been so focused on the murders we hadn't paid much attention to them."

"Tanner, huh." Lexi rocked back on her heels with a smirk.

"Not you too." He stepped away and placed the call and, unsurprisingly, Tanner agreed to come straight away. Whenever someone was in need.

Meeting back up with Lexi and Bob on the deck, he followed as Bob led them up the exterior ladder and onto the bridge, where two men lay dead on the floor.

Declan surveyed the scene, knowing he wanted Parker on the case. The Coast Guard Investigative Service crew was already in place, but once they made their initial assessment, they typically turned the case over to local authorities, or in this case—with a dead federal officer—to the FBI, which meant Lexi and him. CGIS's work was impeccable—Declan had no major concerns with them—but Parker was *the* best. "Run me through what happened here?" he asked.

"Row"—Bob signaled to one of the CGIS men—"can you spare a minute? These are the federal agents I called in."

The man—tall, at least six-two, with short cropped hair and a muscular swimmer's build—joined them.

Bob said, "This is Special Agent Grey with the FBI and his partner, Special Agent Kadyrov."

Declan extended his hand. "Declan."

"Noah Rowley." That explained the Row nickname. Somehow fitting, given his profession.

"Lexi," she said, shaking his hand in turn.

Declan rolled his eyes at her flirtatious tone.

"Rowley," Bob said, "is the CGIS Special Agent in Charge."

"So you're leading the investigation?" Declan asked, just so he knew exactly who Rowley was and where he stood in the hierarchy. It was always good to confirm every person's role when multiple agencies were involved.

"For now," Rowley said. "But we'll turn it over once we've finished our assessment."

"Can you run me through it?" Declan asked.

"Of course. The ship was five nautical miles out of the harbor when a fishing vessel heard shots fired on board. They radioed the Coast Guard immediately, and when our men boarded, they found two dead on the bridge, the captain unconscious, a crew in disarray, and twenty-four refugees in the hold. They then directed the ship into Terminal Six and called Customs and Immigration. We're still waiting on an Immigration rep to arrive."

"You said one of the deceased is . . . was a federal agent?" Lexi asked.

"His name is Steven Burke. He's an agent out of Houston. Had no ID on him. We ran his prints. He was dressed like a crew member."

"Was he undercover?"

"Not according to his superior. Apparently he asked for personal leave almost two months ago. Was due to return to duty next week."

"So what was he doing on a merchant ship flying a Malaysian flag, and who killed him?" The federal agent's presence and circumstances made no sense. Had the guy just decided to ask for a two-month leave to sign on to a Malaysian merchant crew? *Nuh-uh*. Steven Burke was up to something. Perhaps something personal, but definitely something investigative.

Bob slipped his hands into his trouser pockets. "That's why we called you two."

Declan's gaze tracked from Steven Burke lying on the floor to a man lying a bit closer to the door.

"The first mate," Noah said. "Joseph Contee. Citizen of Tanzania."

Declan spun around looking for someone in custody and not

finding anyone. Perhaps they'd moved the killer belowdecks. "And the shooter?"

"The captain claims Burke opened fire on the first mate and then moved to shoot him," Noah explained. "But the captain pulled a revolver kept on the bridge in case of pirates and shot Burke before slipping backward and conking his head on the control panel. He says no other crew members were present, and that has been corroborated by the crew members we have spoken to so far."

Declan surveyed the bridge. "May I speak to the captain?" Undoubtedly the man seated next to the control panel with the icepack on his head and a medic at his side.

He and Lexi strode to the man, Bob Matthews following, and Noah returned to his work.

"Captain Randal Jackson, federal agents Declan Grey and Alexis Kadyrov," Bob said.

Jackson nodded.

"Are you American?" Lexi asked.

"Kentucky born and raised," Jackson said, a hint of Kentuckian accent remaining.

"Later you're going to have to tell me how you ended up captaining a Malaysian merchant ship, but for now I need you to tell me what happened here," Lexi said, squatting beside him.

"That man"—Jackson lifted his chin, indicating Noah— "just did."

Declan purposely stood over the man rather than squatting to his level. "So you're sticking with that story?" Because he just couldn't see it playing out that way. Not without some pretty extreme extenuating circumstances.

"It's not a story," Jackson said heatedly. "It's the *truth*."

So the captain had a hair-trigger temper. Even more

interesting. No sense pressing the issue just yet though. Ballistics would either confirm or contradict Jackson's story.

Jackson removed the icepack from his head, and Declan leaned over to survey the gash and dried blood on the back of Jackson's head. It was an awful lot of damage for a slip and knock. Looked more like someone had whacked him over the head—with what, he wasn't sure. But why claim he fell if he'd been hit over the head instead? Unless he wanted to be hit over the head.

"Any idea why Agent Burke would want to shoot you and your first mate?" he asked, extremely curious about Jackson's assessment of what led up to the shooting.

"Because the first mate discovered his true identity," Jackson finally said.

"And . . . ?" Declan left it there. Better to let Jackson try to fill in the pieces.

"And he panicked."

Now he knew Jackson was lying. Federal agents didn't panic when their cover was blown unless they had a serious reason to.

"Did he have cause to panic?" Lexi asked.

"What do you mean?" Jackson scoffed, tenderly touching his wound.

Was he intentionally trying to draw attention to his injury, to remind them *he* was a victim?

"Had Burke been threatened? Had he discovered something he wasn't supposed to?" Lexi pressed.

Jackson frowned. "Like what?"

"The refugees in the hold for one," she said, disgust for their mistreatment evident in the heightening of her typically throaty voice.

Declan studied Jackson. "Did you know Burke was a federal agent when he joined the crew?"

"No. How would I know something like that?"

"So you just thought he was one of the crew?"

"Yeah."

"How did it make you feel when you learned Burke was a federal agent?" Lexi asked.

Jackson shrugged.

"That's not an answer," Declan said.

"I don't know. Guess I haven't thought about it."

Yep. The captain was most definitely lying. The question was why and to what extent?

Bob Matthews cleared his throat. "Agent Grey, your associate is here. They are holding her at the tape line until one of us escorts her in. I thought you could accompany me."

He looked to his partner, and Lexi gave a nod, signaling him to go. She had this.

"Of course," he said, moving to Bob's side.

They climbed back down the ladder, the metal hot beneath Declan's grip.

"You think the captain's lying, don't you," Bob said.

"It crossed my mind."

Bob straightened his jacket and tightened his tie as he stepped onto the deck. "All I care about is bringing the man or men responsible to justice."

He wanted a quickly closed case—not a publicity nightmare for the port's image.

Declan spotted Tanner on the other side of the yellow-and-black crime-scene tape, her hair blowing in the stale breeze. Even the slight wind coming off the water felt hot in the humid August air. It was a blistering weekend.

Tanner shifted from one foot to another and back again.

Curious. Was she simply anxious to help, or was something else going on? A few more steps in her direction and he spotted the source of her shifting. She was wearing paper-thin flip-flops. Her feet had to be burning on the scalding asphalt.

"She's with me," he said, approaching the officer guarding that portion of the line.

The officer gestured her in under the tape.

"Thanks," Declan said, and the officer nodded.

"Tanner Shaw, Bob Matthews."

Bob shook her hand. "Thank you so much for coming, but I'm not certain how much help you'll be able to offer. It appears none of them speak English or they simply aren't talking."

"It could be either case, but I do speak a number of languages. Hopefully one of them fits."

"Well, I appreciate you coming down on such short notice." Bob looked across the parking lot to the gathering reporters. "If you'll excuse me, I have a statement to make."

"Of course," Declan said.

"I'm surprised you called," Tanner said.

"I'm surprised you wore what are basically sheets of paper on your feet when you were coming on a ship. Your feet must be burning."

Now that Bob had excused himself, she was practically hopping.

"I'm fine. Besides, I was at a friend's when you called. We were heading to the beach for the day."

So that explained the tank top, shorts, and shoe choice.

"Would you like me to carry you? We've still got a lot of ground to cover." He indicated the looming remains of the parking lot with a nudge of his chin.

"Nope. I'm fine." She shuffled her feet. "Let's just move faster."

"Sorry to ruin your beach plans." He wondered who the friend was and if it was a he or she, but that was none of his business.

"I'm glad you called," she said. "Seriously. It meant a lot."

He arched a brow. "It did?"

"Yes. That you trusted me to help."

Right. Help. As she burned her own feet.

This was ridiculous.

He reached over and swooped her up in his arms.

She wriggled. "What are you doing?"

"Saving your feet."

"I'm fine."

"Stop being so stubborn and enjoy the ride." He winked.

She rolled her eyes.

He chuckled. "I'm just messing with you."

"So Mr. Serious has a sense of humor after all."

"So that's how you see me? Mr. Serious?" *Ouch.*

She finally relaxed into his hold as they covered the remaining stretch of parking lot. "Well, yeah."

Good to know.

"I mean, it's not a bad thing. We're just different," she said.

Different as could be, and yet there was something about her. Like a magnet pulling another to it or repelling it. He still hadn't figured out which of the two they were, but he suspected the former, which confused him to no end.

"Lexi here?" she asked, something he didn't understand lingering in her eyes. She liked Lexi, liked everyone, but there was *something* there. No way was she jealous of Lexi. That would mean . . . Now he was just being foolish.

"Yep," he said. "Up on the bridge. I'll take you to the refugees." He set her to her feet on the boat, missing the feel of her in his arms, the sweet scent of coconut tickling his nose.

"Thanks for saving my feet."

"You're welcome."

They entered the hold where the refugees were being held, and Tanner rushed for them.

A Customs agent blocked her path.

Declan showed his ID. "She's with me. She's a crisis counselor."

The Customs official nodded and stepped aside. "Great. We can definitely use her. They're terrified."

Declan took in their dazed and frightened expressions. Their hair matted, their clothes tattered. What had they been forced to endure? "I don't blame them." He prayed God would work through Tanner to provide some comfort to the poor souls so far from their homeland, just looking for a better way of life.

He needed to call Parker. Needed another sweep. They had to catch whoever was responsible not only for the murders, but for this atrocity, and he had a strong suspicion the captain knew far more than what he claimed.

17

Parker and Avery snapped several pictures of Skylar's photograph from Charm City Investigation, their headquarters for the case, and climbed back into the car for the trek back to Megan Kent's. Unfortunately, no one else had been at CCI while they were at Megan's, so they'd had to lose time making the ride in, but at least Megan had promised to talk.

A few minutes into the drive, Parker's phone rang. He clicked it on. "Mitchell?"

"Hey, Park," Declan said, the sound of squawking seagulls in the background.

"Where are you?"

"Down at the port. Terminal Six."

"Okay. Why?"

"I've got a merchant vessel with a dead first mate, a dead federal agent, and two dozen smuggled refugees in the cargo hold. The CGIS is finishing up their sweep. When they are done, I'd really love to have you do a second one, just to be extra thorough."

"Okay. Call me when they're done. Avery and I are on our way to an important stop in Skylar's case."

"Will do. Thanks."

"Thanks for going to Megan's with me," Avery said as Parker disconnected the call.

"This is important, and like Declan said, CGIS isn't finished yet."

"After we're done at Megan's, you can drop me back at CCI and I'll head to Sebastian's location."

"Even if she can tell us where he is, I don't want you going without me."

"What? We're finally making progress on finding Skylar, or at least in finding Sebastian."

"I understand, but it's not safe." He had a very bad feeling about Sebastian Chadwyck. "I know you can hold your own, but if he's the one who took that picture, there's something dark inside of him."

This time, with the photos on Avery's phone, Megan actually allowed them inside. She led them the few steps from the front door to the living room.

A brown leather sectional took up the majority of the floor space, and a flat-screen TV filled much of one wall, but it was the images of death surrounding them that jarred the breath from Parker's lungs. Images of women, the majority of them Megan, posed in a variety of ways, but all appearing postmortem, alongside cemetery markers, dead flowers, and rotting leaves.

"Sebastian has a gift for finding the beauty in death," Megan said.

"Is that what this was?" Avery asked, holding up her cell with the first image of Skylar's portrait on the screen.

Megan stared at it, bewildered, hot angry tears tumbling down her freckled cheeks. "I can't believe he actually did it."

"Killed her?" Avery said, anger and concern heightening her tone.

Megan looked up in shocked confusion. "Killed her? What are you talking about?"

"What were *you* talking about? What can't you believe he did?"

"*Photographed* her. Why on earth would you think Sebastian killed Skylar Pierce?"

"Because Skylar has been missing since before the showing, and as far as we can tell the last person to see her was Sebastian. Not to mention in that photograph she looks like she's already dead."

"Duh," Megan said. "That's kind of the point. He must have gotten a slot in the Black Dahlia display after all. I can't believe he didn't tell me." She looked at the portrait image, squinting. "I know why he didn't tell me. Because it was of *her*."

"Can I show you what we're concerned about in the portrait?" Parker asked.

She nodded.

Avery handed him her phone, and he zoomed in on the details that led to their concern that Skylar was already dead when the portrait was taken.

Megan's coloring paled, and she raked a hand through her mousy brown hair. "That's why he was acting so strange."

"Sebastian was acting strange?"

Megan nodded.

"When was this?" Avery asked.

"Yesterday."

"When you say he was acting strange . . . ?" Parker nudged.

"He was buzzed but edgy. Said he had to take off. When I pressed where, he said he was going to scout some locations, but he had this weird energy about him. Way more restless than usual, and for Sebastian that's really saying something. I thought it was just because he was upset he wasn't in the show, but obviously he was."

"Not legitimately." Avery explained the swap.

"Oh." Megan bit her bottom lip. "Maybe *that* explains his edginess."

"Did he give any indication of what area he was planning to scout locations in?" Avery pressed, praying for an answer, a lead, any lead to where they could find Sebastian.

Megan shook her head. "No. He didn't say."

"And you didn't ask?" Avery pressed.

"No. I knew better. Sebastian is very proprietorial when it comes to his work. I admire it, and completely left him to it, except when it came to *her*."

Avery's eyes narrowed. "Her? You mean Skylar?"

Megan's jaw tightened. Clearly there was no love lost between Megan and Skylar. Avery had hit a tender spot. Time to prod.

"How'd Sebastian meet Skylar?" Parker asked.

Megan's dry, cracked, pale pink lips thinned. "He saw Skylar around. For some reason he just became obsessed with photographing her. But he's a peon in the art scene. Don't get me wrong. He's brilliant, but there's a pecking order and he's on the bottom of it, so naturally, a girl like her—she wouldn't give him the time of day."

"That must have made Sebastian frustrated, angry?"

"Angry? Ha! It only enthralled him more. The elusive model he had to win over. I can't believe she finally let him shoot her." Megan glanced back at the image, her brown eyes narrowing. "You really think she was dead? I mean for real?"

"We fear so," Parker said.

"Sebastian may have a penchant for morbid photos or an obsession with the beauty of death, as he says, but he wouldn't kill anybody."

"Just photograph her after she's dead?" Parker asked.

Megan didn't respond.

"I'll take that as a yes," he said.

"I didn't say that."

"You didn't say otherwise."

"I don't know, but I do know he'd never kill anyone."

"Not even if he were obsessed? Not even if she ignored him one too many times?"

Megan continued gnawing on her bottom lip, which explained the chapping. After an uncomfortable moment of silence, she said, "I'm done talking."

Parker exhaled. "If only it were that easy."

She frowned. "I'm not talking anymore about Sebastian."

"That's fine. We need to talk about you," Avery said.

Megan frowned. "Me?"

"Yeah. We're going to need you to explain why your fingerprints were in Skylar Pierce's trailer."

Megan's eyes widened. "Wh . . . wh . . . what?"

"We found your fingerprints in the trailer. Based on our chat here, you two clearly weren't friends, so why were you in her place?" Avery asked.

Megan fixated on a loose button on her black short-sleeve blouse, twirling it between her black painted nails.

"Megan, we need an answer," Parker said.

Megan swallowed, lowered her hands to her side, and exhaled. "After Sebastian took off . . ."

"You mean yesterday?" he asked, needing there to be no confusion.

Megan nodded. "Yes. Like I said, Sebastian was so buzzed, so antsy, something in my heart said he was going to visit *her* again."

"And did he?" Parker probed at the venom in Megan's voice. Had she visited Skylar instead? Taken out the competition?

"No." Megan shook her head. "But I didn't know that. I tried following him, keeping up with him, but it's impossible when he's on his bike. He just weaves around traffic."

"Bike?" Parker asked.

Megan shook her head. "Motorcycle."

"What kind?" Avery asked.

"Blue."

"Sports bike or a Harley style?" Parker tried.

"Sports bike." Megan pulled a four-by-six photograph off the mantel and handed it to Parker.

Parker glanced at the Ninja. Now that they knew what Sebastian was driving, Declan or Griffin could put out an APB.

"So you went to Skylar's place, guessing that's where Sebastian would be?" Avery surmised.

Megan gnawed on her bottom lip. "Yeah."

Avery arched a brow. "How'd you know where Skylar lived?"

Megan's cheeks flushed. With embarrassment or anger, Parker wasn't sure.

Her shoulders dropped. "Because I'd followed him there before."

"To Skylar's?" Parker asked, just to be 100 percent clear.

"Yes."

"When you say *before*? When do you mean?"

"When Sebastian went to her trailer last week to ask if she'd pose for him. He'd brought his portfolio, hoping if she saw his talent she'd change her mind, but she wouldn't give him the time of day, wouldn't even let him inside. She was only interested in landing the top guys. Poor Sebastian was heartbroken. I waited until he left and then banged on her door. When she opened it, I barged in and told her to stay away from Sebastian."

"And then?" Avery asked.

"Then she told me she had no intention of posing for an amateur."

18

Avery hardly felt sorry for Sebastian Chadwyck. "Poor" Sebastian had most likely photographed her friend dead—may have even killed her to do so, since she'd made it clear she had no intention of posing for him.

"It had to make you happy that Skylar refused to work with him," Parker said.

"I've seen plenty of girls like her," Megan said. "Contrary to what she said, you put a photographer and a model like *her* together and stuff happens."

"'Stuff' happened with Sebastian and other models?" Avery asked, picking up on the resentment in Megan's tone.

"I don't want to talk about it."

It didn't matter. Their focus was on Skylar, and she apparently hadn't been the least bit interested in Sebastian.

"When you went back to Skylar's—last night—was she there?"

"No."

"What time was it?"

"Maybe eight thirty."

So before she arrived and got bowled over.

"How'd you get in?" Parker asked.

There'd been no sign of a break-in when they arrived.

"I found a key under—"

"The duck," Avery finished before Megan could. She'd told Skylar that was an awful idea. Maybe that's how the intruder who'd bowled Avery over had gotten in as well. Why hadn't she thought of that sooner?

Because it'd been almost a decade since she'd last used the key beneath that duck. Since Sky first started living there on her own. "So you broke in?" Avery prompted. "And?"

"And I went in, but no one was there," Megan said. "The girl was a slob. It looked just like the first time I'd been there—stuff still flung all over the place—but I do know Sebastian was there at some point after that first visit."

Now they were getting someplace. "How?" Avery asked.

"I found this." Megan strode to the coatrack by the front door and grabbed a lightweight gray-and-red-plaid scarf—the kind one wore as an accessory rather than for warmth. "It's Sebastian's favorite. I found it there in her living room in a pile of clothes. He had to have left it there after that first visit, because he wasn't wearing it last night." Megan linked her arms across her chest. "Skylar obviously changed her mind about letting Sebastian in the next time he visited her."

"Maybe she did. Might they have done the photo shoot at Skylar's place?"

"No . . . I can't imagine Sebastian doing that. He insisted on doing those sorts of portraits at his studio, so he had more control."

"Studio?" Avery said, hopeful for a new lead.

"He recently set up a new one at an old abandoned building he found. He showed it to me soon after he discovered it, all excited about how he was going to transform one of the rooms into his studio. A week or so later he said the place was working great, that he was happy with the lighting, but I've never gone back. The place gives me the creeps."

Man, it had to be bad if she—who lived surrounded by disturbing photographs and with a guy obsessed with "the beauty of death"—got creeped out by it. "Where's the building?"

She didn't answer.

"Megan, there are already charges that could be leveled against you. You really want to hold out on us?"

Megan exhaled. "It's down in Fort Howard."

"The abandoned military bunkers?"

"No. The old VA hospital that shut down a decade ago."

"Oh, right. I forgot that was there."

"Most people have, which makes it perfect for Sebastian—he got a studio rent free."

"What floor is the studio on?"

"Don't know. I didn't let him show me the actual room." She shuddered. "Too creepy."

"Can you think of anything else?"

"No . . . but just for the record, I wasn't the only one there last night," Megan quickly said.

"Last night? At Skylar's?"

Megan nodded. "While I was in there this guy and chick came in, so I hid in the shower. They were looking for something. Saying 'Where'd she stash it?'"

Okay . . . "Did they find what they were looking for?" Avery asked.

"No, but not for lack of effort, and they certainly came prepared."

Avery's gaze narrowed. "What do you mean *prepared*?"

"I peeked around the shower curtain from where I was hiding and they were both dressed in black, wearing gloves, carrying flashlights even though it wasn't fully dark out yet, but it was dim enough in the trailer I suppose. Anyway, they were hurrying like they were worried Skylar might return any moment."

"So they didn't know she was missing?"

"Nuh-uh. Anyway, the dude said she'd figure out he wasn't going to show soon. Like they'd texted or called her, telling her to meet up with him someplace just to get her out of the house so they could sneak in."

"What else did they say?"

"The girl was ticked. Sounded like her guy had hooked up with Skylar and now Skylar had something on him."

"How old were they?"

"Early twenties. College age. Richies."

Avery would have asked how Megan knew they were rich college kids, but the type wasn't hard to spot.

"Anything you can tell us about them? Hair color? Height? Build? Did they mention each other's names?" Parker asked.

"The chick was little. One of those super-thin types. Long blond hair pulled into a low ponytail beneath her black ski cap. I never saw her full face, but she was pretty."

"And the guy?"

"Tall, lean. I caught a glimpse of his face in her flashlight. Handsome, if you like the yuppie type."

They had worn gloves, which meant it was unlikely there was any fingerprint evidence—and therefore would be virtually impossible to identify. And the guy didn't have the right build for whoever had bowled her over. Man, Sky's really had been a revolving door that night.

"Any chance you saw their car?" she asked.

"Yeah. When they were in the kitchen, I got out of the bathroom and snuck out the bedroom window. They were parked right underneath it. It was one of those cutesy cars."

Parker arched his brows.

"Kind of like a bug, but different."

"A Fiat?" Avery asked.

"Yeah, I think that was it."

Avery looked at Parker. A Fiat had been following Gary, with a blonde driving with her hair pulled back in a long ponytail. What did Skylar have on them? "Did they find what they were looking for?" Avery asked.

Megan shook her head. "No, and they were super frustrated. The chick kept nagging under her breath at the dude that this was all his fault."

"But she never said what? I mean what Skylar had on him?"

"No."

"Thanks, Megan. That was really helpful. If you think of anything else or if Sebastian comes home, please call us or have him give us a call. I just want to find my friend," Avery said, handing her one of her business cards.

Megan took it and nodded before shutting the door.

"What do you think Skylar had on the *dude*?" Avery asked, using Megan's word.

"I don't know. Something worth money?"

If Skylar was working another con—though Avery prayed she'd left that all behind, like she claimed—it would definitely involve money.

"Why do you think Megan assumed they were rich college kids? I get assuming that being early twenties it's likely you could be in college, but rich?"

Avery settled back in her seat. "It's really not that hard to tell, especially when you come from where I do. You learn to spot people of different classes quite easily. I'm guessing Megan grew up someplace similar to me and Sky."

She half expected Parker to take that as a cue to inquire

further about her past, but he didn't. Maybe he wasn't ever going to ask.

"Any chance they were college kids who were high and just goofing around?" Parker tossed out another option. "Illegally and not at all funny, of course. I'm just saying college kids have been known to do stupid things when they're high."

"Doubt you're high if you put enough thought into wearing gloves."

"Ah. True."

The blonde must have come back. There'd been no guy in the car with her when she'd been tailing Gary. Perhaps she'd dropped her male companion off and returned for one more look, finding them at Skylar's instead. Then, seeing Gary tearing out of the parking lot, she'd followed in pursuit just as they had. At least until they'd spotted her. Assuming for certain it was the same blonde, but what were the chances? And, if so, why the interest in Gary? Avery shifted, ready to hit the next spot.

"So you'll drop me off at my car on your way to the harbor? I can head for the abandoned hospital and keep you posted."

He glanced over at her with a smile. "Yeah, about that—I'm thinking no."

She rolled her eyes. "Don't tell me you're going to go all overprotective again? I can hold my own. We've been over this."

"I know you can hold your own, but they teach you in self-defense classes not to put yourself in dangerous situations to begin with, right?"

She remained silent. She'd taken more than enough self-defense classes to know he was right.

"It's unsafe. Come work the ship with me. We'll get it done quicker together, and then we'll head to the hospital. I promise I'll work as fast as I can while still doing the job right."

"It could be dark by the time you're done. Even if you're 'fast.'"

"Really? Air quotes?"

"We both know your version of *fast* and mine aren't the same."

"So I'm thorough at my job."

"And I totally admire your level of dedication, but I want to find Skylar, and this is a huge lead."

"Which we will follow together."

She grunted and shifted in her seat.

"Did you seriously just grunt at me?"

"Yes. You're that vexing."

He chuckled.

"That wasn't a compliment."

"Agree to disagree." He winked.

"You're impossible."

"And you're stuck with me."

That hit her hard. How she wished that were true, but after Skylar was found they'd go back to their separate ways. "What if I ask Griffin to go with me?" she said, quickly trying to distract herself from the reality of the situation.

"Declan put Griffin to work on the safe-deposit-box angle with Kate, and before you go there, Declan's on the ship. Face it, beautiful, you're stuck with me."

She fought a smile, trying to look fierce. "Flattery only irritates me more."

He didn't bother to squelch his smile. "I know."

19

Terminal Six was a flurry of activity. Immigration, the Coast Guard, and Customs officials were all present and all clamoring for control of the situation.

"Super," Parker said under his breath as he climbed from his car and grabbed his kit. This situation was precisely why he'd chosen to become a freelance crime-scene investigator. He got to choose whom he worked for and when.

Avery walked down the pier by his side, the humid harbor air and crabby scent bringing with it memories of his hometown, Chesapeake Harbor, though his harbor was a much cleaner inlet off the Chesapeake Bay, the water far fresher and the scent less pungent. It'd been a few weeks, more like a month, since he'd seen his folks. He needed to make a point to get down for Sunday dinner next week.

They approached the merchant ship, and Parker frowned as he gazed up at the Malaysian flag flapping in the wind.

"What?" Avery asked beside him. The past six months without her had been beyond miserable. He prayed this case or— he glanced up at the merchant ship they were about to enter standing more than six stories over them—*cases* wouldn't just be a one-time occurrence. He prayed Avery was back in his life for good.

"Malaysia," he finally said, tracking back to his initial thought and Avery's question.

"What about it?" she asked. "Why the frown?"

"Isn't Malaysia where Kate said the possible photograph of Luke was taken? I'm pretty sure Griffin said Malaysia when he'd relayed the information."

Avery slipped her wind-blown blond hair into a black hairband. "Kate asked me to take a look at the photograph when I had a chance."

"Did she? I suppose that's not surprising. You are the photography expert. Probably wants you to confirm it hasn't been photoshopped."

Avery shifted her ponytail, pulling it to the side and flipping it over her right shoulder, exposing her supple neck that he wished to kiss his way up. . . .

"I'm hesitant to look," she said.

He snapped himself out of it. Sooner or later he was going to have to tell Avery how he felt, but how did he move forward when he still had one foot in the past? "You're hesitant to look because it might not be Luke in the photograph?"

"Yeah. Because I might not be able to give her the answer she so desperately desires. I don't want to be the person who dashes her hopes."

He prayed she didn't dash his. That is, if he ever got the nerve to man up and tell her. He just had to figure things out first. He'd been praying, and God kept answering *Avery*, but what about Jenna's memory? How could he respect and preserve Jenna's memory and still have a future? He cared so deeply for Avery. Beyond cared, but . . .

Waves pounded harder against the ship the closer they drew to the water's edge, the spray of the bay lashing their faces as recreational boats bounced out in the harbor. He was thankful for the jolt back to where his present focus needed to be—the ship before them.

Walking up the *Hiram*'s gangplank, they then proceeded up the series of steep, narrow ladders to the bridge, where Declan said he and Lexi would be awaiting them.

Declan caught sight of them as they entered and moved straight for them. "Thanks for coming, man."

Parker set his kit at his booted feet. "Anytime. You know that." He lifted his chin in greeting to Lexi, and she returned the gesture, switching up to a smile for Avery.

"Appreciate you coming too, Avery," Declan said.

She slipped her hands into her pockets. "Always happy to help when I can."

Another man—six-foot-two, one-hundred-and-seventy-five pounds, with cropped hair—joined them. Parker bet coast guard.

"Guys, this is Noah Rowley with CGIS," Declan said.

Parker extended a hand. "Pleasure. Parker Mitchell." He turned to Avery. "This is Avery Tate. My crime-scene photographer." And friend and . . .

He exhaled, cutting off that thought. She wasn't anything more, and yet she was *everything*.

"Nice to meet you, ma'am." Noah tipped his coast guard cap.

"Tate will be fine," she said, preferring to use her last name when working.

Noah smiled. "Tate it is." He looked back to Parker. "I hear you're quite the genius when it comes to crime-scene investigation."

"I just do my job."

"So do my boys. We've finished with the bridge."

"I'd love to hear what they've found."

Noah gestured toward the crime scene. "Let me show you." He went through each step, explaining what his team had processed thus far—and it was all wrong. Not the Coast Guard team's work, but the crime scene itself.

"It's been staged," Parker said.

Noah placed his arms behind his back, standing at parade rest. "That was our estimation as well."

"The question is why?" Parker knelt down by Agent Steven Burke's body, examining it in greater detail. Who was Steven Burke, and what was a federal agent doing on a Malaysian merchant ship?

It took them several hours to fully process the crime scene, including Steven Burke's berth upon Declan and Lexi's request, but Parker and Avery's work was finally complete. At least what could be done on the ship. He would do further work in the lab later, but his priority was to Avery and Skylar's case.

Rowley's men offered to handle the tedious task of fingerprinting the rest of the crew. It would take multiple man-hours to finish, and Avery had been patient to hold off on such a big lead in Skylar's case.

Before leaving, though, he did a quick overview with Declan, Lexi, Avery, and Rowley to go over his preliminary findings.

"So?" Declan said, always so impatient when it came to investigations.

"There is no way the shootings happened as the captain claimed. The trajectories don't fit his explanation of where everyone was standing—Burke and the first mate were shot from behind—and there is no gunshot residue on Burke's hands. Also the captain's wound was not caused by slipping and hitting his head—there is no blood or tissue residue on the control panel, and the wound itself doesn't fit. I am guessing he shot the bridge gun to set up his story, and someone else hit him over the head to make him appear the victim. And . . . I believe both men were shot by that other person."

"Any idea who the other person is?" Lexi asked.

"I've got so many fingerprints that it's going to take days to work through them all." He turned to Rowley. "Have your men started fingerprinting the crew?"

"Yes, it shouldn't take long—I have several men on it."

"Excellent. I'd love a copy of your report, so I can compare it to mine."

Rowley nodded. "Of course, and I'd like a copy of your results as well. Just in case you found anything my boys missed."

Parker nodded. He liked Rowley, or "Row" as his men referred to him. It wasn't often he got to work with someone who excelled at his job and cooperated so earnestly on top of it.

"One more thing," Parker said before leaving. "Has your team fingerprinted the refugees?"

"Why would we?" one of Rowley's nearby men responded. "I doubt any of them would be in the database."

"Parker's right," Rowley said. "*Everybody* on board needs to be fingerprinted."

The man nodded, his face flushed with the reprimand.

"It might be a good idea to have them take a photograph of each refugee, and note their name," Parker said. "Once Immigration takes them, you'll quickly lose access. Avery and I would stay and do it, but we have another case we're working, and we've got a major lead waiting."

"Understood." Rowley nodded. "We'll finish up here." Parker assumed they would have regardless, but it never hurt to communicate expectations. Fortunately, everyone involved in the investigation was playing nice.

"Just a quick question," Rowley said as Parker stood to leave.

"Sure."

"I agree everybody on board needs to be fingerprinted, but you seem to be focused on the refugees. Any particular reason why?"

"For exactly the same reason your guy didn't think that they were worth fingerprinting. They are off the grid. Those are often the ones you have to worry about most."

20

After Parker and Avery departed, Declan and Lexi made their way down to the mess hall, where the refugees had been moved. They were seated around the long, narrow tables where the crew took their meals.

Tanner had seen the refugees were fed and given much-needed water. Declan admired the heck out of her. Her tenacity and compassion were both fierce, and he'd gotten to witness them firsthand today.

"Though it is likely the shooter is a crew member, as Parker said, the chance exists that the unknown suspect is one of these refugees," Declan said under his breath to Lexi, but clearly not quietly enough.

"Unknown suspect?" Tanner said, popping up beside him. "I'm glad you two came down. I may have some information you'll find helpful."

Declan arched a brow. "Oh?" What was coming now?

"As you know I've been talking with everyone . . ."

He scanned the refugees' faces. While they didn't look good, by any means, they looked far better since Tanner had been with them. "How are they doing?"

"They're terrified. It's a legal and logistical nightmare with all the agencies being pulled in, but that's an entirely separate situation. What I thought you might like to hear is what Hana had to say." She pointed to the elderly lady huddled at the front table, a blanket across her feeble shoulders. Poor thing was skin and bones. "So far she's been the only one willing to really talk to me."

"You speak Malay?" he asked. The woman kept surprising and impressing him.

Tanner nodded. "I speak a number of languages. It's critical for the work I do—or did—overseas. You can't help people if you can't sit down and talk with them."

He turned his gaze to the lady Tanner pointed out. "So what did Hana have to say?"

"That she's thankful the 'evil man' is gone."

"What evil man?" he asked, his attention captured.

"She said he was a man who came on the boat with them. Supposedly one of them . . ."

Lexi's eyes narrowed. "Supposedly?"

"Hana said he was dressed like them, but he wasn't one of them."

"Meaning?"

"He wasn't Malaysian. He was Indonesian."

"All right," Lexi said. "Can she describe this man?"

"Black hair, dark eyes, a thin moustache and beard, which he stroked along his chin frequently."

"Thin beard? Like a goatee?" Declan pulled out his pad and pen and drew a rough sketch of a man with a goatee, showed it to the woman, and she nodded. "Great. What would she estimate his height and weight?"

Tanner asked and Hana replied, then Tanner relayed her answer. "He was about the size of that man."

Declan followed Tanner's outstretched hand to a man in his

thirties seated at the table across from theirs. "So five-sixish—and weight?"

"Hana says about the same as him."

"One hundred and fifty pounds," Declan said, studying the man, "depending on build, of course."

"Anything else unique about him that she can think of?" Lexi inquired.

"She mentioned that he always wore a black knit hat pulled to his ears and never interacted with or responded to the others. Just turned away if they tried to converse with him."

"Like he didn't speak their language or like he didn't want to talk?" Lexi asked.

"Both."

"If we got a sketch artist down here, would Hana be willing to describe the man? And would you be willing to translate?" Declan asked.

"Yes on my end." Tanner asked Hana and got the same response.

"Great," Declan said. "I'll call it in. My guess is it'll take the sketch artist under an hour to arrive. Please thank Hana for us."

Tanner relayed their thanks, and Hana nodded with a smile.

He smiled back, feeling horrible for having to put the woman through any more distress, but the question needed to be asked and, he prayed, answered.

"Is she able to tell us anything about the man in question's habits? Where he slept? For how long? Any strange behavior?" Sometimes the smallest or seemingly most inconsequential clue could be exactly what they needed to catch the suspect.

"She says at the start he was treated like one of the refugees, but after being on board for a day, things changed."

"Changed how?" Lexi asked.

Rowley entered with two of his men, both carrying finger-printing kits.

Tanner's eyes widened as a terrified murmur riffled through the room. "What's going on?"

"These men are going to fingerprint the refugees," Lexi said calmly.

"Why? They aren't criminals."

"That we know of," Rowley said. "That's the point. We don't know anything about them, other than that the ship's paper-work says all cargo belongs to Max Stallings."

"Max Stallings?" Declan said, adrenaline pumping through him. He looked to Lexi and saw the same fire in her eyes.

The Bureau had long suspected Max of bringing in illegal immigrants, but they'd never been able to catch him in the act—until now.

"You actually think one of these terrified people killed those men?" Tanner said, outraged.

"Keep your voice down," Declan said, his gaze scanning the room. "Your tone is scaring them."

"These *men* are what's scaring them."

"Once Immigration takes over, we'll lose track of them. We need to fingerprint and photograph each one so we have a record of them. That's all."

"Fine." Tanner tried calming the refugees as Rowley's men did their job—fingerprinting and photographing each one. She was speaking with them in soothing tones, but he had no idea what she was telling them.

Declan felt horrible about the turmoil they were causing, but they were just doing their job. He prayed Tanner would explain that to the refugees—and that she understood as well. What she thought of him was becoming more and more important, and yet he feared none of it was good.

21

arker pulled to a stop at the end of North Point Road. The area had played a significant role during the War of 1812, and over the years it came to be known as Fort Howard and served a number of uses, with a variety of buildings being built up and torn down. The only sign of the fort's early history still evident were two concrete coast batteries erected in 1902 in commemoration of the fort's wartime history. Though now both were crumbling shells of their former glory.

The Veterans Administration acquired the title in 1940 and built a five-story, three-hundred-and-seventy-seven-bed hospital, which remained in operation until 2002, when its doors were eventually and dishearteningly, to the community and the veterans it served, closed.

Fort Howard was across the Patapsco River from Sparrow's Point, and the sound of a train rumbling over the railroad tracks echoed on the wind across the dark water.

As Parker and Avery walked the grounds, the dusk shifted to night, and the wind shifted to a calm, eerily silent breath. The only sound was the water lapping against the concrete base of the small red-and-white lighthouse thirty or so feet offshore.

The hospital sat dark, the grounds overgrown, a meadow where a basketball court had once been, the entire area a hub for illegal urban exploration and ghost hunters who believed the empty hospital halls were haunted by spirits.

It took a little time to find an entrance that wasn't boarded up, but they did and without too much struggle were inside within half an hour of their arrival.

A rank odor assaulted Avery's senses as they moved down the hall littered with trash and old medical equipment. "Dare I ask what that smell is?"

"I think we're better off not knowing. Doesn't smell like decomposition to me."

They passed a number of red gurneys and a defibrillator cart, before the hall ended and they turned right, taking the only available passage past an abandoned nurse's station, dusty filing trays and empty bulletin boards still littering the space.

Examining each room they passed, their flashlights bounced off dark walls, desk chairs, and patient beds.

They stepped in the last room, and Avery screamed at a pair of legs lying feet up in an oversized laundry cart in the corner of the room.

"It's okay," Parker said, stepping closer. "They're prosthetic legs."

"Oh." Her pulse slowly stopped racing.

"Shall we continue?" he asked and she nodded, following him up a flight of stairs, past graffiti-covered walls and empty beer bottles, where they exited onto the second floor at the end of the hall. A different odor wafted down this corridor. One of death.

"This place gives me the creeps." That was usually something she'd keep to herself, but she trusted Parker enough to be open about the heebie-jeebies tickling the nape of her neck.

"Hey," Parker said, placing his hand on her arm and gesturing to the closed door with a deadbolt lock installed on it.

"That's odd."

"Looks recent," Parker said, moving to bust it open with his Maglite.

"Hold on." Avery stepped forward, pulling a small case from her bag. "Allow me." She picked the lock and swung it open.

"Not even going to ask how you know how to do that," Parker said.

Avery smiled. "Best you don't."

Parker lifted his flashlight, illuminating the room . . . and they both stilled. Before them was the staging from Skylar's photograph. A white sheet draped over a sofa with burgundy velvet pillows, which Avery recognized as the ones Skylar kept on her bed.

That's why Sebastian had been in Skylar's place. He'd been taking props for his photograph. What else had he *taken*?

Parker spotted a small generator and turned it on. Lights flashed on, revealing boarded-up windows with blackout curtains hanging over the plywood for extra concealment.

Photographs of Skylar hung on the walls—clearly taken when she wasn't aware she was being photographed—and they were surrounded by hand sketches of her in various poses, all of which were morbid or at the very least disturbing in nature. Whoever had drawn them had taken great care in getting all of Skylar's features just right. He'd been studying her. Fantasizing about her. Planning the perfect portrait.

A sound, soft and rhythmic, caught Avery's attention.

She spun around, facing the door. Parker quickly followed. Both still and listening.

Something or someone was shuffling down the hall, the noise growing louder, closer. And then a new sound joined the shuffling.

She looked at Parker. *Was that . . . ?*

Humming.

Parker pulled his gun and positioned Avery behind him.

The noise shifted, moving away from them, and from what Avery could tell toward the stairwell.

What if it was Sebastian? What if he'd detected their presence and was leaving? The one person who Avery believed held the key to Skylar's disappearance.

She looked to Parker and he nodded. "Stay right behind me."

They stepped into the hall, Avery glancing up and down. It was dark compared to the lit room they'd just exited. It was going to take a moment for her eyes to adjust, but they didn't dare turn on the flashlight for fear of scaring Sebastian or whomever it was away.

They moved quietly down the corridor, the humming growing louder again. They were headed in the right direction, getting closer.

Avery's heart thudded with a mix of trepidation and anticipation, her chest squeezing so tight she could barely catch a decent breath.

Parker's arm swung out, landing on her stomach and pressing her up against the wall. The sound was so close it was almost on top of them. Parker held at the corner of the wall and at just the right moment swung around to the intersecting hallway, aiming his gun at a very startled man's center mass.

"Wh . . . who's there?" The man squinted. "Lizzy? Is that you?" an elderly voice quivered.

Parker indicated for her to turn on the flashlight.

The elderly man shielded his eyes from the light. Clearly he was used to the dimness of the building. His face was scruffy and unshaven, his clothes a size too big.

"Who are you?" Parker asked.

"Edward."

"What are you doing here, Edward?"

"I live here. Have since '69."

"They closed this place down more than a decade ago."

"No. No!" Edward shook his head, running a shaky hand through his thinning gray hair standing nearly on end. "Lizzy told me to wait for her, that she'd be right back after her surgery."

Oh. "Is Lizzy your wife?"

"Yes." His countenance brightened. "Have you seen her? She's beautiful as a sweet summer day."

Avery's heart broke for the poor man. "No. I'm sorry, I haven't."

"Oh." Anguish blanketed the brief glimpse of joy that had surfaced on his dirt-smudged face. "That's okay. I'm sure she'll be along soon enough."

Avery's gaze settled on the McDonald's bag clutched in his hand, the fresh scent of warm fries wafting through the otherwise stale air.

"Where'd you get that?" she asked.

He clutched the white paper bag to his chest. "It's mine."

"Of course. I'm not trying to take it. I was just wondering . . . where I could get some of my own."

"Oh. Sebastian brings it. I keep an eye on the place and he brings me stuff."

Her muscles tightened. So Sebastian had recently been in the building, maybe still was.

"Do you know where Sebastian is now?" She tried to keep the adrenaline coursing through her system from her voice, tried to keep her tone even when she felt anything but centered.

"In his storage room," Edward said, opening the bag and pulling out a fry, then popping it in his mouth.

"Where he takes the pictures?" They'd just been in there. If he'd come and seen the light on, surely he would have left. They would have already lost him.

"No. That's his studio." Edward rolled his eyes, rocking back on his heels. "His storage room is in the basement."

"Could you show us?" Parker asked.

"I don't see why not. Sebastian likes pretty girls."

"I bet he does," Parker whispered under his breath as they headed for the basement.

22

Rowley's men finished fingerprinting everyone and exited the chow hall, leaving Declan and Lexi alone with Tanner and the frightened refugees.

Lexi hung back as Declan approached Tanner. Why, he wasn't sure. The two got along just fine, but both seemed hesitant about encroaching on the other's territory. Not that he was either's *territory*. He didn't get women. Taking a deep breath, he stepped to Tanner's side. She was busy helping the refugees wash the black ink off their hands with a handful of wet dishrags she'd procured from the kitchen.

"Can you finish talking with Hana about the evil man?" he asked.

She finished wringing out a washcloth and then looked up at him like he was nuts. "Seriously? I'd just convinced them that you were here to help, and then you guys treat them like criminals."

"We're just doing our jobs. I'm sorry if you don't understand all that entails, but we have a murderer on the loose and the re-mote possibility exists that he or she may be in this very room."

"Hana said he left."

"She said an 'evil' man left, but how do we know for certain he's the killer? And if he is, where is he hiding? If you could please ask Hana about the man, it may just help us catch a killer."

Tanner's heart was full of compassion, but she had to know the murderer's presence onboard was a very real possibility—whether hiding among the crew, the refugees, or somewhere in the ship.

"When you put it that way . . ." she said, moving back to Hana to finish their conversation, picking up where they'd left off.

Hana spoke and Tanner interpreted. "Hana says the man started receiving special treatment rather quickly. Full meals, water, even better sleeping quarters."

"By who? Who gave him all this stuff?" Someone who knew he was different.

"Hana said a number of different crewmen came to bring him food and water, and then when he moved to different sleeping quarters she was thankful because he was away, but whenever the ship made port he came back into the hold with them. Whenever he was in there, he was antsy and twitchy."

"And today? Was he in the hold with them or in his berth?"

"He was in the hold with them, but someone let him out, and shortly after they heard gunshots. He returned not long after, grabbed his stuff, and left."

"His stuff?"

"She said he had a knapsack."

"When she says he left . . . ? What does she mean exactly? Left the hold? Left the ship?"

"Only that he left the hold in a hurry, and she hasn't seen him since."

Declan signaled Lexi. "We need to account for all the lifeboats and fast rafts."

"I'll go pull the ship records to find out how many boats they have and then ask Rowley to have his men do a count of how many there currently are."

"Smuggling ships also always keep a count of their 'cargo.'" He looked at Tanner. "I apologize for the horrific nickname."

Tanner nodded. "Thanks, but unfortunately, I've heard the term before."

"I'll see if we're missing any refugees as well," Lexi said.

"Thanks." Declan nodded, then turned back to Tanner. "And, thank you. Because of you and Hana we may have just figured out who our unknown suspect is. Now we just need to figure out *where* he is."

Avery and Parker followed Edward down the cement-block stairwell to the basement.

Avery's breath hitched as they opened the stairwell door— the metal hinges creaking something awful with the forced motion.

She prayed if Sebastian heard the noise he'd assume it was simply Edward.

They followed Edward through the furnace room, the hefty piece of equipment long unused, and past rusting machinery to a door at the far end marked *Biohazards* in big red letters painted on the once white, now faded yellow, peeling sign.

"This way," Edward said, opening the door. "In there." He gestured at the closed door up ahead on the left with light emanating underneath.

Please let it be Sebastian, and please let him have the answers we need.

Edward hung back.

Avery frowned. "Aren't you coming?"

"Sebastian doesn't like folks in his space. I keep an eye on his rooms, but I don't go in. 'Never go in,' he says."

"Okay. Why don't you wait here for us?" Parker said.

"Wait here?"

"Yes, please," Avery said. They were going to want to ask him more about Sebastian and what he'd seen taking place in the building.

"Wait here." Edward nodded.

She followed Parker to the door.

"Ready?" he said under his breath, gun drawn.

She nodded.

Parker opened the door, and her heart lurched.

23

Can you ask Hana if she has any idea where the man slept once he was moved?" Declan prayed she knew. If they were really lucky, maybe they'd find the man, if not perhaps something—*anything*—to help uncover his identity. Speaking of identity . . . where was that sketch artist?

"Hana says they put him in one of the crew's quarters."

"Can she show us which one?"

Please, Lord. They needed a break.

"Hana said she never saw the man go in a berth."

Declan struggled against asking Tanner to press Hana for more information, but what was the use? She either knew or—

Hana tugged Tanner's arm, speaking urgently.

After listening for a couple minutes, Tanner turned with a smile. "Hana says her grandson, Adam"—she pointed to a boy Declan estimated to be about eleven who was seated at the nearby dining table—"sneaks out of the hold at night to scrounge for food. Hana told him it was too dangerous, but he'd just wait and go after she fell asleep. She'd wake up and there'd be a chunk of bread in her pocket or a few crackers.

She said Adam saw the man in question come out of a berth one night to use the head. Adam hid, fearful of being seen, and waited until the man went back into his berth."

"Can Adam show us that berth?"

"Sure," Adam said from the table.

Surprised the boy spoke English, Declan smiled at him and then looked back to Tanner. "I owe you a big kiss. You may have just given us our suspect."

He followed as the boy sprinted down the narrow ship corridor to the room nearest the hold, which made perfect sense. If the man ever needed to rush back into the hold, he could do so in a matter of seconds.

What didn't make sense were the words that had just come out of his mouth. *"I owe you a big kiss"*? Had he seriously said that? Perhaps he'd fantasized about kissing Tanner a time or two—who was he kidding? *A lot*—but it made no sense, and if nothing else, he was a sensible man.

He ducked, stepping inside the berth as Adam darted back, no doubt to Tanner, where he felt safe.

Tanner.

Kissing Tanner.

Get your head in the game, man.

What on earth was going on with him?

The berth. Focus.

It was a small berth, as most were, consisting of a double bunk and metal wardrobe.

He'd have to ask Adam if he saw which crewmember shared the berth with the man.

Declan moved to the wardrobe, praying he'd find something inside, but there was zilch. Hana said their unknown suspect took his knapsack, but what about his roommate? Surely the man hadn't gotten a berth all to himself? Not in such tight quarters. Not with such a large crew. Not unless he was a man of great importance to someone high up.

Lexi ducked her head in. "Hey."

"Hey. We need to have another chat with the captain."

"That might need to wait," Lexi said, her tone holding an urgency Declan recognized immediately.

"What is it?"

"This ship is missing a fast raft, and one was reported floating adrift in the harbor about eight hours ago."

"You're kidding me?"

"No."

"That's a half hour before we arrived on site. Why are we just finding out about this now?"

"The couple who spotted the empty raft notified the harbor master. He had no idea it had any connection to this investigation until Rowley put out a call for any sighting of a fast raft matching the description of theirs. Based on the coordinates the sailboat couple gave, along with the time the call came in and the currents, it is Rowley's estimation that our suspect exited along Canton's shoreline. Most likely in the area between Holabird Avenue and Lazaretto Point."

"Let's send a team to canvass the area," Declan said. "Starting with the businesses in that particular section, though most are well past closed." They'd need great luck to locate anybody who witnessed their suspect come ashore.

"A big kiss?" Tanner took a minute to sit back and let the words sink in. Had they actually come out of Declan Grey's typically subdued mouth?

And had a tremble of delight really just ricocheted through her at the notion of a kiss from Declan?

What in the world was going on? It must be the case they were working. The thrill she felt whenever she was able to help people, the secret thrill she felt when danger was nipping at her heels.

She'd never sought it, but danger seemed to follow her, and she loved combating it. Combating evil through God's enabling. Maybe today with Declan and Lexi, through God's enabling, they'd get to bring another evil man to justice.

Avery rushed across the room to Skylar's red sweater fitted over a headless mannequin. It was the sweater she had bought Skylar for her birthday the year before last—one of her friend's favorites.

Avery stood there, disbelief and confusion swirling inside, trying to grasp why Skylar would have chosen to be photographed here. By *him*. It had to either have been against her will or, as Avery had feared for a while, Skylar had been murdered and then photographed.

What kind of sicko were they dealing with?

24

He watched them tear apart his storage room from the hidden shelter of the tunnels, but it didn't matter. Nothing else did. He'd found her—an angel clothed primarily in black, which was ironic because she actually deserved to wear white. She was perfect. Better than perfect.

The soft curve of her cheeks, the full ripeness of her lips, the creamy velvet skin along her supple throat—just aching for his hands to wrap around. To feel her pulse beneath his fingertips, but it was no good anymore.

Dead was so much better. Then he could mold them to his needs. Have them pliable, posable. *Like putty in my hands.*

He hadn't planned it that way. Hadn't intended that outcome for Skylar, but there was no turning back now. Not when he'd tasted euphoria. Not when he'd found his next subject: the lovely Avery Tate.

⟡

The room was a smorgasbord of evidence, almost overwhelmingly so. Skylar's sweater was just the start. Her jewelry. Her outfit from the portrait hung neatly in a wardrobe, shoes resting on the floorboard of it. Everything was preserved with a level of care that bordered on obsession. Avery found Sebastian's camera and, with gloved hands, began scrolling through the images. Her heart stopped the third image in. Skylar was lying limp against the chaise lounge sitting not two feet from Avery's leg. She glanced over at it, and tears beaded in her eyes.

Parker moved to her side, put his arm around her shoulders. "What is it, love?"

He took in the picture as she did. Skylar's head tilted back—bruising and ligature marks around her bare neck. She'd been strangled. Her eyes were open and lifeless, her fingertips bruised and cut. No doubt trying to fight her assailant.

Avery swallowed. Had it happened in this very room? Had Sebastian lured Skylar there and then pounced?

She clicked to the next image, but it was a video. Swallowing hard, terrified of what she might see, she clicked Play.

It was Sebastian in the upstairs studio, prepping Skylar's body for a photo session. Parker tightened his grip on her shoulder. Sebastian talked to Skylar as if she were alive, but she clearly wasn't. She was a rag doll in the beginning, and then her limbs stiffened before he'd finished—rigor mortis beginning to set in. When he had her "just right"—his words—he walked to the camera, his face bearing elation, and shut it off. Avery feared she'd get sick.

Disturbing. Vile. Perverted. It horrified her to have watched what her best friend had gone through, even though she'd clearly been dead at the time. She clicked to the next image and straight on through the photo shoot.

Parker engulfed her in his embrace when she put the camera down. "I'm so sorry."

She tried to fight back the tears, but she couldn't hold them in. They splashed down her cheeks, dripping off her chin and onto her hands, balled up in front of her.

Parker didn't say anything, just let her expend the sorrow crushing in on her. She was so thankful for this man, for his steady presence. For his care. Finally, knowing she needed to stop for them to get on with processing the room, she stepped back and swiped her face, trying to brush the tears away.

The anguish on Parker's face was startling. He was that upset for *her*? For what she was going through?

"I better call Griffin," he said. "We're definitely dealing with a homicide."

She nodded, thankful Skylar's case would be fully pursued by one of the best.

"Shoot," Parker said, holding his cell up and moving around. "No bars."

She lifted her chin toward the open door. "Try the hallway."

"Come with me. I'd rather not leave your side."

"I'll be right here. I think it's okay to go ten feet into the hallway. I'm going to start shooting." She retrieved her camera from the counter she'd set it on when she'd rushed for Skylar's red sweater. The best way she could help Skylar and make sense of it all—or at least not be crushed by the pain—was to get straight to work. To prove this psycho was Sky's killer.

Parker hesitated, pausing at the door with a reluctant expression on his ridiculously handsome face.

"I'm fine. You'll be within eyesight. Go call Griff."

Parker nodded and, on a long exhale, stepped into the hall.

She set to work, systematically photographing the evidence, quickly finding her rhythm.

Parker must have reached Griffin, because she could hear his voice not far away.

She turned to photograph the next piece of evidence, and the door swung shut.

Avery spun around, her heart thudding. "Park?"

"Avery," he hollered from the other side of the door. "Let me in."

She moved for the door, but it wouldn't open. Some sort of lock had been engaged. "I can't open it."

"Step back. I'm going to try and kick it in."

She did as instructed and heard Parker's efforts, but no results came. "Whatever's keeping it locked is strong."

She ran her fingers along the door edge. "I see multiple dead-bolts across the door, but no corresponding knobs."

"Someone must have remotely triggered it."

Someone. Adrenaline seared her limbs.

"I saw a bottle jack back in the machine shop. I'll be right back."

"Okay." *Please hurry.*

Out of the silence she heard footsteps . . . *behind* her.

She spun around, panic dampening her skin, the cool air hitting her, causing gooseflesh to ripple up her arms.

The footsteps, slow and rhythmic, moved ever closer. Where were they coming from? Was it Edward, perhaps? They stopped, and just as relief started to swell inside Avery, a panel in the wall slid open and Sebastian stepped out.

"Hello, Avery."

25

It wasn't long before Declan and Lexi got a firm hit on where their mystery man came ashore. An employee at Lehigh Cement had stepped outside to take a smoke on his break and saw a man climb out of a fast raft and race through the company's parking lot.

Declan headed over to speak with the eyewitness personally, calling for a sketch artist to join him, and Lexi stayed with Rowley while his men sifted through the numerous sets of prints and partials they'd found in the suspect's berth.

The warmth of the day lingered despite the moon shining high in the sky as Declan stepped from his vehicle at Lehigh Cement. He was directed to Tom Fisher, a man in his late forties, about Declan's height but a good twenty pounds heavier. A thick brown-and-gray mottled beard covered his neck and jawline.

"Mr. Fisher." Declan extended a hand, so thankful they'd caught him before his twelve-hour shift ended.

"Tom, please." He shook Declan's hand, and they both took a seat at a table in the otherwise empty break room.

Declan pulled out his pad and pen. "I appreciate your help.

We have a sketch artist on the way, but in the meantime, can you describe the man you saw?"

Tom described a man very similar in appearance to the man Hana had described to Tanner as the evil man.

"Did you speak with him?" Declan asked, wondering if their unknown man spoke English.

"I tried. I asked what happened. If he'd lost his way."

"And?"

"He simply asked where the nearest payphone was. I offered him my cell, but he didn't want to use it. He just kept asking for a payphone, so I directed him to the nightclub over by the Royal Farms."

"Which one?"

"The one on Ponca Street."

"Just a block up from Boston?" Not far from the railroad tracks or the traveler's truck stop, where he could no doubt hitch a ride, but he'd wanted a phone, so he may have already had a ride set up.

"Yeah, that's the one." Tom nodded. "The nightclub there has a payphone out back. One of the younger guys talked us all into going over there one time and having a beer. Too loud and shiny for me, if you know what I mean."

"Yeah, I do."

"But I saw the payphone. Couldn't believe they still had one in operation."

"There's still a few left in the city." Declan needed to keep the man focused. They had a possible murderer on the loose. "So you told him about the payphone . . . ?"

"Right. Sorry. Got off track."

"It's no problem."

"So he asked directions on how to get to it, and then took off. Just like that. No thank you. No nothing. Oddest thing."

"How long ago was this?"

Tom glanced up at the black-framed analog clock ticking on the wall. "Around two. That's usually when I take my first smoke break."

"Thank you so much." Declan stood and shook the man's hand. "The sketch artist will be by soon. We really appreciate your time and assistance."

Tom stood. "Just out of curiosity, what'd the guy do?"

"I'm afraid I'm not at liberty to say, but you really have been an enormous help in a significant investigation."

Tom smiled.

Declan rushed back to his Suburban, calling Lexi with the news as he moved. He was going to head for the payphone Tom Fisher had directed the man to. See if he could find another eyewitness, though as late as it was, they were racing against the clock. "We got a location and another description," he said, starting the ignition and pulling out of the lot, turning right.

"And we just got a hit on one of the fingerprints you're going to want to see ASAP."

"Okay." Declan pulled a U-turn and headed back for the *Hiram* as he called in a team to check out the payphone and nearby Royal Farms. If the man had called for a ride, he'd have to wait for it to arrive. Perhaps he'd gone in for a drink or snack while he waited.

Lexi met him on the pier and handed him a printout of their suspect.

Anajay Darmadi. Born September 9, 1985, in Jakarta, Indonesia. Wanted for terrorist bombings in Jakarta, London, and Israel. Suspected affiliation with a highly dangerous Indonesian extremist sect.

"He's a terrorist." Declan had to say it out loud, just to let the reality fully sink in. They had a known terrorist loose on American soil.

Had Federal Agent Burke discovered his identity and been killed for it? Had he been undercover, and Burke's boss had lied to them?

Taking a deep breath, Declan called *his* boss, who initiated a nationwide manhunt, focused on the I-95 corridor, putting Declan in charge.

Declan and Lexi strode to the MPA office where they were holding Randal Jackson, the *Hiram* captain. He slammed the FBI's profile sheet for Anajay Darmadi in front of Jackson.

"You transported a known terrorist into your own country," Declan said, straddling the empty chair beside him, his face less than a foot from Jackson's as he clutched the printout of Darmadi's crimes. "What I want to know is if you knew you were transporting a terrorist onto American soil."

Jackson looked away. "I have nothing to say."

Declan stood. "Maybe a change of location will help with that." He was taking Jackson into custody. He handed the cuffs to Lexi. "Would you like to do the honors?"

Lexi stepped to Jackson, hauling him to his feet and turning him around to cuff him. "My pleasure."

Parker located the bottle jack and a discarded piece of rebar and rushed back to the room. If his plan worked, he'd pop it open. If not, he'd find another way. He was getting through that door whatever it took.

"Avery, I'm back."

No answer. *Was that a scuffle?*

"Avery!" he hollered, panic squeezing his airways nearly shut.

Still no answer. But he was definitely hearing something from the storage room.

Please, Father, I don't know what's happening in there, but

*please not again. Don't rip another woman I love from my life
because I couldn't protect her.*

Love. He loved Avery.

Positioning the rebar and the jack in the frame, he began to
extend the jack. After a moment, the deadbolts disengaged and
he was able to kick the door in.

He rushed in, finding Avery on the couch, her jaw swelling,
blood dripping from the corner of her mouth.

He raced to her and knelt in front of her. "What happened?"

"Sebastian."

"What? How?"

"The wall." She stood, and he reached for her hand.

"Hold on. Sit here a bit longer."

"There's no time. There's a door in the wall. He came out and
tried to drag me through it, but I fought him off long enough
for you to return. He heard you getting the door open and fled
back into the secret door. We need to follow him."

After a moment's searching along the section of the wall
Avery pointed out, Parker found the door and rammed it open
to discover a long tunnel running the length of the building.
"Come with me." He grabbed Avery's hand and they ran.

His breathing was still shaky even as the fear of losing Avery
dissipated. They followed the tunnel to its end and burst out a
hidden door in time to see motorcycle taillights speeding away
into the distance.

"Get in the car," he said, rapidly climbing inside.

Avery jumped in.

He was not losing this guy. "Call Griffin on his cell. Tell him
we're in pursuit."

Avery did as instructed, but by the time he and Avery reached
the first major intersection, there was no sign of Sebastian.

They'd lost him.

26

Much to Parker's chagrin, Avery insisted on still working the rooms despite the fact they'd both been up for close to forty hours and despite the fact the victim was her friend. Because of the personal tie, the horror of what her friend's body had been put through, he'd tried to talk her into letting another crew handle this one, but *stubborn* wasn't a strong enough word to describe Avery's unwavering determination.

Parker's cell dinged, and he glanced at his phone. "Griff and Jason are here. Let's go meet them. They'll need our help to find this room."

It took some trekking, but Parker and Avery finally made it out to the parking lot—well, what had at one time been a parking lot. Now grass and weeds cracked up through the crumbling asphalt.

"Thanks for coming," he greeted Griff.

"No problem."

Jason Cavanaugh, Griff's partner, stepped out of the car. "Parker." He nodded, then shifted his gaze to Avery. "Miss."

"How many times have I asked you to call me Avery or Tate?"

"Sorry, miss. It's either going to be miss or ma'am. Your preference."

"Great."

Finley's car rounded the corner.

"Finley?" Avery said.

Griffin shook his head. "She was with me when Parker called and insisted on coming to make sure you had support."

"That's kind of her, but unnecessary, especially at this late hour."

Griffin raked a hand through his hair with a smile. "You try arguing that one." It was crazy to think in less than two weeks the two would be husband and wife.

Finley stepped from her car and hurried to Avery's side.

"How are you?" Concern creased her brow. "What happened to your face?"

"She fought Sebastian off," Parker said, pride imbuing his words. She was a fighter, and he loved that about her—loved so many things about her. The instant he thought he might lose her, it had all come into focus. He loved Avery Tate. Not just cared about. Not just admired. He *loved* her.

"I think I have an icepack in the car," Finley said. "I'll be right back."

Two patrol cars pulled down the drive.

Griffin inclined his head in their direction. "Cavalry." He moved to relay to the officers what had occurred and what they would be focusing on in the building.

Finley gave Avery the icepack, and she winced as she set it against her jaw.

Parker inhaled sharply. He wanted to kill Sebastian for hurting her.

The wind had picked back up, skimming over the dark water

behind them, the somewhat-cool breeze actually refreshing after the stale air of the long-abandoned building.

They were closing in on Sebastian. They'd located where Skylar had been photographed, confirmed she'd been dead at the time, and the cause of death had most likely been strangulation. So far Parker had collected hair, clothing fiber samples, and a small spot of residue on the sheet draped over the sofa. He wasn't certain if it was biological or chemical—if it had been on the sheet to begin with or if it had come from Skylar's body or clothing. He was betting the latter, but he'd have to wait until he could fully analyze it at the lab.

He just prayed when their time here was done that Avery would allow him to comfort her, to shelter her in his embrace and let her cry on his shoulder again. He was there for her, always. He hoped she knew that.

"This place looks like something out of a horror movie," Finley said as they approached the side entrance he and Avery had come through. It didn't help it was pitch-black and the sound of bats echoed through the rustling trees.

He pulled the rotting plywood back, holding it for them. "Wait until you see the inside."

"You weren't kidding about the inside of this place," Griffin said, holding a flashlight in one hand and Finley's hand in his other, helping her maneuver over and around metal chairs tipped on their sides, piles of trash, and random gurneys.

"If someone were purposely making a haunted house for a carnival, this place would make a fantastic source of inspiration," Finley said.

"Two more floors up," Parker said.

He so wished they'd found Skylar alive, but at least they

were finding evidence and viable leads. At least Skylar's case wouldn't become a cold case like Jenna's.

Jenna.

The horrific images of her remains on the shoreline they'd grown up playing on still ripped at his soul. If only they could find *her* killer. Bring Jenna justice. It was so unfair.

He climbed the next flight of stairs, fearing he'd never see justice happen for Jenna's brutal murder. But he knew one day justice *would* prevail. One day, if it didn't happen on earth, her killer would stand before Almighty God and answer for the evil he'd done.

Parker wanted, ached, to deal out that punishment, but earthly punishment for murder was the court's jurisdiction and in eternity, God's.

It was infuriating at times not to take matters into his own hands, most certainly in regards to Jenna's murder, but at least God had seen fit to bless him with the drive and skill required to help bring truths to light, to expose the deeds of evil men and women, deeds they thought they'd hidden so well. And they had not just let Jenna's case remain cold, not any longer. They, as a team, were still working her case whenever they had the chance—evenings, weekends, days off—with each focusing on their area of expertise to hopefully, finally bring Jenna's killer to justice. No matter how long it took, they weren't giving up. Not until Jenna's killer was behind bars.

"What's your profile of Sebastian?" Griffin asked, holding the stairwell door open for Finley and Avery, Jason bringing up the rear.

Parker swallowed. "There's darkness in this guy, a penchant for dancing with death." Just like whoever killed Jenna displayed by his brutal actions.

"So you believe he killed Skylar?"

He blinked back to the present, fully focusing his attention on Skylar's case before them. "There are no signs of a struggle here, but in pictures of her body I saw signs of her having fought back. We know Sebastian was at her trailer and took props for the photo, but there were no signs of a struggle there either. I don't know where he killed her, but so far everything points to him as our man."

Parker remained by Avery's side as the cops canvassed the place. Edward was nowhere to be found—but they discovered that the tunnel system went throughout the entire complex.

"Dude, this guy is beyond creepy," Finley said, studying the photographs and sketches of Skylar on Sebastian's studio wall.

"Hopefully someone will spot him."

"And if not?"

"We go back to his home? Come back here? I think he's too attached to this place to leave it for long."

"And in the meantime?"

"We search the grounds for Skylar's body."

27

Declan entered the interrogation room at his Bureau office followed by Lexi. The *Hiram*'s captain, Randal Jackson—an American citizen—sat cuffed to the table, waiting with a smirk on his full face. Declan dropped a file on the table, and both took a seat opposite Jackson.

"Well, I imagine you can guess my surprise when your records showed you were a boatswain mate with the U.S. Navy." Declan scanned the file. "You served your country for a decade until you were honorably discharged due to injury."

He sat back. "And now you're smuggling not only illegal immigrants but also a known terrorist into America. What do you have to say for yourself?"

Jackson's jaw shifted, and he shook his head before leaning forward, rattling the cuffs with the jerky motion. "My *country* betrayed me."

Declan arched a brow. He hadn't read anything about that in Jackson's file, nor anything about reprimands or poor performance on Jackson's part, so where was this coming from? "Betrayed?" he asked.

Jackson sat back, propping one foot on his knee. "Yeah, betrayed. They *conveniently* discharged me after a mooring line snapped while we were in port in Okinawa, and I lost my right leg. This"—he stomped his right foot on the floor, his left knee bouncing as his left foot still rested on his right knee—"is a fake leg. Very pirate-like, don't you think?"

"So that's why you turned smuggler? A pirate leg?" He was being crass, but he needed to push Jackson's buttons and get him to give away the details he needed to get to the heart of his actions.

"Something like that," Jackson said smugly.

Man, he wanted to knock that look off the captain's face.

"I'm sorry to hear about your leg." That was a raw deal. "But it's no excuse for illegal activity, and most certainly not for treason."

"Treason." Jackson shrugged.

Was this a game to him?

He looked Declan straight in the eye. "My country betrayed me. I betrayed it."

"By smuggling in a known enemy?" Lexi said, her throaty voice heated with irritation.

"What's it to me who wants a ride on my ship? And for your information, I am a man without a country. The sea is my home."

Declan looked back to the file. "It says here you were married and have a son, Randy. I'm guessing named after you. What about them?"

"My *wife* left me, took my son away, and remarried some hotshot attorney out in Vegas. Just like I got no country, I got no family."

"So you don't care if the man you smuggled in blows up your family?" Might as well lay a worst-case scenario on the line.

"Vegas ain't exactly a terrorist hot spot."

So he did care about his family, or at least about his son. Declan could use that to his advantage.

"So you know where Anajay's target is located?" Lexi asked.

That dimmed Jackson's haughty attitude. "I never said that."

"But you seem pretty confident it isn't Vegas, where your boy lives, so that tells me that you do love your son," she said, resting her arms on the table, leaning in.

"Of course I love my son. I'm not a monster. I just hate his cheating momma and her lover." The edge to his voice was dark and full of rage. Declan half wondered if part of the deal Jackson had made with Anajay involved a hit on Jackson's ex and her husband in return for passage. Or perhaps Jackson was planning to simply hire a hit man with the money he was paid. They'd need to look into his financials and check the burner cell they'd found in his cabin.

"I'm curious. Did you set out with the intention of smuggling a terrorist into the country as payback for what it did to you?" Lexi asked.

"I didn't set out with the intention of smuggling anyone, but merchant marines don't exactly make a whole lot, and neither do wounded soldiers. A man came to me, offered me ten thousand dollars to help some hurting people get to America for a better way of life."

"Well, doesn't that sound like a generous sacrifice on your part," Lexi said, "but here's the problem: There's nothing generous about treating refugees like animals."

"I didn't treat them like animals. I offered them a better way of life."

"It's funny you keep saying 'a better way of life,' but you've been very clear that you hate America, so how is bringing refugees here offering them a better way of life?" she pressed.

"It's better than where they were at."

"Ah, how generous of you." Lexi sat back, arms crossed. "All for the price of ten grand."

"Nothing wrong with being an entrepreneur."

"It is when it involves illegal activity. Speaking of which . . ." Declan shoved Anajay's wanted release in front of Jackson—including sketches from the descriptions given by both Hana and Tom Fisher, which had come in, matched remarkably well, with only subtle differences. In Fisher's sketch, Anajay had more facial hair, a fuller face.

Anajay had aged a bit since the photo the Bureau had of him was taken.

"Smuggling refugees is one thing. But smuggling a terrorist is a completely different concern," Declan said.

"Smuggling is smuggling." He pushed the picture back to Declan as best he could with cuffed hands. "I gave him passage just like the rest."

Declan shook his head. "Not just like the rest. You gave Anajay the same meals the crew ate, full water privileges, even a private berth."

Jackson shrugged. "So?"

"So, I'm betting you made more than ten thousand dollars to smuggle Anajay Darmadi into the country. I'm also betting the money for Anajay's passage didn't come through Max Stallings."

Jackson shifted uncomfortably.

"That's right. We know who paid for the *cargo*, as you call the refugees. Agents are bringing Max Stallings in as we speak," Lexi said.

"That's his business to work out with you."

"But someone else paid you for Anajay's passage. We may not know who yet, but we'll track your financials," Declan said. They'd track the money trail right back to the person or organization who funded Anajay's passage into the country.

Jackson pressed his lips together and stared at the ceiling.

Declan leaned forward, resting his forearms on the lacquered tabletop. "What I'm curious to discover is how many times this person or organization—which we *will* find—paid you. If it's more than once, then we will investigate on the premise that you've already smuggled in other terrorists."

Jackson swallowed, his fingers twitching. "I want a lawyer."

So there had been others. *Dear God*. How many other terrorists had Randal smuggled into America?

"Grey, Kadyrov." A fellow agent opened the door.

"Yes, Matt?" Declan said.

"We have something you're both going to want to take a look at."

Declan looked back to a now panicked Randal Jackson and smiled. "The case against you is already building. If I were you, I'd cooperate. Might save you the death penalty for treason."

"I want a lawyer now!"

Declan stood. "Matt, you heard the man. Call a lawyer, and in the meantime, put him in a holding cell."

Matt nodded.

Declan and Lexi followed him out.

"So what do you have?" Lexi asked.

"Techs confirmed Anajay Darmadi's fingerprints were on that payphone, among a good number of others."

"Have we traced his call?" Declan asked.

"The only call placed on that phone on Saturday was to the Islamic Cultural Institute of the Mid-Atlantic."

A center they'd been investigating for years. A center they

highly suspected of extremist ties. He and Lexi would be paying them a visit first thing Monday morning.

"Agents canvassed the area and found a gas station attendant across the street from the payphone who saw a black sedan pick up a dark-skinned man less than half an hour after he placed that call."

"Good memory."

"Said the payphone is pretty much never used, so he noticed the man making a call and then pacing anxiously until the sedan arrived."

"Any markings on the car he can recall?"

"Nope."

"You know who I bet has black sedans like that?"

Matt smiled. "The cultural institute."

"It appears I'm going to need a couple of warrants."

28

It was nearly two in the morning when Parker followed Griffin, Finley, and Avery into Charm City Investigations, where Kate, Declan, and Tanner were waiting.

Kate took one glance at him. "Rough night?"

"You have no idea." He'd thought he'd lost Avery. He couldn't get his heart to stop pounding in his ears. What would he have done if he'd lost her? He dared not think.

"I made cookies." Tanner held up a plate of chocolate espresso cookies. "Fresh out of the office oven."

"I'll take a handful," Avery said. "I can't remember the last time we ate."

"Chick-fil-A. About a dozen hours ago," Parker said, taking a handful for himself.

"Glad I made a double batch," Tanner said, setting the plate on the coffee table while everyone took seats around it.

"So you have your guy?" Declan, who looked strung out on caffeine and exhausted, asked.

"All the evidence points to Sebastian Chadwyck," Parker said.

"His prints were all over the place. Skylar's hair was there, along with the portrait set and the clothes she'd been photographed in."

"We *need* to find him," Avery said as urgently as her exhausted state would allow. He needed to get her home.

He sat down beside her, rested a hand on her knee, and exhaled, hating himself for letting Sebastian get away. "We nearly had him."

Declan arched a brow. "At the abandoned hospital?"

Parker explained what happened with Avery.

He was still thanking God she'd been able to fight him off until he'd broken through and Sebastian fled.

"So what's next?" Declan asked.

"I take Avery home," he said. "It's been a long couple of nights."

"You *take* me home?"

"You can't seriously think I'm going to let you go home alone when you've been threatened by Gary and nearly abducted by Sebastian. We've already talked about this."

"Fine," she said, clearly too tired to fight.

"I'll fill you in on what Kate and I learned in the morning," Griffin said.

"No," Avery said. "Go ahead. I want to hear."

"You sure? You look spent."

She linked her arms across her chest. "I'm positive."

Parker settled back. He too was curious what Griffin and Kate had discovered before he had called Griffin and Jason to the hospital.

"We interviewed Connor Davis," Griffin began. "He admitted to knowing Skylar. Well, he said he hooked up with her once. Met her at a bar but couldn't remember which one."

"That's convenient."

"But not impossible if they were doing a pub crawl."

"True." From what Parker had seen, by the end of the night most couldn't remember which Fell's Point bars they'd even been to—the drunken night a hazed blur. It was surprising Connor even remembered Skylar's name if it was just a one-night hookup. So why did he remember her, and was he lying about how often they'd been together? Perhaps he was lying about the nature of their relationship entirely. "Maybe it wasn't a one-time thing?"

"No . . . he seemed to be telling the truth," Griffin, who was the master at reading body language and facial expressions, said.

Kate jumped in. "But it seems to me like he wanted it to be more. Like Skylar moved on from him before he was ready to end things."

"I concur," Griffin said.

"What gave you that impression?" Avery asked.

"His expression when he said Skylar slept around a lot."

"How would he know she slept around a lot if it'd just been a drunken one-night thing? Ewww, by the way." Avery cringed, though she didn't protest Skylar's virtue, so clearly the possibility of that sort of behavior on Skylar's part wasn't out of the question.

"Exactly," Kate said. "So we asked if he knew any of the other guys she'd been with, like had he heard rumors or something . . . ?"

"Which would make sense," Parker said.

"Yeah." Kate nodded with a smile. "But his response was odd."

"How *did* he respond?" Parker asked, curious.

"Connor immediately glanced to a picture of him, his roommate, and a woman we are guessing is the roommate's girlfriend, though she identified herself as Connor's friend."

"Talk about a piece of work," Kate said, shaking her head.

Avery frowned. "You mean the roommate's girlfriend? She was there?"

"Yeah," Griffin said, clearly sharing Kate's opinion of the woman.

Kate continued, "Her name is Amanda King, and she came in right when we were asking Connor if his roommate, Kyle, had slept with Skylar."

"Based on his instant trajectory to the photograph of him and Kyle," Avery said. "Smart."

"What did Connor say?"

"Nothing. Amanda walked in and asked who we were talking about."

"Did she know Skylar?"

"She claims not to."

"But you think she's lying."

"She called her a skank. Seemed like she knew her and was not a fan." Kate blushed and dipped her head a bit. "I'm so sorry about the skank comment. I know we're talking about your friend."

"Thanks. But I'm under no illusions that Skylar is some kind of saint. She's just my oldest friend. I never could bring myself to give up on her."

Avery was still referring to Skylar in the present. Despite what they'd found tonight, her mind still hadn't accepted that her friend was dead.

Parker studied the determination on her face. Avery wouldn't give up on Skylar until they'd found her body and arrested her killer. He prayed hard that, as difficult as it would be to endure, she got her closure. For the alternative—never catching the killer—was a far worse, enduring torture.

"Sure sounds like Amanda knew Skylar," Declan said.

He looked like he, too, was carrying a heavy weight tonight. They still needed to discuss what'd happened on the ship after he and Avery headed for the abandoned VA hospital and Sebastian's disgusting "studio."

"There was venom in her voice when she referenced her," Kate said.

"You think Skylar slept with Kyle too, and he's Amanda's guy?" Parker asked.

Griffin inclined his head. "If I were a betting man."

"Okay, so we have a ticked-off Connor because Skylar dumped him for his roommate," Parker said, "and a ticked-off girlfriend because Skylar slept with her boyfriend."

"Yeah. It wouldn't be the first time. Skylar had a pretty bad habit of stuff like that," Avery said. "As gorgeous as she was, guys went gaga for her."

"But Kyle's girlfriend, Amanda—if she is in fact his girl-friend—is gorgeous too," Kate said, clearly wondering why Amanda's boyfriend would stray. "She has long blond hair, big blue eyes . . ."

Parker exchanged a quizzical look with Avery. *Rich college kids . . .*

"What?" Kate frowned.

"It couldn't be . . ." Parker said.

"Couldn't be what?" Kate asked.

"I don't suppose you saw what kind of car Amanda King drives?" Avery asked.

"Yeah. A burgundy and white—"

"Fiat," Parker and Avery said in unison.

"Yeah." A curious expression danced across Kate's face. "How'd you know?"

They explained about their tail, or rather Gary Boyd's second one, and what Megan had said about Skylar's nighttime visi-tors—that the young couple had broken into Skylar's place and argued about how "*his* cheating had gotten *them* in this mess."

"So are we thinking it was Kyle Eason who broke into Skylar's trailer with Amanda?" Griffin wondered.

"Based on her referring to 'his cheating,' that's my guess," Kate answered. "But his cheating got them into what kind of mess? Clearly more than within their relationship if they were breaking and entering into Skylar's trailer."

"Megan said they were there looking for something. Something Skylar must have hidden well."

"Hidden?" Parker said. "Did they find it?"

"Nope." Avery shook her head. "If Skylar wanted to hide something . . ." she began, then her eyes lit. "The safe deposit box?"

Kate smiled. "Exactly."

"Any luck on tracking its location down?" Parker asked.

"Ask and you shall receive." Kate handed him the printout.

"Wells Fargo on Bel Air Road. Skylar made quite the trek for that box." It was easily a forty-five-minute drive without traffic, and around the beltway there was always traffic. There had to be a closer Wells Fargo to her.

"She was probably worried if anyone found out she'd gotten a safe deposit box, they'd search the closest bank to her home," Avery said.

"I should be able to get a warrant tomorrow, so Jason and I will head there first thing Monday morning," Griffin said. "Avery, why don't you meet us there? I'd like to have you accompany us since you can verify Skylar's signature on the forms. I could compare documents, but I'd prefer having the word of someone who knew her well."

"No problem." Avery leaned forward, resting her hands on her knees. "I'm curious. Do you think someone else might have rented the box in her name?"

"No. I just like to dot my I's and cross my T's."

"Of course you do." Parker smiled. Griffin was the most thorough person he knew, which is what made him so good at his job. "Okay, if we're done here," Parker said, standing and gesturing to Avery, "I'm taking this girl home."

Everyone arched their brows in a teasing manner.

"Not like that." *Children—the lot of them.* Though, when it came to teasing, he was often the worst of the pack.

"Let me just help Tanner clean up the kitchen first," Avery said, seeing Tanner moving to do so alone.

"Of course. Can I help?"

"No. Just sit. With the two of us it won't take long."

"Three of us," Kate said, jumping up to join them in the kitchen. Declan picked up his phone and excused himself.

Griffin and Finley, instead of moving for the kitchen, moved to sit on either side of Parker.

Okay, whatever was coming was going to be fun. *Not.*

He raised his eyebrows. "Yes?"

"What are you doing?" Griffin asked.

"About . . . ?"

"Avery."

"What about her?" He ached for Avery to be his, but what about Jenna? He had no intention of spending the rest of his life alone. . . . It was just that Jenna's loss took such a chunk out of his heart, he wasn't sure he'd ever be whole again. And Avery deserved whole.

"Please," Griffin said. "You are clearly into the woman."

Wonderful. "Is it that obvious?"

"Oh, honey," Finley said. "You have *no* idea."

"What's holding you back?" Griffin said, leaning forward and interlocking his hands. "Is it Jenna?"

Was he seriously going to have this conversation with Jenna's big brother about caring for another woman? They really had come a long way in repairing their relationship if they were going to have this conversation.

Griffin stared at him, waiting for an answer.

"Yes." He exhaled.

"It wasn't your fault Jenna died," Griffin said quietly. "Trust yourself that you can protect Avery, that you can be there for her. Especially with everything that's going on now."

Parker swallowed hard. That meant a lot coming from Griffin.

"Still . . ." Parker fell back in his seat. "Avery deserves someone whole, and after what happened with Jenna . . ." He didn't know how to explain it.

Finley shifted forward. "Maybe to be whole, you need someone else to fill that hole."

"But isn't that killing my memories, my love for Jenna? She deserves better." She was his first love. "And so does Avery. She deserves all of me, and I want to give it to her, but I want to honor Jenna too."

"You will always have those memories and that love," Finley said softly, "but it doesn't mean there isn't room for a new love in your heart, which, by the way, is already clearly there."

"It's obvious you love her," Griffin said.

He'd fallen hand over fist in love with Avery Tate and totally missed the fact until she'd nearly been taken from him. For the first time in seven years, he *loved* a woman. Not just wanted, not just longed to date or spend time with, but completely *loved* a woman. And not just any woman, but a strong, vulnerable, brilliantly quirky mess of perfection.

"So how long are you going to sit there with that goofy expression on your face before you go tell her?" Griffin asked.

Tell Avery I love her? "She's skittish. I don't think she believes I could love her *fully*, and until now neither did I."

Reaching over, Finley clasped his hand. "Tell her the truth."

Finley was right, but the notion choked the air from his lungs.

29

Rain lashed down as Avery fumbled out front of her townhome with her keys. The intense heat of the day had finally triggered the thunderstorm threatening to let loose with a fury.

Raw, restless energy coursed through Parker's veins as he scanned the dark street and thin copses of wooded areas surrounding them. They were fixed targets.

He placed a steadying hand over Avery's shaky one. "Allow me."

Not only did he want Avery safely inside ASAP, but he *needed* to share the words burning like embers in his throat.

Unlocking the door, he followed her inside, scanning the perimeter once more before shutting the door, the feeling of being watched prickling the nerves along the nape of his neck.

Avery sloughed off her drenched raincoat, tossing it over the stair rail. "I'm going to make something hot to drink. You want something?"

You. "I'll take coffee if you have it."

"Yep. French press, just like you prefer."

"Sounds great."

She kicked off her Docksiders at the end of the hall and padded barefoot into the kitchen.

He moved through her family room, the townhome more than a hundred years old. It was one of the first built in Federal Hill, back in the days of Francis Scott Key. The place was gorgeous, the hand-carved crown molding, gleaming refurbished hardwood floors, and turn-of-the-century light fixtures exquisite, just like the woman who owned the place.

Her personal touches were so evident. She'd worked hard—saved almost everything she earned and bought the place the year before last. It suited her to a T.

Avery could never be labeled a girly-girl, so there were no hints of pink or lace or flowers. Instead, she'd gone with rustic nautical. Decorating in crisp white, dark navy, and deep red. And thanks to hanging around the ladies far too much, he knew all about shabby-chic distressed furniture.

Kicking off his shoes, he sat down on her cushy navy sofa.

"One coffee with Irish creamer," she said with a smirk, stepping into the room with two blue-and-white-speckled ceramic mugs. No doubt from Ten Thousand Villages, the store Avery loved near Finley's house.

"Nice touch with Irish cream, lass." He thickened his brogue in playfulness. Having immigrated at the age of four and grown up in a home full of strong Irish accents, his lingered. He was proud of his heritage. Proud of the beautiful area of Ireland on the southwestern coast they'd come from.

"Same to you with the accent." She sat down beside him, resting her head back against the sofa, her blond hair splaying out about her beautiful face.

"I love listening to you talk," she said sleepily, and then jerked

upright as embarrassment flashed across her face. "Sorry. I mean
. . . I-I'm just exhausted." She raked a hand through her hair.
"I can't believe I just said that."

He nudged her foot with his. "Because you didn't mean it?"

She smiled, softly—lighting her whole face for the first time
since Skylar's disappearance. He loved that he could bring her
even a moment's respite from the heartache that was coming.

"Because I did," she whispered.

He smiled, shifting to face her, resting his arm beside her
head on the sofa, his fingers longing to run through her silky
hair. "Well," he said, refraining, "while we're sharing confes-
sions . . ." He took a deep breath and let it fly. "I love you."

"Very funny." Un-amusement fixed on her face. "Way to
make fun of my exhausted confession."

Of course she'd assume he was joking, but he'd *never* been
more serious.

He scooted closer, so close he could almost hear her heart
beating. "I'm not joking. It took me a while to sort through
things, but tonight I realized I've been in love with you since you
first walked through my door all feisty and determined not to
take no for an answer on the photographer's listing I'd posted."

He chuckled. She was staring at him like he was crazy, and
maybe she was right, but as his mom liked to say, he was full-in.
There was no turning back now.

He thought back to that first day. To the first ray of light
in his life in so many years . . . "You were so surprised when I
said yes and hired you. Come to think of it, your face held the
same shocked expression that day as it does right now." A face
he wanted to cup and . . .

Stay on topic.

The woman was a flight risk if ever he'd met one. He swallowed, reaching for her hand, and to his surprise she didn't pull

away. "That love has grown each day since, until it's engulfed me. You"—he slipped his fingers into her hair, finally running them through her silky golden lengths—"have engulfed me."

With that, he engulfed her, kissing her with all the pent-up passion that'd been boiling inside for nigh on a year.

Her lips were even softer than he'd imagined, her kiss equally fervent.

"Avery," he whispered as he reluctantly came up for air.

He moved back to kiss her again, wanting to never stop, but she pressed her flattened palm to the center of his chest, halting him.

His breath ragged, he looked up into her eyes and saw what he feared most.

～～～

He shifted his position, zooming in with his binoculars, and he still couldn't get an angle on them. The blasted sofa was blocking his view.

What were they doing?

Anger raked through him.

She was *his*.

That man, whoever he was to her, better not be touching Avery, spoiling her. He wanted *this* subject pristine. Angelic. And Avery Tate was.

～～～

Disbelief. Avery was staring at him in guarded disbelief. Parker reined in the nearly excruciating urge to pull her back into his arms. Taking a focusing breath, he behaved as the gentleman she deserved him to be. "I'm sorry. That came out way faster than I expected," he said.

"You think?" She ran her finger along her full bottom lip.

Leave it to Avery to be just as blunt.

He shrugged. "Subtlety is not my strong suit."

"But Jenna?"

He smiled. "Subtlety is far from your strong suit either, love." He sighed. "I loved Jenna. She was my first."

Avery's eyes widened. "You and Jenna . . . ?"

"No, of course not." But he needed to be completely honest with her. To share something he'd never shared with anyone—wanting to protect Jenna's honor and the privacy of their relationship—but Avery had asked, and if this relationship was going to work, he needed to be an open book. He rubbed his thighs. "But . . ."

"But?" She shifted to face him better.

"The night before Jenna died things went too far."

"But you just said . . . ?"

"We didn't have sex. We both believed in purity before marriage. I still do, but that night we came dangerously close. We were so young and in love, and you know the desperation that goes with that." The desperation and urgency he felt for Avery, but now he was a different man—grounded in his faith and far more mature and self-disciplined. He knew how to be a gentleman.

"I know," she said, stroking his hair. "It's hard to resist the temptation to rush. God never promised it would be easy, but it would be worth the wait."

"You're worth the wait, and Jenna was too, which is how we managed to stop." He'd somehow raggedly found a restraint he barely possessed and stopped. Jenna was half hurt and half impressed, and even more in love with him for wanting to protect her virginity, for knowing she deserved that to be for her husband—who he'd hoped to be one day.

One day.

It was amazing and brutal how twenty-four hours could alter one's life. But it was equally, if not more, amazing how God was taking the shell of the man he'd become and made him able to fully love again. And, the fact that it was with a woman as remarkable as Avery flat-out boggled his mind.

"What?" She tucked her chin in, studying him.

"I was just thinking how grateful I am that God brought you into my life."

"And?" She bit her bottom lip.

He smiled. He loved her bluntness and tenacity. "And I can no longer imagine life without you in it. Without you at my side."

"As your photographer?"

He cupped her face, careful of her bruised jaw, and stared into her gorgeous green eyes. "Much more than that, love, so much more," he whispered, lowering his lips to hers.

She kissed him back, and joy filled him. He tentatively brushed his fingers along her jaw, so in love, so in awe of the restoration, the hope, and the renewed life Christ had brought into his life. His love and memories of Jenna would always be a part of his past, but Avery was his future, the half to his whole. One day she'd be his wife, God willing.

She narrowed her eyes. "That's quite the mischievous smile on your lips. What's going on in that handsome head of yours?"

"You find me handsome, do you?" He smirked.

"Tall, dark, and Irish. *Please* . . ." She rolled her eyes. "Of course I do."

His smile widened. "I like that."

"I bet you do. Now back to my question. What's going on in that head of yours?"

"You'll just have to wait and see." The moment he proposed needed to be perfect.

"I don't like surprises."

"Trust me, love, not all surprises are bad." He tugged her onto his lap.

She studied him again, this time far more intently.

"Now, what's going on in that beautiful head of yours?"

"You think I'm beautiful?" A flirtatious smile danced across her lips.

"Please, you know you're gorgeous. Now answer my question. What are you thinking so hard about?"

"I want to know why you love me."

"Because I don't make sense without you. You're part of me." He placed his hand over his heart. "It beats for you."

***

Finally, they moved into view. She was sitting on his lap.

Rage burned through his limbs.

She was right there. Ripe for the taking. If only it were simply him and her—an artist and his subject.

Her creamy white neck called to him.

How would he do it?

Every fiber of his antsy being screamed "take her," but he was no fool. He knew he had to wait—now was clearly not the time.

She was the one, but she wasn't alone. He'd wait and take her when he could ensure he'd have plenty of time with her. He'd start by combing her hair. He bet the teeth would just glide through her silky golden tresses. Then he'd dress her. Evergreen would match her eyes and be a striking contrast to the white sheet he'd place her on. Then came the best part—posing her. He'd place her on her back, her golden hair fanned out around her pale skin bordering on blue but not quite there. Her arms outstretched, her legs bent slightly at the knee.

He'd photograph her after her breath had left her body, but

before the blood drained fully down, pulling life from her angelic face. She would be his angel of death. His perfect peace. *Finally*.

Waiting was going to be excruciating, but he needed time to acquire and set up a new location. It would be a fresh start. New studio. New subject. It was only a matter of where and when, but he'd work fast. He couldn't hold out much longer. He was itching for her.

30

The sun shone brightly Monday morning as Avery followed Griffin and Jason toward the Wells Fargo branch across the street from a much-needed Starbucks they'd be hitting afterward.

On Sunday, Parker had insisted on crashing on the couch, and after sleeping late, Avery and Parker had attended church together. They spent most of the day talking—processing through the case, touching base with the gang, and even talking a little bit about *them*. She was still in shock. Parker loved *her*.

Thank you, Lord.

When she was with him, in his arms, it felt so right—in her heart it felt right and in her prayers it felt right—but her gut kept tugging at her. Could he really love her fully? And, more importantly, could she fully be herself with him?

She still hadn't told him. Not the deepest, darkest part of her past, and there was no way she could spend her life with a man without being fully open. Could she share? And, more importantly, could she trust him to embrace her despite the ugliness of her past?

Not needed for the bank visit, Parker waited in his car, but she so wished he was at her side. She was walking in to see why her oldest friend, who'd been murdered—based on what they'd found in Sebastian's disgusting storage room—had rented a safe deposit box the week before her death. What secret did the box hold? And had it played a role in Skylar's death?

Griffin held the door open for her, and she stepped inside.

"Just act like you're supposed to be with us," Jason said under his breath to her as they approached the bank manager's office.

Griffin knocked on the open door with the back of his hand. "Mr. Phillips?" he asked.

"Yes?" The middle-aged man with strawberry-blond hair and sleek frameless glasses looked up.

Griffin showed his ID. "Detective McCray," he said. "We spoke on the phone."

"Yes, of course," Mr. Phillips said. "I went ahead and pulled the box records for you." He grabbed them from his locked desk drawer and slid them across the glass-topped desk to Griffin.

Avery leaned forward, studying the form beside Griffin, noting the date the box was opened, Skylar's name, and her signature.

Griffin glanced at her, and she nodded her indication that the signature was valid.

He flipped to the second page, where visitations were noted. There was only one instance when the box had been visited since its opening, and while the signature read *Skylar Pierce,* it was most definitely not Skylar's signature.

It was close. To someone who didn't know Skylar or wasn't paying careful attention, it was easy enough to miss, but the *S* was most certainly wrong.

Skylar always looped the bottom of hers a special way, had

ever since elementary school. Avery remembered practicing cursive alongside Skylar as Skylar worked to put her own personal spin on her name, always wanting to stand out and be special. The memory—the days of their youth, growing up side by side—diverted Avery's train of thought for a moment, but she shook off the emotions and forced herself to focus . . . for Skylar. Whoever had attempted to forge Skylar's signature had gotten it close, but not close enough.

"That's not her signature," she said, pointing at the forgery.

"I beg your pardon?" Mr. Phillips straightened. "We always compare signatures." He flipped between the pages, clearly looking for a glaring error.

"I'm sure you do, and they are quite alike, but here . . ." Avery held out her hand, and Mr. Phillips complied, handing her the forms. "May I?" she asked about separating the pages. He nodded his consent, and she carefully removed the staple and laid them side by side. "If you look closely, you can see the *S* is different. The original *S*, which is Miss Pierce's," she said, wanting to sound professional no matter how personal this felt, "has a special swish at the bottom curve."

Mr. Phillips' eyes widened, and then he sat back, clearing his throat. "I see, and I must apologize, profusely. This"—he tightened his tie knot—"was extremely lax on our teller's part." He looked at the initials beside Skylar's forged signature. "I will have a talk with Miss Westin regarding this matter. I assure you it will not happen again."

"We'll need to see the box," Griffin said. "We have a warrant."

"Of course." Mr. Phillips nodded and stood, moving for his office door. "Right this way, please."

He gestured to a man sitting with a toolbox at his feet. "This is Glenn Talbot, who will be drilling the box open for us since we cannot access it without Miss Pierce's key."

Mr. Phillips led them through the lobby to a waist-high glass door, which he held open for them. They stepped beyond the sign-in area to a locked glass door.

Pulling his keys and directing a darting glare toward a woman who Avery assumed was Miss Westin, he unlocked the door and led them inside. Gray metal boxes lined the walls, and a separate row running halfway down the center of the space divided the room. Private rooms in the right corner of the room sat with doors open. So at least they had the place to themselves.

Mr. Phillips retrieved Skylar's box and Mr. Talbot made short work of getting it open. Without opening the lid, he stepped back.

"Feel free to use either of our private rooms," Mr. Phillips said. "I'll wait outside. Just signal me when you are finished in here."

"Thank you," Jason said as Mr. Phillips and Mr. Talbot exited the drab room.

Gray shelves, gray metal boxes, gray carpeting. It was beyond depressing. Avery wasn't a big decorator, but the room looked more like a prison than a bank space, though she supposed the bank wasn't exactly going for a "hang out in here" or a particularly fancy look. They'd gone with the bare-bones approach instead.

The three of them moved into one of the rooms and closed the door, though she was surprised by the lack of privacy, with wood-framed glass doors. Anyone could see in, but she turned her attention to the box, her heart rate elevating much as it had the other night when Parker told her he loved her. Today it was racing for very different reasons.

Please let it hold some answers. Some link to Skylar that will lead us to her body and her killer, Lord.

She ran her gloved fingers along the cool metal lid, and then taking a deep breath, opened the box.

Nada. It was empty.

She looked at Griffin and Jason, perplexed.

"Well, that's disappointing," Jason said.

"Extremely." She exhaled. "I was so hoping . . ."

"I know." Griffin squeezed her shoulder. "I was too. But this is not unexpected, considering the unknown visitor. He or she must have emptied the box."

"What now?" she asked.

"Now we need to figure out who the forger is."

Avery agreed.

Griffin led her back into the bank lobby and signaled Mr. Phillips, who was conversing heatedly with Miss Westin. Jason followed.

Mr. Phillips made one last statement to the woman, and she hurried away, sniffling and dabbing her eyes.

Mr. Phillips rejoined them. "The matter has been taken care of. I hope you found something helpful to your case."

"Unfortunately, no," Jason said. "The box was empty."

"Oh, I'm sorry to hear that."

"Whoever forged Skylar's signature must have removed the box's contents."

Mr. Phillips pushed his glasses up the bridge of his noise. "That is disturbing news."

"We need to speak with Miss Westin," Griffin said, "and we're going to need video footage of the sign-in area on the date in question." Griffin surveyed the lobby. "I will also be sending a crime-scene investigator here to dust for prints. I assume the forger wore gloves when handling the box, but we might get lucky."

"Yes, of course. We will cooperate fully. Miss Westin is in the break room." He gestured to the red door on the opposite side of the lobby area. "I'll go speak with security about the footage you need."

"Thank you." Jason nodded.

They moved through the lobby seating area, which consisted of a few red leather chairs and a modern-styled rug with red, purple, and yellow circles. At least the lobby had some color to it.

They found Miss Westin sobbing at a break room table, her back to them. She quickly swiped her eyes and wiped her nose with a crumpled tissue before turning to see who had entered. "Yes?" her voice quivered.

"Miss Westin." Griffin showed his badge. "Detectives Mc-Cray and Cavanaugh, and this is Avery Tate."

Tears pooled in her eyes. "I'm so sorry. I looked at the base signature and compared it. I can't believe I missed the difference. We're understaffed, and I'm sure it was hectic, and . . ." She bit her lip and then shook her head. "It's no excuse, though. I am so sorry for any trouble I have caused."

Avery sat down beside her. "We're not here to reprimand you." Clearly Mr. Phillips had seen to that. "We just need to ask you a few questions."

She sniffed and wiped her nose. "All right."

Avery pulled Skylar's picture from her purse and handed it to Miss Westin. "Do you recognize this woman?"

"No." Miss Westin shook her head.

"Do you recall what the woman who signed in for Box 206 looked like?" Jason asked.

"We see so many people normally I wouldn't recall, but I remember complimenting her on her necklace. She said she'd gotten it at Four Corners, and I'd just returned from a trip to the Southwest so we chatted for a moment."

Thank you, Lord.

At least they wouldn't leave completely empty-handed.

"What did the woman look like? Can you describe her?" Griffin inquired.

"She had long brown hair. She was slender, but her eyes and nose were different than hers," she said, gesturing to Skylar's picture.

"How so?" Jason asked.

"The woman's eyes were more . . . almond-shaped, I think you call it. I remember they were large and pretty."

"Anything else?" Avery asked, overstepping her bounds in the investigation, but they needed more to go on, and the words had come rushing out before she'd realized what she was doing.

"She had a cute button nose. Must be nice. I got born with this old honker." Miss Westin swished her tissue at it.

"Anything else you can think of?" Jason asked.

"The littlest detail could be helpful," Griffin said.

"I'm sorry. That's all I recall."

"Thank you for your help." Griffin handed her his card. "Now if we could just ask one more thing of you . . ."

"Anything."

"Could you accompany us to the security booth to identify the woman on the footage from that day?"

"Of course."

Mr. Phillips greeted them in the lobby, his frown focused on Miss Westin, but he remained on task. "We don't have footage of the deposit box room. It would clearly be a violation of privacy and would defeat the whole principle of a *private* safe deposit box, but we do have footage of the sign-in area."

Avery looked at Griffin. "Let's just pray the woman looked up."

They entered into the security booth.

"This is Aaron, our security guard on duty," Mr. Phillips said, pointing at a man about their age—dark hair and eyes, handsome, tall and lean—a runner, Avery guessed. "Aaron, this is Detectives McCray and Cavanaugh, and I apologize . . ." He looked to Avery, his eyes narrowing. "I don't believe I caught your name."

"This is our associate, Miss Tate," Jason said.

"And you know Miss Westin," Mr. Phillips said with a shaming edge to his voice.

Aaron nodded.

"If you could run the day and time we discussed," Mr. Phillips said.

Aaron played the footage.

"There," Miss Westin said after a few moments. "See the large necklace I was telling you about."

Mr. Phillips' light brows arched, but he remained silent.

"Can you zoom in?" Jason asked.

Aaron did so.

"And freeze right there."

A shot of her face. Her eyes were cast down, but it was her full face.

"Can you zoom in a little more?" Avery asked, her heart lurching. "I know that face. Crystal Lewis," she said. "That thieving, lying . . ."

31

Avery took a deep breath and calmed herself as they exited the viewing booth with a picture in hand of Crystal Lewis signing into Skylar's account.

Gary had probably broken into Skylar's jewelry box to steal her ring but found the safe deposit box key instead. He'd tracked it to the right bank, made Crystal a fake ID—some things never changed—put a wig on her and sent her in to take whatever was inside the safe deposit box. It was likely whatever Skylar had on the college kids.

"So?" Parker rubbed his hands together as Avery climbed in his car. "What was in the box?"

"Nothing," she said, still deflated on that point, but at least they had the next lead.

"What?" he said, pausing to wave to Griffin and Jason as they drove past them out of the bank's parking lot.

"So . . ." Parker reversed out of their slot. "Skylar emptied the box already?"

"No. Someone else did."

Parker arched a brow. "I'm guessing by that determined scowl you know who."

"Crystal Lewis," she said, waiting for Parker's reaction.

Not a lot fazed him, but that certainly did.

"You're kidding."

Avery shook her head. "Nope."

"Any idea what she took? What was in the box?"

"No. She entered with a large purse, so I'm guessing she put whatever it was in her purse, but we have her on camera." She handed Parker the picture.

Parker clutched the image. "Time to pay Crystal another visit."

"Yep. Griffin and Jason are headed there now. They said we could join them since I know Crystal and she might respond better with me present."

"Sounds like a plan."

"I also think we—or rather, they—need to dig a little deeper into Amanda King and Kyle Eason. I'm betting whatever Skylar was hiding was dirt on Kyle Eason."

"Which is why they couldn't find it at Skylar's place."

"Right."

"So now Crystal Lewis has it?"

"Yep."

"What do you think she's going to do with it?"

"Knowing her and Gary, if they're bright enough to figure out what they have, they'll probably try to take advantage of it."

"If Skylar was able to dig up dirt on Kyle Eason, then so can we."

"Or maybe we'll be lucky and Crystal will just hand it over," she said as they crossed Bel Air Road and pulled into Starbucks' drive-thru line.

Parker arched a brow.

"What?" She shrugged. "It could happen. You're awfully charming."

"Charming, eh?"

"Please, you know you are."

"Mmm." He leaned over while he waited in line. "How far will my charm get me?"

She kissed him on the cheek.

"Not exactly what I had in mind."

"I know what you had in mind. Now drive." She pointed at the line moving forward.

He stole a kiss on the lips and then did as instructed.

⟶

Now he was kissing her? Defiling her? Didn't he realize Avery Tate was *his*? He'd already found a new place and was preparing it just for her. It would be ready soon, very soon. He could almost taste it.

32

Declan and Lexi entered the Islamic Cultural Institute of the Mid-Atlantic and were quickly greeted by a man who introduced himself as Jari.

"Special Agents Grey and Kadyrov, I presume?" he said.

Rather than just show up, Declan had called the minute the Institute opened and scheduled an appointment with the cultural center's head, Dr. Khaled Ebeid.

Jari was dressed in a stylish and—from what Declan could tell—expensive, perfectly tailored gray suit, a tweed-style navy vest, and white shirt with matching navy tie. "Right this way." He led them down the light blue halls, along the black-and-white-tiled floor to two large doors.

Jari knocked and, upon a positive response, turned the gold door handles and pushed in both doors. A dignified man in his early fifties, of Egyptian descent, if Declan was correct, sat behind a large antique desk.

"Dr. Ebeid," Jari said, "may I present Special Agents Grey and Kadyrov."

"Please have a seat," Dr. Ebeid instructed. "Thank you. That will be all, Jari."

Jari nodded and excused himself from the room, closing the doors behind him.

"Thank you, Dr. Ebeid, for making time in your schedule to speak with us."

"Certainly. I am always happy to entertain those interested in our organization. This is why you are here, to learn about the work we do?"

Declan knew a fair amount about their organization, thanks to the agent assigned to learn everything the Bureau could about it. On the surface the organization functioned as a center to celebrate the Islamic culture, to be a focal point in Baltimore's thriving and growing Muslim neighborhoods. Declan's colleague described Dr. Ebeid as an unofficial Islamic diplomat to the region, an Islamic cultural attaché. Beneath the surface, however, the Institute had ties to extremist groups. The Bureau had a man deep undercover, but they were too far into the investigation to risk compromising his identity now. Thankfully, Declan had other sources to call on, and he had a feeling he'd need to.

"Actually we are looking for someone."

Dr. Ebeid arched a thick brow. "Oh?"

"Yes. An Indonesian man newly arrived in America."

"And you wish to recommend our institution to him?"

"We believe he's already been in contact." Lexi slid Anajay Darmadi's wanted picture across the gilded desk to Dr. Ebeid.

Ebeid's face hardened before he fixed a congenial smile on it. "I'm afraid I don't know what you're talking about." He handed the picture back to Lexi.

Lexi cocked her head. "That's odd."

Dr. Ebeid didn't bother asking why. He clearly wanted this conversation over with.

"We have an eyewitness placing Anajay Darmadi at a pay-phone in Canton on Saturday, shortly after he fled the merchant cargo ship he was smuggled in on."

"Perhaps your eyewitness was incorrect. I'm sorry to say that, for many, people of Indonesian descent are indistinguishable."

"No. We know it was Anajay. His fingerprints were on the phone," Lexi said.

Whenever she spoke, a tiny muscle in Dr. Ebeid's jaw flickered. He clearly did not appreciate a woman questioning him.

"I see," he said.

"And can you imagine our surprise when the call he placed was to the Institute." Lexi smiled.

"We receive many calls. Perhaps someone else used that phone to call the Institute."

"Perhaps the Institute gets plenty of calls, but that payphone rarely gets used. There was only one call placed Saturday and it was to the Institute."

"Well, he did not speak to me."

"May we find out to whom he might have spoken?"

"I'm sorry, but I'm not going to expose my employees to federal questioning."

"I had a feeling you might say that, so I brought this." Declan handed Dr. Ebeid a warrant allowing him to question all employees and to check the Institute's phone records. He had a second warrant to check their organization-owned vehicles, but he wouldn't play that card just yet.

Dr. Ebeid set the warrant down. "I don't believe that will be necessary."

"Oh? Why is that?" Lexi said with raised brows.

"As I recall now, there was a man who called here this weekend and spoke with Jari, asking about recommendations for a place to stay. Jari got the impression the man was in some sort of trouble, so he promptly ended the call."

Amazing how his memory came right back. "Four minutes and thirty-two seconds doesn't seem prompt."

"He may have put him on hold for part of that time."

"I see. And did Jari get his name?" Declan asked.

"He did not."

Now it was time to play the second card. "Then why did you send a car to pick him up?"

Dr. Ebeid cleared his throat. "I beg your pardon?"

"A black Lincoln Town Car, like the ones you have sitting out front, picked Mr. Darmadi up within a half hour of his call."

"Do you know how many Lincoln Town Cars there are in this city? You can't possibly assume it was one of ours."

"Fortunately, I don't have to assume." Declan pulled out the second warrant and handed it to Dr. Ebeid, knowing the rest of their team was in place just around the block, waiting for the call to proceed. "I'll notify my team to begin their search. I assume Jari can give us the keys?"

Dr. Ebeid practically choked out his response. "This is an outrage." He pressed the intercom button. "Jari, call Nidal down here immediately."

"And Nidal would be?"

"The Institute's lawyer."

"Interesting a cultural institute would feel the need to keep a lawyer not only on payroll but physically on the premises."

Dr. Ebeid didn't respond.

33

After a much-needed stop at Starbucks for a caffeine boost, Avery and Parker made the drive back to Crystal's place, where Griffin and Jason were already waiting.

She and Parker climbed out of his Land Rover, the day promising to be equally as warm and humid as the past few, and moved for Griffin and Jason, both leaning against their unmarked car.

Avery shielded her eyes from the sun with her hand. "What's up?"

"She's not home," Griffin said.

"Did you try Gary's?" Avery pointed to his trailer.

"I will now." Griffin strode over to Gary's trailer, Jason at his side.

He knocked several times, then shook his head. "No answer."

They walked back to their cars.

"What now?" Avery asked.

"We're waiting on a warrant to come through. In the meantime, we're going to talk with Megan Kent."

"Okay. Thanks," Avery said. She knew they were doing their

job, but she also knew Griffin was working the case as a friend too, and she deeply appreciated it.

"While they're talking to Megan, why don't we swing back by Modell's, since Vinnie hasn't gotten back to you?" Parker suggested.

"Sounds like a plan." One she wasn't looking forward to, but a necessary one all the same. She still couldn't believe Parker hadn't asked about her less-than-savory past. If the situation were reversed, her curiosity would be sky-high.

Parker and Avery entered Modell's pawnshop.

Vinnie looked up from the customer he was attending to and scowled at the sight of them.

"This ought to be fun," Parker murmured to Avery.

She had a sinking feeling he didn't know the half of it. She'd seen that scowl on Vinnie's face before, and it never boded well. She had the option of turning on the charm like the old days, flirting with a man who now revolted her, but she no longer played those games.

They waited until Vinnie finished ringing up his sale and the patron exited the store before they approached him. He was wearing jeans and a red shirt with *Modell's* scrolled across the front in white block letters. Modell's shop attire hadn't changed in a dozen years, and neither had her past. She'd changed but her past remained the same—frozen in time, a horrible reminder of her life before coming to Christ.

"I told you I'd call," Vinnie said, his tone gruff.

"And yet you didn't," Avery said, striding toward him but keeping a fair amount of distance—the width of a display case was not far enough.

"Were you able to call around?" Parker asked.

"Yeah, but as you can see it's been busy. Didn't have time to call you."

"Or maybe Stallings didn't want you calling us."

"Stallings sends business my way, but I run my own shop—and life, for that matter."

She doubted that. Whenever Max Stallings was involved, there were expectations, and Vinnie no doubt had to dance to them just like all of Stallings' lackeys.

"So what'd you learn?" Parker asked.

Vinnie glanced at the other customers milling about the shop and then leaned in.

Thankfully Parker leaned in to meet him, as she would never be that close to Vinnie Modell again.

"I talked with all the pawnshops in the area, and Boyd hasn't pawned anything in the past few months. Last thing he hawked was a knife about three months back at a place called, cleverly enough, The Pawnshop."

"Thanks, Vinnie."

He looked at Parker and then at her with a cocky grin. "How about you thank me like you did in the old days?"

"How about I knock that smug grin off your face?" Avery retorted.

"Seriously?" He laughed.

"You'd be surprised," Parker said. "But I think we'll just be leaving."

"So you're missing the gym," Parker said as they stepped outside.

"No. Just hated hearing him talk to me like that. It brought back a lot of bad memories."

"I'm sorry."

"It was my own fault."

"We all make mistakes."

"I've made more than my fair share."

"And all that got wiped away with Christ's sacrifice, so stop beating yourself up for something He's already taken care of."

She exhaled. "You're right."

He held the car door open, and she climbed inside as he moved around the Rover and climbed in the driver's side door.

He kicked the air on and shifted to face her. "You wanna talk about it?"

"No." *Yes.*

He clasped her hand. "I'm not here to judge. Heaven knows I'm in no place to judge anyone, but I've got a great listening ear if you just wanna vent."

He was offering her the chance to finally voice everything she'd wrestled with for years, and if he truly loved her, he'd keep his word and not judge. If he did judge, she knew he wasn't the one.

She swallowed hard. "All my life I didn't think I was worth anything."

"Is that why you ended up with Gary?"

She nodded.

"But you must have ended it at some point. You left the trailer park when you were sixteen."

"I had to." She left it at that. At least for now, but she had to tell him sooner or later.

"It was incredibly brave of you."

She shrugged.

"It was." He shifted closer. "And Jesus? Where did he find you?"

"On my own, at nineteen. Skylar had moved back to the trailer park to take care of her mom, and I went to an outreach center for a meal. A lady took time to sit down and chat with me. Before I left, she prayed for me, a total stranger, but her words were so kind. I didn't know what to do with that.

Something inside changed that day. I kept going back and talking with Sue, the director of the outreach center. She led me to Christ, and eventually I accepted Him as my Savior. She still goes to my church."

"That's so awesome."

"Indescribable."

"Then you know you're a new creation. Your past is in the past."

"I know."

"But?"

"But all that pain doesn't instantly go away. It gets better, and I know it's in the past, but . . ."

"Now you're smack back in it."

"Yeah."

"But it's different now."

She arched a brow.

"Because you're a new creation. A different person. That changes everything. Look at how you stood up to Vinnie."

"True."

"But I'm so sorry you have to be around all this. Is there anything I can do?"

She leaned into him, resting her head in the crook of his neck. "Just love me." That's all she'd ever wanted in a partner, in a husband. Someone who truly loved her as described in the Bible.

She was in love with a man for the third time in her life, and the first two relationships had crashed and burned. Gary abused her and Joshua dumped her when she got ousted from the art community, his reputation and position in Baltimore's high society more important to him than her. Would Parker truly stand by her side no matter what?

He stroked her hair as she nuzzled into his hold. "Done, lass." He kissed the top of her head.

Father, Parker's right. I am a new creation. I need to let this go. Part of me thought I had, but I'd just been stuffing it down. Being back here, back around Gary and Vinnie . . . it's raised it right to the surface. You aren't like anyone from my past. You are trustworthy and you deserve all of me—battle scars and all. Not just the parts I'm willing to give.

She took a deep breath and blew it out slowly.

I give myself fully to you, Lord, and I pray so desperately for the healing only you can bring. I know the journey may not be easy. How could it be? But thank you for giving me Parker to walk through this at my side. Thank you for bringing a good man into my life. Please let him prove true. I know he is, but I've been let down so many times, deep down I fear when I tell him everything, he'll bail. Please don't let that happen. Let him be the man I believe him to be.

"I know what might help relieve some of that tension," Parker said, rubbing her shoulder.

"Oh?" *Neck rub?* She could go for one of those.

"A little time in the ring."

That always helped. But . . . "Do we have time?" They were on a case.

"Sure. Instead of grabbing lunch out, we'll hit the gym and bring takeout back to the lab."

That sounded perfect.

34

Avery cricked her neck from side to side, loosening up, muscles still tense from the bumps and bruises of the last few days. "I can have someone else spar with me," she offered.

"Only if it makes you feel more comfortable," Parker said, dropping his gym bag—which he always kept in his car, knowing he had to hit the gym when he had free slips of time—to the ground.

"No. I'm good." She wanted to see what he had. "But you have to promise not to take it easy on me."

"As you wish." He climbed in the ring, shaking out his arms, his colorful tattoo of evergreens running from his wrist to just below his elbow.

They started tentatively, sparring slowly, but soon they both moved full-steam into the session.

Perspiration drenching, Avery did another roundhouse kick. This time Parker anticipated it and ducked low under her leg.

She swung a right hook, and his hand barely made it up in time to block it.

He was good, but he was also taking it easy on her. It was so obvious.

"Come on, lad," she said playfully. "Let me see what you got. Stop holding back."

"Okay." In one quick move he swept her legs out from under her. She quickly reciprocated the favor—both laid out on the mat, both crazy enough to laugh.

Parker rolled on his side, propping his weight on his elbow, and leaned down low to kiss her. "Truce?"

"Truce." She smiled as his lips melded to hers.

━━━➤

Declan paced the Islamic Cultural Institute of the Mid-Atlantic's parking lot, waiting as the techs worked the last Town Car. Lexi leaned against the car, drinking a Coke.

Please, Father, Declan prayed. *If Anajay Darmadi was in that car, let us find evidence or we're back to the drawing board.*

"I've got something over here," Sam, one of the techs, said.

"Yeah?" Hope rose at the tone of Sam's voice.

"You're going to want to see this."

Declan and Lexi moved to the tech's side, and he handed Declan the electronic fingerprint reader. They had a hit. Anajay Darmadi had been in the back of the Town Car parked beside them.

Thank you, Lord.

"Any idea who was driving?" Lexi asked.

"One of the employees. Jari Youssef."

They reentered the building and Jari greeted them, his smile fading as he took in their countenance.

"We're going to need you to come with us, Jari," Declan said.

"I don't understand. What is this about?"

"We just need to ask you some questions."

"Then ask them here," Dr. Ebeid said, rounding the corner.

Jari wouldn't be able to speak freely anywhere in the building. No. Their best bet was to take him to the Bureau. To offer him a plea. He knew Jari would never go for it, but perhaps they could get something out of the man.

"I'm afraid we need to take him in for questioning." Declan indicated for Jari to stand, and he cuffed him before leading him toward the front door.

"Interrogation? Handcuffs?" Dr. Ebeid said, blocking the door. "This is an outrage."

"Khaled," the Institute's lawyer, Nidal, said, "they have the right. Let them go. I'll meet Jari over at the Bureau office."

Declan stepped past Dr. Ebeid and put Jari Youssef into the back of his car as Lexi climbed in the passenger side. They pulled out of the lot and headed for Route 40, banking west on 40 en route for 695 North and their office.

They stopped at the light by the Shell gas station at the corner of Route 40 and Swann Road. It was just about to turn green when Declan's rear passenger window shattered. He floored the gas, speeding through the intersection with lights flashing.

Lexi looked back. "He's been shot in the head."

Declan called it in, and emergency personnel met them in the Westview Shopping Center parking lot, but it was too late. Jari Youssef was dead.

35

Kate greeted Parker and Avery as they entered Parker's lab at CCI. It was weird because every other case Avery had worked with him had been at his old lab in the ME's office. This one looked very similar and not at all like a lab. It was clean and professional, the walls painted a rich hunter green and the cabinetry a rich cherrywood. Inset track lighting lined most of the ceiling on either side of the at-times-required fluorescent light. It looked like Parker—masculine, unique, and a clear love for the outdoors in color choice and wood accents. The man had good taste.

"Good to see you guys," Kate said from the doorway.

"You too. Got you some lunch. I set it in the kitchen. I was just taking a quick assessment of things before we eat," Parker said.

"Awesome. Thanks. I'm starving and the kitchen's bare except for peanut butter and pickles. Oh, and ingredients for chocolate chip cookies."

"Cookies for lunch don't sound so bad." Avery smiled.

"Please. Kate bake something?" Parker laughed.

"I'd argue, but you're right. So what'd you get me?"

"Mission barbeque."

"I love you."

"I know. I'm just that lovable."

Kate shook her head and moved for the kitchen.

"We better follow or she'll get into ours," Parker said.

They all grabbed their food and headed for the leather chairs in the lounge area.

Kate took a bite. "Yum." She wiped her mouth with a napkin. "Hey, Avery, maybe after lunch, you could take a look at Luke's photo."

"Sure," Avery said, praying she'd be able to give Kate some good news and not dash her hopes.

After lunch she studied the image file that had been e-mailed to Kate, searching for any signs that the image had been photoshopped or altered in any way, but she couldn't find any trace of corruption.

Kate hadn't stopped pacing since Avery sat down at the computer.

She pushed back from Kate's desk.

"Well?" Kate finally paused her pacing.

"Well, I can't say it's Luke, as I've never met him, but I can say the image is legit. It hasn't been altered or photoshopped in any way."

"I knew it." Kate's smile beamed.

"Katie, it's impossible to say that's Luke for certain," Parker said. "I'm not trying to quash your hope, but—"

"Funny. That seemed to be exactly what you were doing."

"I'm sorry. I just want you to be careful."

After they finished lunch and entered his lab, Avery closed the door behind them, giving them privacy and the freedom to speak without concern of hurting Kate's feelings. "You seem so sure it's a scam," she said.

"No. I just hate to see her get her hopes so high on such a slim piece of evidence."

"You don't think it was Luke?" She lifted Skylar's sweater, her gloves in place, trying to hold on to the little bit she had left of her friend.

"I think when people have been gone that long without a word, they aren't coming back." He turned and looked at her, his gaze shifting to Skylar's sweater. "I'm so sorry." He stepped toward her. "That was horribly insensitive of me to say given the circumstances."

"No." Tears stung her eyes. "You're right. That's always been my experience, and clearly from the video we saw, Skylar's already gone. It's just . . . I wish . . ."

He stepped to her side. "Wish what?"

She clutched the sweater tighter. "That I'd been able to reach her in time."

"Reach her . . . for Jesus?"

She nodded, the gravity of her guilt in the situation pressing down on her again. "It's my fault."

"That she wasn't a Christian?"

"Maybe if I'd tried harder, been there more . . . But actually, I was referring to leading her down the wrong path to begin with."

Parker's brows furrowed.

"I'm the one who pushed Skylar into committing her first crime when we were twelve. *Twelve.*" Her eyes stung with hot tears, but she fought them.

"I don't know the exact circumstances of what happened," Parker said. "But people make their own choices."

"But she was younger than me, by a whole six months, but she still idolized me—why, I'll never know . . ."

"Because you are so strong."

"Not when it counted."

He tilted his head and she froze. She needed to tell him, but the words wouldn't form.

"Av?"

"The point is, Skylar followed me down that path because I pushed her into it, but I could never manage to pull her back off of it." She went into detail, explaining the first trespassing, then shoplifting, then drugs, then using guys to numb the pain when in the end that only caused more pain.

She looked down, scared to see the judgment that had to be in Parker's eyes.

"Love." He tipped her chin up. "Skylar made those choices. No one can make you do anything. And no one can make you accept Jesus as your Savior. You can only share the good news with them."

Good news. It was, and yet being surrounded by her past made her feel like a sheep among wolves.

Please, Father, protect me fully.

She'd never been in a more dangerous situation since she'd joined the criminal justice field as Parker's crime-scene photographer.

"There's more. I can read it on your face."

Of course he could. Well, might as well go for broke. He'd either be the man she believed he was or he too would let her down, but it would be before things went any further in her heart.

"I—"

Parker's phone rang, but he ignored it.

"Aren't you going to answer it?"

"This . . . you"—he cupped her face—"are far more important."

"But it could be a call about the case. Please answer it."

He glanced at the number. "It's Griffin."

"Answer it."

Reluctantly he did so and listened for a moment. "Okay," he said. "Thanks." He hung up.

"That was quick."

"Griff said they are swinging back by Crystal's place for one more try today."

She grabbed her purse. "Let's go."

He rested a hand on hers. "Let's finish talking first."

"It can wait."

"Are you sure? It seemed pretty important."

"Positive." It'd buy her more time.

"Okay, but whatever you have to tell me, please know nothing you could say could change my love for you—other than deepening it. The more I see and learn, the harder I fall. You're a warrior, and that's flat-out hot."

She laughed. How on earth did he have the ability to make her laugh in such circumstances? "You're a mess."

"Ah, but now I'm your mess." He placed a kiss on her lips. "And only yours."

<hr>

Still in shock, Declan entered the Merritt Athletic Club off Boston Street in Canton, not far from where Anajay Darmadi had come ashore. His mind was racing down a million possible angles, but taking this time out to meet with Moha was exactly what he needed.

The meet had been set, and after Jari's murder—no doubt by his own people—Declan wanted to not only catch Anajay Darmadi but also bring down Dr. Khaled Ebeid and his supposed cultural institute for abetting an international terrorist.

He followed the meet drill, dropping his gym bag in a locker with the padlock both knew the combination to and heading for the treadmills. He climbed on the one at the end, the two machines to his right still available. Moha had been an informant—well, more of a consultant—for Declan for close to a year now, whenever matters grew heated in the Islamic community and intersected with a case Declan or one of his fellow agents was working.

Declan started running, keeping his pace slow and steady, knowing after their talk he'd finish a strong run. He craved a release of pent-up energy and frustration.

Why hadn't he just left the Bureau and signed on with the private investigation firm Kate had founded after her own departure from the Bureau three years ago? It would distance him from the politics he hated. But when it came down to it, he loved his job with the Bureau. Loved his job but certainly didn't love the bureaucracy or politics.

Moha entered and climbed on the treadmill beside him. He started slowly, walking and offering a nod in Declan's direction.

Declan nodded back. The overhead TVs were loud, and nearly every man and woman in the place had headphones in their ears, no doubt listening to music or audiobooks.

Dr. Moha Natsheh, PhD, was the curator of Islamic Art and Armor at the Walter's Art Gallery and an associate professor of history at Hopkins's Krieger School for the Arts and Sciences, teaching courses in social and art history of the medieval Middle East. He was a brilliant man with amazing connections in the Islamic culture of the city and among the growing communities within it—Middle Eastern and Southeast Asian being the two primary areas of growth. Declan had no doubt that Moha had met Dr. Ebeid, PhD, as Dr. Ebeid held a particular interest in the arts and medieval Middle Eastern history. He hoped Moha could shed some much-needed light on the situation and, if at all possible, on the undercurrents and inner workings of the Institute.

"As always, everything I say is strictly confidential," Declan began. They hadn't alerted the public to Anajay Darmadi's presence in the United States for one very simple yet important reason: They didn't want panic to ensue. The chances of someone helping them find Darmadi based on his face being plastered all over the news were slim, and the massive panic such news would instill, sky-high.

"As always, I risk my life by talking to you, so I trust you will keep my name out of all communications."

"Of course." He'd given Moha his word many times. "We have a known terrorist in town. At least he entered Baltimore Saturday, and intel leads us to believe he's still here."

"Tim McVeigh or 9/11?" Moha asked, clearly working hard to keep his expression neutral.

"Foreign, highly dangerous. Responsible for several overseas bombings."

"Any leads?"

"Actually, yes. Anajay Darmadi, the terrorist in question, phoned the Islamic Cultural Institute of the Mid-Atlantic upon his arrival, and they sent a car to pick him up."

"You know this for certain?"

"Yes."

"Did they try to explain their actions?"

"I was in the process of transporting the man who drove Darmadi to my office for interrogation when someone shot and killed him through my car window."

Moha placed his feet on the sides of the treadmill, instantly stopping, and stared at him with concern. "You are okay?" He looked him over.

"I'm fine . . . but ticked. I'm going to find who did this, but I have a strong feeling I already know who ordered the hit."

"Who?" Moha moved back to his run, scanning the crowd to see if anyone was watching them.

"Dr. Khaled Ebeid."

Moha shook his head as sweat drizzled down his neck. "Then you are in a very dangerous position, my friend."

"You know Dr. Ebeid?"

"I've spoken with him on numerous occasions."

"And?"

"He's a well-spoken and highly educated man."

"With ties to extremist groups."

"So the rumor goes."

"Has he ever discussed his affiliations with such groups with you?"

Moha chuckled and wiped his face with his running towel. "No. A man like that . . . he does not go about bragging and voicing his private business."

"But there are rumors?" He knew there were. The agent undercover had told them as much.

"Yes. People talk."

"About what specifically?"

"About how well connected and well financed Dr. Ebeid and his organization are."

"Well protected too. Dr. Ebeid keeps his lawyer on the premises."

"I'm not surprised."

"What are your thoughts on Anajay's motives for staying in the area?" If they were right that he was.

"If he hasn't moved it's either because he's lying low until he can find a way to move without notice, he's a sleeper, or Baltimore is his target."

36

Parker and Avery climbed from Parker's Land Rover as Griffin stepped from his vehicle, Jason following suit. They were trying Crystal Lewis's place for a second time, because both he and Avery, in particular, believed Crystal Lewis was the next step in the investigation.

Parker and Avery approached, both wearing a nice shade of pink lip gloss on their lips.

Griffin chuckled.

"What?" they both said.

He shook his head, trying to smother his laughter as Jason did the same. "Nothing. Let's do this."

Parker narrowed his eyes, staring at Griff as he climbed Crystal's metal steps. "Seriously, what was with the chuckle?"

Griffin glanced at the pink sparkly shine on Parker's lips and took pity on the man. "You got a little something . . ." He pointed to his own lips. "Right there. Nice shade on you, though."

Parker licked his lips, clearly tasting whatever fragrance the gloss held, and smiled.

Of course Parker wouldn't be embarrassed. Avery, on the other hand, blushed for the first time since he'd met her.

Griffin rapped on the door, and it swung open. He frowned, and Jason pulled his gun.

"Police, Ms. Lewis. We're coming in," Griffin said.

Griffin and Jason swept the place, finding no one, and signaled Parker and Avery to enter.

"The place has been tossed," Griffin said.

"Someone must have come while we were away," Avery said in frustration.

"On the bright side, it means we're on the right trail."

"Which is?" Jason said.

"Blackmail."

"Whatever was in the safe deposit box," he said.

"That's my bet." Avery rested her hands on her hips. "Now the question is whether or not it's still here."

"Let's spread out. I'll take the kitchen," Griffin said.

"I've got the living room," Jason offered.

"I'll take the bedroom," Avery said.

"Need help?" Parker asked with a wink.

The second blush Griffin had ever witnessed flared on Avery's cheeks.

"I've got it handled. Why don't you work the other bedroom she used as a catch-all?"

Parker smiled. "Yes, ma'am."

An hour later they'd searched the entire trailer and come up empty-handed on what Crystal had taken from the safe deposit box, but Griffin had found the safe deposit box key in the sugar bowl.

"Amateurs." Avery rolled her eyes. "I found the fake ID Crystal used, along with the rest of these." She tossed a handful of false driver's licenses on the kitchen counter.

"Good work," Griffin said, "but the question remains—what did Crystal take from Skylar's safe deposit box?"

"And, better yet—" Parker said.

"Where is it now?" Avery finished for him. "I wonder if Gary and Crystal are already attempting to blackmail Amanda and Kyle with what they found in Skylar's box."

"Or are they sitting on it?" Griffin said. "We need to question Gary and Crystal if they ever show."

"Parker and I will stay until they show."

"A stakeout?" Parker smiled. "I'm game."

Avery smirked. "I bet you are."

"You two kids have fun, and behave," Griffin said as he and Jason headed for his vehicle. "Call if you want a break, and I'll send an unmarked patrol car."

"We'll be good," Parker said.

"Uh-huh." Griff shook his head and opened the trailer door, Jason beside him. "Let's go have another chat with Gerard Vaughn. This all started with him, and he hasn't been investigated fully on our end. It's time we correct that."

37

Being the gentleman that he was, Parker offered to wait at the trailer lot while Avery ran to the 7-Eleven up the road for stakeout supplies. Clearly you couldn't do a stakeout without supplies.

She grabbed snacks, drinks, the latest copy of *Outside* magazine, and a few Marvel comics and headed for the counter, where she inquired about Crystal on the off chance the teen working the register knew her. When Avery had been living in the park, everyone in the area knew everyone. The teenager knew both Gary and Crystal but said he hadn't seen either of them since Gary came in last night near the end of his shift for cigarettes.

When she returned to the spot they'd deemed the least likely to be seen from either Gary or Crystal's trailers while still being able to keep an eye on them, Parker climbed into the passenger seat and smiled.

Maybe he had some good news. "Anything?"

"Nope," he said, breaking into the bag of Doritos she'd purchased and smiling at the Marvel comics.

"Then why the nice smile?"

"Just happy to see you." He popped a cheese-covered chip into his mouth.

"I was gone all of ten minutes."

"Far too long."

She chuckled and reached for the Doritos. "You better share."

They read the comics, ate the Doritos, and chitchatted for over an hour, and then Avery grew quiet. She needed to tell him, if she could just muster her courage.

Please, Father, give me the strength and don't let him look at me differently.

"What is it, love?" he asked, concern marring his brow.

"How do you do that?"

"Do what?"

"Always know when something is bothering me?"

He shrugged. "God-given gift."

"This could cause real problems long term," she half joked.

He intertwined his fingers with hers. "What is it?"

She swallowed, so nervous her entire body felt like it was trembling. She slipped her hair behind her back, fidgeting it into a braid—something, anything to keep her distracted from the pain of what she was about to share.

"What I was going to share back at the lab . . ."

"Yes?" he said softly after she was silent for a moment.

"There's something else about my past that you should know."

Genuine concern filled his handsome face, his full attention rapt on her.

"I . . ." She shifted, embarrassed she was actually trembling.

"Honey, what is it?" He rubbed her arms. "Are you cold? I can turn down the air."

"No." She looked down, shaking her head. "It's not that."

"Then, what? I've told you, nothing you tell me is going to make me love you any less. It's not possible."

"I hope that's true."

He clasped her hand. "I promise."

She looked up at him. She'd heard the word *promise* before—not from him, but from others—and it always had come back void. "How can you promise before you've even heard?"

"Because I know you."

She bit her bottom lip. "Not all of me."

"Then tell me."

At the lab he'd told her that she wasn't defined by her past but, rather, by her identity in Christ, but it still seemed too good to be true. Not on God's end, but on hers. Could *she* really be beloved, protected, chosen?

Please, Lord, I'm so terrified to have this conversation, but Parker deserves to know before he continues a relationship with me. Please help me to get the words out, because I can't do it on my own.

She inhaled and exhaled deeply, starting before she chickened out. "My mom left when I was eight. Just took off one day, leaving me with my stepfather, Fred." The name alone burned acid in her throat, unsure she could even utter the next. "And his son from his first marriage, Peter."

"I'm so sorry. Is that why you left when you turned sixteen?"

"Not because of my mom." Her head dipped, shame rushing over her. "Because of Peter."

"Peter?" he said, clearly clueless as to the direction this was headed.

"Peter was five years older than me and much stronger."

Parker's eyes widened. Now he knew, at least part of it. She could read it on his face. "Did he hurt you?"

She nodded and prayed God gave her the strength to continue. "At first it was just verbal bullying, then he started pushing me around, and when I turned twelve . . ." She swallowed, tears burning down her shame-filled face.

Parker wrapped his arm around her, securing her in his loving embrace. "He . . . ?" He nodded.

She nodded again, so thankful she didn't have to say it out loud. But now Parker knew.

She swiped at her tears, now gushing. "It went on until I ran away, talking Skylar into going with me."

"But Skylar went back?"

"Only when she learned her mom was dying. She ended up staying and has been there since."

"But you never went back."

"Only twice to see Sky, after Fred and Peter moved to Florida."

"Did you ever press charges against Peter?"

And tell the world her shame? She shook her head.

"Maybe it's time you do. Maybe that's what you need to fully heal."

Fully heal? No matter how many hours she spent in prayer or in the gym punching the bag until her hands bled, she doubted she'd ever be whole. Peter took a part of her and replaced it with hot shame.

"It would be my word against his," she said.

"I'm not trying to push you by any means. I just thought. . ." He clutched her tighter into his embrace. "I'm just shifting into protective mode, where I want to kill Peter, but that's something only you can decide. Pray about it. See where God leads you, but pray, for Peter's sake, that our paths never cross."

God had been leading her to hand it all over to Him, to stop fighting it, repressing it, trying to forget, but the weight had only grown heavier.

"Have you given it to Jesus?" Parker asked, beyond perceptive. "What I can only imagine involves pain, anger, hurt, fear . . . ?"

Tears bounced off their joined hands. "I want to. I've tried."

"But?"

"I'm terrified." Letting go equaled vulnerability. Something she swore she'd never be again for anyone. But this wasn't anyone—this was her Savior.

Parker engulfed her deeper into his embrace, and for once she didn't stem the tears.

She'd told the man she loved her dirty secret and his eyes were filled with nothing but love. How was that possible?

He watched from the woods. What were they doing in there? Hugging? Was she crying?

Had he made her cry? What the devil was going on?

Avery he'd handle, though she'd no doubt put up another fight. She was stronger than he realized, but he was prepared now. He just needed to get Parker Mitchell out of the way.

38

After receiving a quick update on the progress of tracking Anajay Darmadi, Declan moved into his office, realizing he hadn't eaten lunch and it was nearly time for dinner.

He was too preoccupied to eat. He pulled up Anajay's record and photo on his computer, staring into the man's dark eyes. "Who are you?"

"Tanner Shaw. We've met before."

He looked up to find Tanner standing in his office doorway.

"Tanner. I was just . . ." He pointed at his computer. "Never mind. What are you doing here?"

"I wanted to talk to you about Hana and her family."

"Hana . . . from the ship?"

"Yes." Tanner strode in and sat opposite Declan. "Immigration won't tell me anything, and I want to know what's happening with them."

"That's really thoughtful of you—"

"But?"

"I didn't say *but*."

"But you were going to."

Yeah, he was. "However . . ." he began with a smile.

She looked the complete opposite of amused.

"However, once Immigration takes the refugees, it's out of my hands."

"That's convenient."

"It's just the way it works."

"Just because something is the way it works doesn't make it right."

As quickly as she'd entered his office, she left.

He sat back in his chair, knowing he needed to focus the rest of his energy on the manhunt for Anajay Darmadi, not chase after Tanner's wishes.

He tried to focus. Really tried, but Tanner's big eyes, her passionate plea, the image of her getting Hana and Adam to laugh and smile under such awful circumstances replayed over and over through his mind.

With a grunt, he lifted the phone and called an old friend at Immigration.

Six hours later, with no sign of either Gary or Crystal, Parker looked to Avery curled up in the seat beside him, using the blanket he always kept in the rear as a bunched-up pillow. She wasn't asleep, but she was exhausted. It'd been a very long, very crazy few days.

"I think we should call Griff and have him send that patrol car over," he said, knowing they were reaching the limit of their effectiveness.

"And if Gary or Crystal return?"

"Griff will let us know."

She yawned. "All right."

That had been far easier than he'd imagined. She really must be exhausted.

Parker called Griff, and within twenty minutes another officer was in place.

Avery looked over her shoulder as they pulled out of the park. "Are you sure we shouldn't just stay?"

Parker stifled a yawn. "I'm sure."

"Getting too old for an all-night stakeout, are we?" she teased through another yawn of her own.

"Something like that." He smiled, knowing she needed her rest. They'd been going for hours—days, actually—and Avery was carrying a burden he couldn't fathom.

Please, Father, help her hand the burden over to you and to finally let go of it instead of trying to shoulder the weight. I know being strong and self-sufficient is important to her, given what she went through, but please help her to realize you are waiting with open arms to carry this for her and that you can be trusted to take this. That she can be vulnerable with you. That you are safe. That I am safe. Show her who you are fully and let her be consumed by your overwhelming love.

Parker held the door of Charm City Investigations for Avery. He just wanted to wrap her in his arms and never let go. And he wanted to take her straight home. She was exhausted, but Griffin had called as they were leaving the trailer park—said the word *pizza* and explained they were all meeting up to discuss where they were at on the case—so Avery insisted on going, but he wouldn't let her stay long. She needed her rest.

"Hey, slowpokes," Griffin said, walking by with a Styrofoam plate piled high with pepperoni pizza.

"Thanks for waiting for us," Parker said jovially.

"The stomach waits for no man," Kate said, biting into her slice of Hawaiian. Always Hawaiian pizza with her.

Parker placed a sheltering hand on the small of Avery's back, and instead of jolting out of his hold, she sunk into it, making his heart soar. "We better get in there before Kate finishes off the food. She may be little, but her appetite is far from it."

Kate stuck her cheese-covered tongue out.

"Real ladylike." Griffin shook his head.

"Yeah, that's what I'm known for," Kate said, plopping down in one of the five leather chairs encircling the coffee table and dangling her legs over the side.

Avery wondered about Luke, and particularly about the dynamic between him and Kate before his disappearance seven years ago. Kate's latest photograph offered little more than a sliver of hope. But a little hope was better than none.

"Avery," Finley said, practically barreling across the floor. "It's so good to see you again." She gave her a big hug.

"You just saw her two days ago," Parker said, but he totally knew the feeling. He loathed every minute Avery was out of his sight. He wasn't him without her. Not the *him* that came fully alive in her presence.

"Hence, good to see you *again*." Finley smirked. "Griff has been catching me up to speed."

"Why don't we all take a seat in here so we can go over everything together?" Declan called from the conference room.

Everyone got their plates and took a seat for the second time in close to as many days. Despite the awful circumstances, it felt like a family gathering together for dinner, and it made Avery feel a part of something good and healthy, which she'd never experienced before.

"So run through the updates, Declan," Kate said, tossing Declan a dry-erase marker. "You've got the board."

"First, did you tell everyone about the shooting?" Parker asked Declan, catching the story while grabbing his pizza.

"Shooting?" Griffin said.

"I'll take that as a no," Parker said.

"We're here to go over Skylar's case, not mine."

"We have time for both," Avery said. "Please, go ahead."

Declan shared what he could, and when he finished everyone expressed gratitude he hadn't been shot as well.

"You need to be careful. Watch your back," Griffin said.

"Yeah, it made an impression, to say the least," Declan said.

"I imagine a bullet will do that," Kate said, sitting cross-legged and cupping her mug of cocoa she'd made.

Declan shook his head. "I still can't fathom cocoa and pizza."

"Yeah, Katie, that's just wrong," Griffin said.

"I'm not asking either of you to try it. Now, Declan, get back to the board."

Avery settled in to listen.

Working the board was Declan's thing—running logical, known facts. Griffin read people. Parker found stuff, and Kate . . .

Kate. Avery thought a moment. She was a hacker extraordinaire, but in addition to her cyber genius, she somehow kept all the guys in line despite being—at least upon first impression—a rebel. She loved the guys fiercely and steadfastly like brothers. And she loved Luke, a man she hadn't seen or heard a word from in seven years. It made Avery wonder about the depth of love they shared.

"Parker, you start," Kate said.

"We started the day at Wells Fargo and Skylar's safe deposit box."

"There was nothing in it," Avery said, "but we identified Crystal Lewis as the one who forged Skylar's signature."

"We searched her premises and located the safe deposit box key along with her fake Skylar Pierce ID, among others," Griffin said.

"Where are we at with Amanda King and Kyle Eason?" Avery asked.

"I was thinking you and Parker could speak with them tomorrow," Griffin said. "Kate and I think the lot of them are lying through their teeth, but I want to see what kind of read Parker gets off them."

"Sure," Parker said.

"Any word from your guy watching Crystal?" Parker asked Griffin, who shook his head.

"Sorry, man."

Avery fought back a grunt. Gary and Crystal had to show up sooner or later. "But you know what I keep wondering . . ."

"What's that?" Parker asked.

"What does this gig Skylar was supposedly working and the contents of that box—which we're assuming involved the dirt she had on Kyle Eason—have to do with Sebastian Chadwyck?"

"I don't know that it does," Griffin said. "There's a good chance we're looking at two separate things."

Avery inhaled and let it go. If they were going to fixate on anything or anyone in particular it had to be Sebastian Chadwyck. "Where are we on finding Sebastian?"

"I've watched his credit cards," Kate said. "No activity since the night of the showing."

"And no hits on the APB that was put out on his motorcycle," Griffin said.

"I also placed an officer down the street from Megan Kent's place. I have a strong feeling she's the one who's going to lead us to Sebastian, but so far no movement."

"She did make a bunch of calls to one number," Kate said. "I traced it, and it turned out to be a burner cell, so I'm assuming

Sebastian's, though it's already been dumped. But she keeps calling the number."

"Sounds like she's panicking. Tomorrow might be a good time for another visit," Griffin said. "You and Avery made a connection with her. How about you talk to her tomorrow?"

"You got it," Avery said. "And Gerard?"

Griffin shook his head. "I don't believe he had any involvement in this other than choosing the disgusting exhibit theme and being an egomaniac."

That about summed him up.

Declan shifted his gaze to Tanner. "Since we have our next steps figured out on this case . . . on a completely different note, I called a friend at Immigration, and he is seeing what he can find out about Hana and Adam."

Avery looked to Parker, confused.

Tanner straightened, surprise and joy forming on her face. "Thank you."

Declan nodded.

Okay, so something about the refugees, Avery assumed, noting the shift between Declan and Tanner. She couldn't put her finger on it, but something was different, more congenial. Dare she say *friendly*?

"All right," Parker said, squeezing Avery's shoulder. "Time to get you home."

She would have argued, but she could barely keep her eyes open.

He'd spent the entire day readying his new studio for Avery. It was perfect. Just as she was perfect. He'd sketched out a number of poses but decided to go with his original vision. Now he just had to take her from Parker Mitchell.

39

Parker followed Avery down the narrow sidewalk leading to the alley by the rear of her Fed Hill townhome. There'd been no front street parking, so they'd had to go around the rear and then cut through the alley connecting the townhomes. As Avery unlocked her back door, Parker spotted a shift of movement in the shadows.

His muscles coiled.

"Here." He handed Avery his gun and whispered in her ear. "Get inside."

"What?"

The shadow moved and a man raced down the alley.

"Go!" Parker shouted. He heard her door slam shut as he rounded the corner after the man. Without his weapon, he'd need to tackle the perpetrator.

The brick alley was dark, cool. It only went through the row of townhomes connected to Avery's before ending at a ten-foot-high fence on the east side.

Sprinting, he made ground on the intruder, reaching out and tackling him just as he started up the fence.

Pulling his knife from its sheath, Parker held it to the man's neck, not risking any chance that he might be armed.

The light from the streetlamp outside the fence hit the man's face as Parker hauled him to his feet.

Parker hitched slightly. "Gary?"

"Gary?" Avery said as she opened her front door, stepping back and passing the gun off to Parker as they moved inside.

Parker slipped his knife back into its sheath and aimed his gun at Gary. He'd patted him down in the alley but found only a pocketknife. If Gary had come to threaten Avery, he'd come sorely under-armed. A pocketknife would hardly faze her.

"Take a seat on the couch," Parker indicated with a wave of his gun.

"What are you doing here?" Avery asked, pacing, arms linked across her chest.

"Looking for you."

That was backward. He was looking for *them*? "Why?"

"Because I want to know why you and those men were searching Crystal's place."

"You saw us?"

"I came around the back side of the park and spotted a parked car I didn't recognize and then saw you guys coming out of Crystal's place. What were you looking for?"

"What she took from Skylar's safe deposit box," Avery said.

"I don't know what you're talking about."

"Really? What about this?" She showed him the photo of Crystal pretending to be Skylar at the bank.

Gary swallowed, his Adam's apple bobbing.

"What were you after?" Avery pressed.

"What Sky had in that box."

"Which was?"

Gary stalled.

"Crystal is looking at federal charges for bank fraud. You're her accomplice. Now, we can put in a good word for you or say you didn't cooperate. It's up to you."

"What? I ain't no accomplice."

"No? You made her the fake ID she used to commit fraud."

"I didn't know she was going to commit fraud with it."

"What'd you think she was going to do? She's over twenty-one. It's not like the old days when we wanted to get into the bars underage."

"I . . . I didn't know what she was going to do with it."

"Sure you didn't. I bet Crystal will say otherwise."

"She's not going to talk to you."

"After how you just rolled on her?" Avery said, pacing in front of him, hands fixed on her hips. "Please, she'll be blabbing off everything you've ever done."

"Like Avery said, we can put in a good word for you," Parker offered. "Sounds like you could use somebody helpful on your side."

Gary huffed and swiped his baseball hat off. "Fine."

Avery took a seat.

"It was some test."

Avery glanced at Parker and then at Gary. "Test?"

"Yeah, Crystal looked it up. It's the one you take when you want to get into medical school."

"An MCAT?" Parker said.

"Yeah, that's it."

This was all over some stupid test?

"Was there anything else in the box?" Avery asked.

"Yeah, another form. A rental agreement. Had the same guy's signature on it, but the signatures were different."

Someone cheated on their MCATs, and Skylar had proof.

"What was the name on the MCAT?" Parker asked, adrenaline coursing, wondering if it was who they suspected.

"Some guy named Kyle Eason."

He strode to Avery Tate's front window. Now there were two men in her home. *Two?* He'd have to wait another day to grab her.

He raked a hand through his hair, the gel sticking to his fingers. This was taking too long. He had art to create. Longings to fulfill. If this went on much longer, he'd use the gun he bought and just take her—no matter who got in his way.

40

On Tuesday morning, Parker and Avery paid a visit to Connor and Kyle's townhouse, where Connor informed them that Kyle was at his parents' home with Amanda for some sort of midweek party. Something to do with an upcoming golf tournament for charity, he thought. Though he didn't seem quite sure. What did seem rather certain was the fact that they'd roused him from a deep sleep.

They made the relatively short drive over to the Easons' neighborhood, and the word *party* seemed an understatement to Avery, considering their entire street was blocked for the festivities, forcing them to park in the gated community's pool facilities lot.

They walked past the third fairway of the neighborhood golf course and banked right onto the Easons' road. The street was packed sidewalk to sidewalk with people for a breakfast block party. The men's button-down shirts ranged in color from pastel hues to traditional navy and whites. All wore different classic shades of Dockers shorts in gray, tan, or white, and nearly every man wore a pair of Docksiders—also in a variety of colors ranging from light blue to dark navy to traditional brown. The women had more variety among their outfits. Some wore sundresses and others fancy blouses with shorts and heels.

The scent of bacon and sausage wafted in the warm summer air. Even though it was only midmorning, it was nearing ninety, and the humidity was quickly rising.

The Easons' brick mansion turned out to be at the end of the cul-de-sac, and the walk gave Parker and Avery opportunity to search the crowd for Amanda and Kyle. Kate had pulled up their driver's license photos, since the only glimpse they'd had of Amanda was when she'd been tailing Gary.

Avery glanced at the cars in the driveway. Amanda's Fiat and a black Mercedes S500. "Nice wheels," she commented and then looked up at the Easons' home. The car looked like a Matchbox toy in front of the grandeur of the house. "This place is bigger than the entire trailer park I grew up in," she said as they approached the door and Parker rang the bell.

A woman in her early fifties dressed in a Lily Pulitzer knee-length flamingo print dress and Jackie O sunglasses answered. "The party is on the street, not in our home." She moved to shut the door.

Parker stuck his foot in the quickly narrowing opening before she could fully shut it. "I'm afraid we're not here for the party," he said.

She slipped her sunglasses up on top of her head, her light brown hair now out of her face. "Well, then what are you here for?"

"We need to speak with your son, Kyle."

She exhaled a bored whiff of air. "What is this regarding?"

A petite blonde walked by and stopped, turning her attention on them.

Amanda King.

Parker waved with a smile. "Amanda, right?"

"Yes." She stepped closer to Parker, clearly smitten with him, as the majority of women were. "Do I know you?"

"Our colleagues spoke with you the other day regarding Skylar Pierce."

Her smile quickly vanished. "I have nothing more to say about *that* woman."

"What is this about?" Mrs. Eason asked.

"Nothing," Amanda said, moving to shut the door.

"I'd hardly call breaking and entering into Skylar Pierce's home nothing," Parker said.

Mrs. Eason inhaled sharply, her hand landing on her chest, her perfectly manicured nails a playful pink. "Whatever are they talking about, Amanda?"

"Nothing." Amanda glared at them. "You both need to leave. Now."

Parker, still smiling, said, "You can either let us in to speak with you and Kyle, or Detective McCray, who you met the other day, said he'd be more than happy to send a squad car to come pick you both up and take you in for questioning."

Mrs. Eason's face reddened as she scanned the packed crowd outside her front door.

"Fine," Amanda gritted out. "Come in, but make this quick. I have a party to attend."

They stepped inside the ginormous entryway that reached up all three stories of the home, an elaborate chandelier hanging down on a golden chain from the ceiling.

"Mandy, are you ready yet?" A handsome young man stepped out of the adjoining room. He was under six feet but not by much. He was lean, maybe one-hundred-and-seventy pounds, with dark brown hair that had that just-out-of-bed spikey look and brown sideburns. He frowned. "Who are you?"

"They are with the detective who showed up at your and Connor's place," Amanda said.

"What are they doing *here*?"

"We're here to ask you some questions," Avery said.

Kyle slipped his hands into his pastel pink boardshort pockets.

Pink, seriously? No wonder Skylar had been able to play this guy. At least he went with a white button-down shirt and, quite to Avery's amusement, Sanuks on his feet. She had no idea richies were into surfer shoes like Sanuks. They were all she wore when not in boots or workout shoes.

"Shall we go into the library?" Mrs. Eason suggested.

They moved into the room to find cherrywood bookcases running the length of the walls and up two stories, leather armchairs, and a gorgeous brick fireplace with cherry mantelpiece.

"I'll go get your father," Mrs. Eason informed Kyle.

"Mom, that's not necessary. Mandy and I can handle this."

Mrs. Eason nodded and excused herself from the room.

Kyle settled into one of the armchairs. "Let's get this over with."

"A direct man," Parker said. "Wonderful. This will go efficiently. Let's start with the reason you and Mandy"—he gestured to Amanda—"broke into Skylar Pierce's trailer on Friday night."

Kyle's cheeks flushed. "W-what? I don't know what you're talking about."

Good defensive. Flat-out denial.

"Amanda?" Avery asked, curious what the cool one in the relationship, by all appearances, would say. "Would you care to chime in?"

"We weren't there."

"And where were you?" Parker said.

Might as well hear their alibi now so they could defeat it with pleasure.

"At a charity auction with Kyle's parents."

"Really?"

"Yes."

"About how many people would you say were in attendance?"

"I don't know. Several hundred," she said, no doubt proudly thinking she was convincing them that two hundred people could confirm their alibi, but that many people only made it much easier to sneak out unnoticed.

"How late did the affair run?" Parker asked, popping a mint from the side table bowl beside him into his mouth.

"Eleven thirty, at least."

"And you left, when?"

"Not until well after eleven."

"And then?"

"We went to Kyle's and went to bed. His roommate, Connor, can confirm that."

Avery was impressed. The girl was cool. She really thought she had all her ducks in a row.

Parker glanced at Avery. "Would you care to do the honors?"

She smiled. "It would be my pleasure." She turned to Amanda. "Then Connor would be lying."

"I beg your pardon?"

"Then Connor would be lying."

"No he wouldn't," Kyle said. "We were at my place."

"We know you're lying."

Amanda linked her arms across her chest. "And how do you presume to know that?"

"An eyewitness places you both in Skylar Pierce's trailer around eight-thirty that night. Well before the charity dinner ended."

Amanda's jaw tightened.

The first sign of discomfort. Good. Now they were getting somewhere.

"So which of you would like to explain what you were doing there?"

"Your eyewitness is wrong."

Of course they'd go that route.

"How did you meet Skylar?" Parker asked Kyle, switching tactics.

"She was a friend of Connor's."

"Oh, she was more than a friend of his."

Kyle looked away.

"But I'm guessing you walked in and all her attention shifted to you."

Amanda's posture was stiffer than a statue.

"Dude . . ." Kyle's gaze darted to Amanda and back pleadingly to Parker. "This isn't cool."

"Neither is a dead woman."

Kyle might as well have said "duh" for the confused expression on his face. "Wait? What? Skylar is dead?"

"She's been missing since Thursday night—at least that's the last time she was seen by anyone we've talked with."

"Missing? I thought you said she was dead?"

"We have evidence that she is."

"Evidence?" Amanda frowned. "Wait? Are you saying you don't have her body?"

"Does that cause you relief?" Avery asked, pressing. Why was Amanda so curious if they had Skylar's body or not?

"No. I mean . . . I was just curious when you didn't say you have her body."

"We have video and photos of Skylar taken after she was dead."

"What?" Kyle gaped. "But you don't have her body?"

"She was moved from the crime scene," Parker said.

At least they were assuming, as there was no clear evidence of her murder at Sebastian's studio.

"She was photographed for a Black Dahlia-esque showing at the Christopher Fuller Gallery, and then her body was moved again."

"Wait. You're saying someone showed a picture of her dead body?" Kyle swallowed.

He seemed more concerned about Skylar's body and where it was and what had happened to it than Avery had anticipated. Sebastian was the killer in her mind, but what if they had it wrong? What if Kyle or Amanda had killed Skylar to make the blackmail go away?

Parker's cell rang. "I apologize, but I need to take this. It's Greg," he said to Avery.

Dr. Greg Frasier was the entomologist they'd sent Skylar's sweater to for processing. Based on trace evidence he'd discovered, Parker believed there had been insects on the sweater, and he needed Dr. Frasier's help in identifying the organic material.

He spoke low by the door, looked up once, and then focused his attention back on the call. "Thanks, Greg," he said, moving back to rejoin them.

"Good news?" Avery asked. He could explain later if it wasn't pertinent to this interrogation, but she wanted to at least know if Greg had found something.

"Yes. After identifying the insect residue I found on her sweater, he's narrowed down the location of Skylar's body prior to Sebastian's moving it to his studio." He looked at Kyle. "Should have her body anytime now, and you'd be amazed the clues a body retains. Clues about the victim's murder."

"And murderer," Avery added.

"Whoa!" Kyle jumped up. "I didn't murder anybody. You've got this all wrong."

Footsteps echoed in the hall, but no one entered. Kyle's mother had likely overheard the word *murder* and rushed to tell her husband. They needed to work quickly. Kyle's dad, no doubt, would tell him to shut up and let their fancy lawyer handle it—she was assuming they had one, since rich folks like the Easons always did.

"So tell us what's right," she said, the urgency ramping in her voice.

Kyle swallowed, looked to Amanda and then back to them.

"Let's start with your and Skylar's relationship," Parker began, resting a calming hand on Avery's forearm, signaling he understood and he had this. "If Amanda would prefer to leave the room, I understand." He looked at her with concern and empathy for how difficult this must be.

He was working them, going in for the kill, and she was simply going to sit back and watch.

Amanda shook her head but glared at Kyle, who retook his seat.

Good idea. He was going to need one.

"How long were you and Skylar together?" Parker asked.

"We weren't together. It was a stupid mistake. It only happened once."

Parker arched his brows.

"Okay, twice, but that's it, I swear. The . . ." Kyle started to form an unpleasant and offensive word but saw Avery's glare and thought better of it. "The lady was crazy."

"Crazy how?" Avery asked.

"She was just a tramp moving from one guy to the next," Amanda said. "Kyle was smart enough to figure that out and ended things."

"And how'd Skylar take that?" Parker asked.

"Fine." Kyle shrugged. "She didn't care."

"Other than the blackmail, of course," Parker said.

Kyle swallowed and glanced nervously to Amanda.

"I think it's time you leave," Amanda said.

"Again, we can have a squad car come, if you'd prefer."

"I didn't do anything wrong. The—" Kyle caught himself again and balled his fists. "*She* was the one blackmailing me. I didn't do anything wrong."

"Oh, I'd say paying some guy to take the MCATs for you is all kinds of wrong."

"What's going on in here?" An older version of Kyle stood in the doorway. He looked to Kyle. "Your mother said these investigators are hassling you."

"It's fine, Dad." Kyle stood. "I got this."

"Not if they are insinuating you somehow cheated on your MCATs."

"You must be Dr. Eason," Parker said, standing and extending a hand.

Dr. Eason ignored Parker's outstretched hand. "I think it's time you left."

"They said they'd send a squad car and take us in for questioning," Kyle said, panicked.

"I highly doubt they'd send a squad car for a kid supposedly cheating on his MCATs."

"We have proof he cheated."

"Well, I'll send my lawyer to the precinct of your choosing to look at said evidence. Now, if you'll excuse us."

"The woman blackmailing your son had that evidence, and now she's dead."

"I don't know what you're suggesting, but unless you have a warrant for my son's arrest, get out of my home."

"Well, he was a peach," Parker said as they stepped outside of the Easons' home and the door slammed behind them.

Griffin and Jason were no doubt going to follow up, but they'd done a good job getting them riled up and off-kilter. That's when people covering up things typically slipped up.

"Men like Dr. Eason think they can boss the world around," Avery said with disgust.

"We got what we needed," Parker said.

"Which was?"

He smiled. "The confirmation they broke into Skylar's, and the fact that he did cheat on his MCATs."

"He never admitted to either."

"Not verbally."

She smiled. "Okay, so what do we do now?"

"I'm sure Griff and Jason will pay Kyle and Amanda another visit very soon."

"Amanda had the strangest reaction to our dropping the news of Skylar's murder."

"Yeah, more fear than surprise."

41

Declan climbed on the treadmill beside Moha, who was already in place. And from the perspiration on his shirt collar, he'd been there for a bit.

He gazed around the room. Again packed on everyone's lunch break. "Thank you for the call. I didn't expect it so soon."

"I can't stay much longer, but I spoke with my Madison Park contact."

"Thank you." He didn't know if Moha had learned anything, but the man was really sticking his neck out, and so was his contact.

"You're welcome. The idea that an organization supposedly representing the Islamic culture and heritage would smuggle a terrorist into our country . . ." Moha had proudly been a U.S. citizen since he was eighteen, his family immigrating when he was a young teen. "It angers me very much, so I reached out."

"And?" Declan hated to press, but he was dying here.

"I have an address for you. My contact couldn't guarantee Anajay is there, but that's where the Institute houses their visiting members."

The Bureau had run the Institute's books and finances. No properties other than the Institute building showed up under their name, but if the property existed to house illegals smuggled in, it's no wonder they'd kept it off the books.

Moha stopped his run and wiped his neck with his towel. "I'll leave it in your duffel for you."

Declan nodded his deep gratitude and kept running, giving Moha time to leave the information, shower, change, and exit the gym before Declan even left the equipment. He used the time to release some much-needed energy and to offer up some much-needed prayer.

Declan and his team surrounded the address Moha's information led him to in Baltimore's Madison Park neighborhood, but they held back at a surveillance distance. The brick home was an end unit, but they still had massive civilian collateral concerns, and the house itself appeared to be sealed tight—all the windows covered with blackout curtains, the doors solid wood. It only furthered his belief Anajay was inside, but without positive intel, without a visual confirmation of Anajay's presence in *that* house, they couldn't move, so they waited.

"We could be here for hours, days," his and Lexi's colleague, Agent Hines, said. "You don't have to stay."

He and Lexi weren't going anywhere. Sooner or later someone had to enter or leave that house.

An hour later, the front door opened and adrenaline shot through Declan. A woman, her head and neck covered with a black hijab, hurried out and headed for the bus station. Declan signaled for the closest agent to follow her.

Twenty minutes later, a man approached the property. He wore a hooded sweatshirt despite the hot temperature. Declan tightened his grip on his binoculars, focusing on the man's face. It took a moment to get a clear visual, but it was most definitely Anajay Darmadi. They'd wait until he was in the house and off the streets before moving in. Likely less collateral damage.

Anajay paused when he reached the house gate, part of the four-foot old-fashioned metal crisscross fence that was common in the older neighborhood. The woman had left it cracked open. He dropped his bag and ran for the alley.

Declan raced from his surveillance position, Lexi close behind him, both flying across the street as Declan held his hand up trying to halt oncoming traffic.

He caught sight of Anajay exiting the alley at the far side. He called over his com to alert the rest of the agents while he and Lexi maintained pursuit.

His thighs burned with adrenaline, his breath coming in metered bursts as he increased his speed to his max, Lexi falling slightly behind.

Anajay looked over his shoulder and crossed into the next alley, raced through, then crossed the street into another alley. Declan caught up with him at the alley's dead end.

Anajay scanned the space around him, eyeing the fire escapes as Declan aimed his gun at the man's chest.

He indicated for Lexi to hold the top of the alley—to prevent any civilians from entering. Anajay must not be armed or he would have responded.

Instead he became eerily still, his dark eyes fixing on Declan. He said something—in Indonesian, he presumed—four short words, and his right hand shifted. Instinct and training told Declan to shoot. He squeezed the trigger as a wall of fire pummeled him back in an explosive force.

He woke to smoke thick in the air, his ears ringing. Lexi was trying to tell him something, her own face smudged black. Sirens roared along with the ringing, everything moving frantically, yet in slow motion.

He was lying on something, men hovering over him. He couldn't breathe.

A bump, and he looked around. He was in an ambulance? What had happened?

The ringing dulled, and he could make out words but not sentences. There was a man standing over him, moving fast, talking fast as the bay doors shut and the ambulance started moving.

"Pneumothorax . . . going to . . . needle decompression . . ."

"Ten minutes . . ."

Spots danced before his eyes, and everything faded away in a swirling haze.

42

"How much longer?" Tanner asked, pacing the ER waiting room. It'd already been an hour since she'd arrived. "What is taking so long?" Why was everyone else so calm?

"Come pray with me," Finley said, patting the empty seat on her right.

Swallowing, Tanner sat down, her heart still racing like crazy.

Declan had been in an explosion. Details were sketchy, but the aftermath was all over the news. The scorch marks on what remained of the brick alley walls, the depression on the ground from an aerial view. A suicide bomber dead.

Fortunately, the two buildings lining the alley were commercial storage rooms, and no one other than Declan had been hurt beyond superficial injuries, but what occurred still rocked Baltimore—and the whole country. Another terrorist act on American soil. And Declan had caught him. Admiration swelled in her heart along with deep concern. Collapsed lung, she'd heard the nurse say.

"Please, Father, we lift Declan up to you in prayer. You are his Maker, you formed his body in his mother's womb. Please heal it today. Amen."

Finley's prayer was short, but from deep in her soul.

"He'll pull through," Griffin said, moving from Finley's left to sit beside Tanner and squeeze her shoulder. "Not to downplay his injuries, but the nurse said his worst injury is just a pneumothorax."

"*Just* a collapsed lung?" Was he crazy? Then again, this was coming from the man who had once used his vehicle to ram another vehicle—one Finley and Tanner were being held hostage in—at a high rate of speed. Tanner shook her head, thinking back to the first case she'd worked with this group.

The doctor entered, and Tanner rose to her feet.

"He's going to be fine. I inserted a chest tube and he's breathing well. He's got a broken leg, a couple of fractured ribs—one of which is the culprit for his punctured lung, but he's rebounding well. You can see him now."

"Thank you, doc." Parker stood, shaking his hand.

"See," Griffin said.

"You called his family, right?" Tanner asked. They weren't here and that wasn't like the Greys. His family was close-knit—as was their hometown, Chesapeake Harbor.

"His parents are on a cruise. We told the rest to wait until tomorrow before they start barraging him, so he can get some rest."

Tanner's eyes narrowed. "How'd you know he was going to be okay?"

"Because there wasn't panic on the nurse's face and because Declan's a fighter," Griffin said.

"I'm starting to get the impression this sort of thing happens often with this group," she said as they took the stairs up to the third floor and down the hall to Declan's room.

Griffin held it open. "It goes with the territory."

She'd remember that.

Declan was propped up in bed and smiled as they entered.

"What? No balloons or pizza?" he asked.

Tanner shook her head. They really were a crazy bunch.

"Ready to tell us what happened?" Finley asked, always the curious one.

"We cornered Anajay, and he decided he'd rather die than get taken alive." He looked to Griffin. "Was anyone else hurt?"

"No." Griffin shook his head. "Lexi and a few pedestrians are receiving treatment for superficial wounds, but the storage warehouses boxed the alley."

"That's a gift from God."

"So is your being okay," Tanner said. "Though you don't exactly look okay."

"Why, thank you."

"You know what I mean." She was worried about him. Far more so than she would have imagined. For an hour she'd feared the worst, that she might never see Declan Grey again, and it had shifted something in her. Despite his grumpy, uber logical ways, Declan also had a caring side. She'd become close friends with Kate, and was getting to know the rest of the gang better, but now she found herself wanting to know Declan *much* better. It didn't make a lot of sense, considering how much he vexed her at times . . . but God's ways often didn't make sense upon first glance—or even upon deeper inspection, at times—but she trusted Him, and His Spirit told her it was time to get to know Declan Grey much better.

"Minus all the medical paraphernalia, and the fact you survived an explosion, you look great," Kate said, pressing a kiss to the top of his head. "Anything besides pizza we can get for you?"

"My laptop."

Kate raised her brows in admonishment. "You do not need to be working now. You can take the remainder of the evening off."

"Says the woman who doesn't understand what *rest* means." He shifted a bit in the bed. "I need to do some research. Anajay said something in what I assume was Indonesian before he detonated the bomb. I just wanted to look up the translation."

"I speak Indonesian," Tanner said.

"Right. On the ship." He shook his head. "I must have got walloped a little harder than I realized."

"What did he say?"

Declan did his best in pronouncing the words, and Tanner thought for a moment and said a possible Indonesian phrase. They went back and forth until Declan said he was pretty sure Tanner was repeating what Anajay had hollered.

Her eyes widened.

"I'm guessing it wasn't a warm, fuzzy statement," Declan said at her expression.

"It roughly means 'The wrath is here.'"

<hr />

"It was nice of Tanner to offer to get Declan pizza and hang with him," Finley said, a smile tickling her lips as the rest of the group entered Charm City Investigations.

"What?" Avery's eyes widened. "You think there's something there too?"

Finley shrugged. "I could be wrong, but I'm usually not."

"Try *never*," Griffin said. "It's most annoying."

"*Please*, you adore me." She smiled, wrapping her arms around his waist.

"Good thing." He chuckled, kissing her tenderly.

"If we're done with the lovey-dovey," Kate said, as she moved to her computer, "I have something I need to show you all."

When Kate pulled up a photo with a wide grin, *something* seemed the understatement of the year to Avery. It was a new picture of Luke. A clear picture of his face.

"Luke's alive," Parker said, staggering back. "I don't believe it. Where'd you get this, Katie?"

"My contact in Malaysia."

"Malaysia?" Parker said, moving back to the image. "I assume this is a crop. Do you have the full image he sent?"

"Ye . . . ah," she said, "but there's just some ship behind him."

"Ship?" Griffin said, urgency pulsing in his voice.

Kate pulled up the full image her contact had sent her. Luke was standing on a pier, talking with a man, a large merchant ship behind him.

Parker looked to Griffin. "What are the chances Luke's on a Malaysian pier by a merchant ship . . ."

"When Anajay Darmadi came in on a Malaysian merchant ship," Griffin said, finishing the statement for him. "Declan's going to want to know about this. I'll go tell him, show him the picture. You guys head home—you both look beat."

Avery rubbed her neck. She was exhausted, but after their conversation with Kyle and Amanda, they needed to make one more stop.

43

Parker pulled to a stop in front of Megan Kent's house. "You got the pictures?"

Avery pulled them from her bag and tucked them beneath her arm, thankful Griffin had contracted Parker's services for the case. That arrangement allowed them to make use of the bond Avery believed they'd created with Megan. If they didn't get the answers they were looking for, then Griffin would pull her in for trespassing and interrogate her.

Megan answered the door, the complete opposite of overjoyed to see them based on her stern expression and tense physique. "What do you want now?"

"Can we come in?"

"What do you want?" she repeated, her tone far more heated than it'd been the other day.

"We just want you to look at some pictures."

"Of *her*?"

"No. Of the couple we believe were in Skylar's trailer that night with you."

"Oh. Okay." She stepped back, allowing them passage inside. The scent of clams and marinara wafted in the air.

"Something smells good," Avery said. Probably didn't help she was starving. She and Parker needed to grab a bite to eat, and then she needed to sleep.

"Linguini and clams with red sauce," Megan said. "The sauce is an old family recipe."

Oregano and basil floated along the hallway along with the scent of fresh tomatoes as Megan led them back into her living room. Seemed like a fancy dinner for one, but according to the officer Griffin had placed out front, Sebastian hadn't shown. Though she supposed, if he really wanted in without being spotted, he could trek through the woods out back and enter through the cellar door, which was blocked from view. Maybe they needed to show Megan the rest of the pictures Sebastian had taken of Skylar, clearly dead. Surely that would convince her of the danger she could be in around Sebastian.

Parker nudged Avery. "The pictures?"

"Right." She handed the top two to Megan. One of Amanda and one of Kyle.

Megan studied them. "I recognize her—she was there." She handed Amanda's back and studied Kyle's, but then shook her head. "Sorry. Like I said I just got a glimpse of him. He's hot like the guy I saw that night, but I couldn't say for certain it was him."

"Thanks, that's helpful," Parker said.

"Easy enough," Megan said, moving toward the living room archway to the hall.

"Wait," Avery said.

Megan turned. "Yes?"

Parker looked at Avery, no doubt quickly assessing what she intended to do.

"Please," she whispered.

He nodded. "Okay, but I don't think it will help."

"What won't help?" Megan asked, her bare feet padding across the floor.

"Showing you these." She was very deliberate about which picture she placed on top before handing them to Megan.

Megan took one look and dropped them, the grotesque images splaying out across her living room floor. "Why would you show me those?"

"Because I want you to see what Sebastian did. He's dangerous, Megan."

"Sebastian took those?" she said.

"We got them off his camera at his studio."

She raced out of the room, and a door slammed. They heard heaving, the toilet flushing, the sink turning on and off, and then she returned to the room.

In the meantime, Avery had collected the photos. "I'm sorry to show you those. I know they were disturbing, but I don't want to see you hurt."

"Please go," she said, tears slipping from her eyes.

Avery wanted to stay, to make sure she was okay, but it was obvious they were no longer welcome. She only prayed showing the photographs had finally broken through to Megan—that if she knew Sebastian's whereabouts she'd call, and that she'd stay away from him at all costs.

"I think you got through to her," Parker said as they walked back to his car.

Avery exhaled. "I pray so."

———

Parker and Avery stopped and picked up takeout from Bill Bateman's, and once home Avery devoured her filet, mashed potatoes, and grilled asparagus. Parker made a huge dent in his second order of crab dip, the extra baguette nearly gone.

"We forgot dessert," Parker said.

As full as she was, no meal was complete without dessert. "I'm out of ice cream and chocolate." It'd been a crazy time, and grocery shopping had gone out the window.

"I'll run down to Vaccaro's and grab us some cannoli."

"That sounds awesome, but you're sure you don't mind?"

"I'm certain." He leaned in and kissed her. "I told you, anything for you, love. But I better hurry, before they close."

She smiled as he shut her front door and she deadbolted it behind him.

Raggedly, she climbed the stairs, a hot shower sounding incredible for her aching muscles. Hoping to be out and freshened up before Parker returned, she headed into the bathroom, turned on the shower, and let it run until it was hot, steam billowing in the air. She turned to undress . . . and froze at the sight of Sebastian Chadwyck.

44

With no street parking available out front when they'd arrived at Avery's, Parker had been forced to circle a few times, finally locating a spot four blocks away. He was a little more than one block from the car when the sight of a motorcycle parked in the alley snagged his attention.

Panic surged as he stepped closer. A blue Ninja. *Sebastian.* He turned and raced back to Avery's.

"Hello, beautiful." Sebastian stepped from leaning against the wall, gun in hand, aimed at her heart. "We'll be needing to hurry."

"Parker will be back any minute."

"Not if he's going to Vaccaro's." He smiled, and fear kicked in. He'd been listening.

"But it still doesn't leave us much time. I'm going to need your car keys."

"What?"

"I can hardly take you on my motorcycle, and take you I will."
He stepped closer. "Turn around." He pulled out duct tape.

She did as instructed.

"Now put your hands behind your back. Hold them out. No
fighting like last time."

He was going to tape her wrists together, which meant . . .

He set the gun down, and she waited until she heard the tape
pull, then swung her elbow back and up into his nose.

Sebastian hollered, and she'd swung around, reaching for the
gun, when she heard the soft mechanical click of a trigger readying.

Terrified Sebastian had reached the weapon before her, she
looked up . . . and relief swelled at the sight of Parker with his
gun aimed at Sebastian's heart.

———

Parker stood behind the viewing glass as Griffin and Jason
read Sebastian his Miranda rights and then began their interrogation. Parker had dropped a fully protesting Avery off with
Kate and Tanner because he didn't want her present for the
gory details of her friend's death. And if Sebastian gave up
the location of Skylar's body, he most certainly didn't want
her there when they found it. She didn't need the last image of
her friend to be her decomposing corpse.

"I'm telling you," Sebastian said, rubbing his nose, which
was still red and tender from connecting with Avery's elbow.
"I didn't kill her, and I can prove it."

"How's that?" Griffin asked.

"I saw the dude that killed her. Well . . . kind of."

"Kind of? Yep. That's a real promising start," Griffin said,
looking back at him with raised brows.

"I mean I didn't fully see his face. At first he had his back to
me and then it was dark, but I did see him."

"Uh-huh." Jason wasn't buying it either.

Parker had seen Sebastian's work. Entered his world at the studio. There was nothing but darkness there.

"How about a license plate?" Sebastian offered.

Parker straightened. He hadn't expected that, but Sebastian could toss out any license plate number to throw them off his trail for a while. Divert their attention.

"And," Sebastian said, his voice strengthening, his shoulders squaring, "I can tell you where her body is."

Griffin glanced back at the glass, his expression one of surprise and interest.

"He's lying," Parker said, though he was the only one in the room. No one who had murdered someone would be stupid enough to give up the body dumpsite, and no one as grotesque as Sebastian Chadwyck—based on what they'd seen at his studio, home, and storage facility—could be innocent of Skylar Pierce's murder.

"All right," Jason said, "tell us who did it, and where Skylar Pierce's body is."

"I said I saw him, but I didn't say I know who he is."

"Well, that's convenient." Jason's curiosity dimmed on his face. "And let me guess . . . you aren't exactly sure where her body is, after all."

"Look, I'm not stupid," Sebastian said. "I know how these things work."

"These things?" Griffin asked.

"Police investigations," Sebastian said. "I'm not giving up the location until I get something in return."

Of course. Here it came. His demands for the location of *his* murder victim. This guy really was off his rocker.

"Yeah," Griffin said. "What's that?"

"Immunity against prosecution in her death."

"You're kidding me, right?" Jason laughed.

"Dude, I told you I know how these things work. I'm not telling you where Skylar's body is unless you exonerate me of her murder."

"Exonerate? Fancy word," Jason said. "I don't know which cop shows you've been watching," he said, echoing Parker's conclusion, "but that's not at all how it works. You can't give me the killer's name, you have no idea who he is, and so far all the evidence points to you. If I were in your place and I actually was innocent—not saying that you are—I'd be doing everything I possibly could to help clear my name. Until you give us something to prove otherwise, you're our number one suspect, so if I were you, I'd start talking."

"I may not know the killer's name, but I can tell you what hotel Skylar met him at, the room he killed her in, and the location where he dumped her body."

Parker looked at Griff. Was Sebastian telling the truth? Was it actually possible that he *wasn't* Skylar's killer?

"And you know all this, how?" Griffin asked, sliding a legal pad and pen to Sebastian to start writing it down.

"Because I followed her."

"When?"

"Last Thursday night."

"To a hotel?"

"Yeah."

"Which hotel?" Griffin asked.

"The Hampton Inn."

Jason linked his arms across his chest, his pinstripe shirt bunching beneath his elbows. "That narrows it down."

"The one off Richie Highway by Glen Burnie."

"Why were you following her?" Griffin asked, doing a great job at getting the necessary details, while also tackling the motivation behind Sebastian's actions. Even if Sebastian *was* telling the truth and hadn't killed Skylar, he was still guilty of a lot. Griff was making sure he didn't get the horse and forget the cart—the basis for the case against Sebastian.

Sebastian exhaled. "I followed Skylar because I was trying to talk her into modeling for me."

"Let me get this straight. You thought following and approaching Skylar Pierce at a hotel while she was meeting with another man was the best place to try and convince her to model for you?"

"I didn't know where she was going or who she was meeting."

"But you just said you followed her to the hotel."

"Yes, but I'd been following her for days."

"So you were *stalking* her?" The muscle in Griffin's jaw tightened.

"No. I . . . I just wanted her to model for me. I tried talking to her at the studio and at her place, but she wouldn't even let me in. I thought if I could just get her to look at my portfolio she'd see my talent and want to model for me. It had to be that night, or I wouldn't have the portrait done in time."

"So you followed her as you'd been doing, and she went to the Hampton Inn off Richie Highway. . . ." Griffin prompted for him to continue.

"Yeah."

"Then what happened?"

"She got out of the cab she'd taken. Texted someone. Waited a minute, looked back at her phone like she was reading something."

"A response text, perhaps?"

"Yeah. She shook her head with a laugh."

"Like it'd been a flirtatious text?"

Sebastian's lips thinned. "Maybe, or maybe she thought

someone was being ridiculous. Whatever. Like I have any clue what it said."

Jason's eyes narrowed, creases puckering at the edges. "You really don't like the idea of Skylar and other men, do you?"

Sebastian slunk down in his chair.

"Don't you have a girlfriend?" Jason asked, already knowing the answer. They all did.

"Yeah."

"I'm guessing she doesn't know about your obsession with Skylar?"

"My relationship with Megan is *none* of your business."

"So she does know." Griffin shifted. "And, let me guess, she wasn't pleased."

"I said that's none of your business."

"Fine." Jason held his hands up. "Let's get back to Skylar. So she gets a text, laughs and shakes her head, and then . . . ?"

"She looks at the side entrance of the building. Shakes her head again and goes in the front door."

"And then you follow her in?"

"Yeah. I kept my distance. Watched her walk down the first-floor hall . . ."

"Headed in the direction of that side door entrance she glanced at?"

Sebastian took a moment to answer. "Yeah, actually. I hadn't thought about it before."

So the killer, if Sebastian's story was even true, was trying to lure Skylar in the side door. Predatory 101. Parker leaned against the frame of the glass.

"Which room did she go in?" Jason asked.

"The one at the end of the hall on the right."

"The hall on the right of the lobby or the door on the right at the end of the hall?" Griffin asked.

Sebastian thought for a moment. "Both."

"Okay." Griffin scooted back and stood, adjusting the waist on his navy trousers. "You want something to drink?"

"Yeah. I'll take a Mountain Dew," Sebastian said, his smug expression saying he was finally getting the treatment he deserved.

"I'll be right back." Griffin excused himself from the room and Parker turned down the sound from the interrogation room as Griffin entered the viewing booth. "I'm going to head out to the hotel to check his story while Jason keeps questioning him. I'll call as soon as I know if Sebastian's story pans out."

"Okay. I'll head over and run the room if it does," Parker said. The precinct, through Griffin, had already contracted him and Avery for the case.

As Griffin turned to leave, Parker put out a hand to stop him. "You don't believe Sebastian, do you?" He'd come after Avery twice.

"His story is believable, but he's got a seriously twisted mind, so who knows. Could be telling the truth or he could just be diverting our attention and wasting our time."

Griffin looked at his watch. "Speaking of time. It'll take me a half hour to get over there, another half hour to question the staff . . . I should call within the hour."

"If Sebastian's actually telling us the truth, the man will have paid cash for the room and used an alias. It won't lead anywhere unless there's evidence of Skylar somewhere in that room."

Griffin nodded. "Or unless someone remembers seeing Skylar enter that night."

"That just proves she was there. For all we know Sebastian rented the room and lured her there."

"Lured how?"

"I don't know. It's just a possibility. I'm curious to see what you discover."

"You know another option exists," Griffin said.

"Which is?"

"The blackmail information Skylar had on Kyle Eason."

"You really think pretty boy is capable of murder?" Parker asked.

"Rather than get exposed for cheating on his MCATs and getting banned from any medical school while his dad is the chief of neurosurgery at Johns Hopkins. That's a lot of pressure. . . ."

All this time he'd been so focused on Sebastian. Was it really possible he might not be the killer?

"Be in touch," Griff said, heading for the door.

Parker turned back to the window and turned up the sound. Sebastian was sketching something on the pad, and Parker was dying to know what.

45

What can you tell me about the man Skylar was with?" Jason asked, continuing as Griffin dropped off the Mountain Dew, excused himself, and headed for the hotel.

Sebastian opened the soda and took a long swig, then swiped his mouth with the back of his hand before proceeding. "I didn't see him when he opened the door to let her in the room. I had the wrong angle."

"So what'd you do?"

"I waited."

Jason frowned. "You waited?" He shifted in his chair. "You said you followed Skylar there to talk her into modeling for you, and instead of talking with her you just waited?"

"I didn't know she was meeting anyone until the hotel room door opened and she went in. Then I figured that I'd just wait until she came out and I'd talk to her then."

Parker laughed, thankful for the glass dividing them. Sebastian was worried the man Skylar was meeting might kick his butt. It was clear as day on his face.

"How long did you wait?" Jason asked.

"Fifteen minutes."

"Fifteen *minutes*?" Jason clarified.

Sebastian nodded. "Fifteen minutes, max. The dude comes out carrying a bulky garment bag over his shoulder and exits out the side door."

"You see his face?"

"He had a cap on and the garment bag was in the way. As he turned, I caught a glimpse of his profile, saw the tips of his brown sideburns."

Jason sat forward. "You said the garment bag was bulky?"

"Yeah, looked like he was balancing a load over his shoulder. The bag looked thick, like something bigger than clothes were in it."

"What about his height, his weight?"

"Five-ten, maybe. He had a long raincoat on, but if I had to guess I'd say one-seventy."

"Okay, so then what happened?"

"I knocked on the room door, hoping to talk with Skylar, but she didn't answer. And then something hit me—told me to follow the dude. I rushed out to the parking lot, spotted him hefting the garment bag into his trunk, so I got in my car and followed him."

"Your car?" Jason said. "I thought you owned a motorcycle."

"I do, but I have an old beater I bought for cash a few months ago. Just to have in case I need extra space."

Jason arched a brow. "Extra space for . . . ?"

"Equipment."

Uh-huh. Parker shook his head.

"What about the man's car?" Jason asked. "What kind of car was it?"

"A red Porsche."

"Seriously?" One of the most standout cars in the most stand-out color? Either the guy was cocky or just plain stupid. "Any chance you got the license plate?"

"Not then. I was too focused on following him but keeping enough distance."

"And where did he go?"

"Sparrows Point, down past the abandoned warehouse area that's mostly been leveled. Out to Wharf Road by a thick copse of trees jutting out into Jones Creek. Nothing around. He parked. I parked a ways back and walked in, watched him retrieve the garment bag from the trunk and head into the woods. He'd left the trunk open, illuminating the license plate, and I repeated it a few times before following him into the woods. I watched him dump the bag in a ditch of some sort not far from the water's edge, then hid behind a tree until he left."

Here came the sick part. Parker could feel it in his bones.

"What'd you do then?"

"I found the garment bag, opened it up, and used the flashlight on my phone to see Skylar's face."

"Was she dead?" Jason asked.

"Yes."

"How could you tell?"

"Seriously?" Sebastian shook his head. "I'm not stupid. I can tell if someone's dead."

"Any obvious cause of death?" Jason asked.

"Her neck was bruised and cut into."

Just as they'd seen on the video. Whoever killed her probably used a garrote. Fairly efficient and little mess, other than the usual DNA under the victim's nails as she struggled.

That's why it was so important for them to find Skylar's body. So far Amanda King seemed the most freaked at the possibility of her body being found, but could she really be the killer? Was she strong enough?

Though Sebastian had described seeing a man with sideburns. Sideburns exactly like Kyle Eason had. Perhaps Amanda knew Kyle was guilty and was just attempting to protect him, or maybe they'd killed her together. That wouldn't surprise him at all.

Jason took a quick break and told Parker he was going to order K9 units to canvass the area Sebastian had described. Even though Sebastian had moved the body, they would likely find evidence, and the sooner they started, the better. When he returned to the interrogation room, he asked about the license plate number.

Sebastian couldn't recall the license plate number and hadn't wanted to risk taking a photo of it, but he claimed he'd written it down as soon as he'd gotten to the studio.

Parker remembered Avery taking a picture of a series of numbers carved into one of the dilapidated wooden bookcases. Why Sebastian had chosen to cut it in with a knife rather than simply writing it on a piece of paper, Parker couldn't fathom, but thankfully there was a ton about Sebastian Chadwick that he'd never be able to fathom.

Time to find out if Kyle owned a red Porsche. He made a quick call to Kate and then turned his attention back to the interrogation room, knowing she would call back soon enough.

The killer most likely approached Skylar from behind before she realized what was happening. No wonder Sebastian had used a scarf to cover her neck. They'd guessed right—he was covering the cause of death for the portrait.

"She was still perfect photograph material. I knew I could cover the bruises with makeup or a scarf," Sebastian said as soon as the thought moved through Parker's mind. With every fiber of decency in his being he fought to refrain from lunging through the glass and throttling the pervert.

Jason cleared his throat. "So you found a dead body and your first thought was how you were going to photograph her?"

"You don't understand." Sebastian lifted his chin. "How could *you*? I bet you don't have an artistic bone in your body."

Or a psychotic one. His smugness rankled Parker. He was discussing a murdered woman as if she were nothing more than some sort of art project.

"I'd been trying to photograph her for weeks. Wanted my work to be the centerpiece of the Fuller showing. My work was—*is*—far superior to Gerard's."

"And you didn't find anything wrong with photographing a corpse?"

"It wasn't ideal, of course, at least not at the time."

A very unsettling feel rushed through Parker.

"At the time?" Jason asked.

Sebastian inhaled. "It's quite addictive."

"Excuse me?" Jason's jaw tightened. "What *exactly* is addictive?"

"Working with a completely moldable subject."

Bile churned in Parker's gut. This guy was beyond disturbed. But he knew enough to know Jason would leave that line of discussion there, for now. The psychiatrist, who would most certainly be called to assess whatever depth of depravity they were dealing with, could delve into the perverse mind of Sebastian Chadwick. Jason's job was to focus on the facts and Skylar's killer, and he did so.

"So you took Skylar and . . . ?"

"I zipped the garment bag back up, hefted it over my shoulder just as the killer had, and put her in my car."

"Where's it at?"

"Where is my car?" Sebastian asked, confused.

"Yes," Jason said.

"I'm not inclined to say for the moment."

"Okay, where did you put Skylar's body in your car?"

Sebastian frowned. "Why does that matter?"

"Details matter," Jason said. "I assumed as an artist you knew that."

"In the trunk," Sebastian said, his jaw tightening. Wow, Jason was really getting under Sebastian's skin. *Good*. It was time to get him unhinged and hear the truth, the full truth let loose. "I didn't want to put her in the trunk, but I couldn't risk someone seeing her in the backseat."

So he had trouble putting her body in his trunk, but not photographing it? Okay, then . . .

"So you took Skylar's body?" Jason said.

Sebastian nodded.

"And?" Jason prompted.

"Photographed her."

"I'm assuming you changed her clothes for the picture first?" Jason said.

"Yes. I dressed her."

Jason continued in that vein of questioning. "And fixed her hair and makeup?"

"Yes. She was my subject. I prepared her for the photograph."

Jason was working hard to hide his disgust. Parker could read it all over his face.

"Where did you get the dress?" Jason asked.

"Her place."

"When?"

"On the way to my studio."

"That night?" Jason asked.

Sebastian nodded.

"So you drove with Skylar's body in your trunk to her trailer, took items from her place, and then proceeded with her dead body to your studio to photograph her?" Jason asked, his tone bordering on horrified disbelief.

"Yes, but you needn't make it sound so crass or repulsive. I took something horrible—Skylar's death—and made something beautiful out of it. Her death wasn't wasted."

Parker swallowed the bile rising up his throat.

"Excuse me?"

"The killer dumped her like a piece of trash. I gave her one last shining memorial."

"Before dumping her back with the trash, I'm guessing?"

Sebastian still hadn't said that's where Skylar's body was now.

"I had to put her back where he'd put her."

"Why?"

"In case her body was found. I needed it to be apparent that he did it. Not me."

"And how does that location tie to him?"

"I don't know, but if he put her there I assume it does. Or he could have just picked some random place. Either way, he killed her. I just borrowed her body for a few hours and put her back as I found her, minus her red sweater."

The sweater Avery had found in Sebastian's storage room.

"I wanted to keep something of hers from everyday to remember her by."

That was literally the most repugnant confession Parker had ever heard, but they'd gotten the general location of Skylar's body, and when they found her, Parker would be on site ASAP.

Jason told Sebastian to write out his story—until they had confirmation otherwise, it was a story. If it was the truth, his confession was what they'd need to put him away for a good number of crimes, not excluding impeding a murder investigation.

Kate called to confirm that Kyle Eason was in fact the owner of a red Porsche. He then asked her to work through Avery's pictures, find the numbers scratched into the wood, and hopefully get a match to Kyle Eason's Porsche.

Maybe this was about blackmail after all.

But Sebastian . . .

46

"C an you tell me who rented Room 110 on August eighteenth?" Griffin asked the front-desk receptionist after calculating the room in question based on Sebastian's description of its location in the hotel.

The receptionist verified Griffin's badge, then said, "Let me look." She typed on the computer, her red nails clicking across the white keyboard. "Room 110 was rented that night by a Mr. Abraham Jeffries."

Surely an alias.

"Any chance you have a credit card on file?"

She looked back to her computer and shook her head, her brown hair pulled up tight into a bun fixed in the center of the back of her head. Griffin only noticed it when she turned, the shape reminiscent of a coffee roll from Dunkin' Donuts.

"It looks like Mr. Jeffries paid cash."

Of course he did. "Does that happen often?" he asked. Wasn't that an alert to the hotel staff of nefarious activity?

"You'd be surprised how often." She leaned forward, her

brown eyes darting both ways to be sure they were alone—
though it was nearly the middle of the night, the lobby stone
silent. "Couples hooking up," she whispered. "If you know
what I mean. The married-to-other-people ones."

"I got ya. Can you tell which staff member checked Mr. Jeffries in that day?"

"Sure. Let me look at the reservation. Okay . . . it was Carla
Jacobs."

"Is Carla working tonight?"

"No. I'm afraid not."

"Okay. I'm going to need Carla's phone number and address."

"I'll get it for you, but you won't be able to reach her."

"Why's that?"

"She's in Brazil with her parents. She might answer her cell,
but I doubt her folks paid for roaming."

He'd at least try. If they could get a physical description, it
would go a long way in either confirming or disputing Sebastian's claim.

He slid Skylar's picture across the desk. "Any chance you
saw this lady?"

"Her I saw."

"How's that if you don't remember Mr. Jeffries, if you didn't
check him in?"

"Because the lady didn't check in with Mr. Jeffries. She entered the front door as I was heading out for the night. I held
the door for her and she winked her thanks."

"You've got a good memory."

"Look at her. She's gorgeous. I mean I'm straight and all—
don't get me wrong—but a woman that striking is memorable."

"Unfortunately, she's also dead."

"What?"

"She was killed that night."

"Oh no. I'm so sorry to hear that."

"We're going to need to examine Room 110."

"You think it happened here?" Her eyes widened, and she paled.

"We need to check the room to be certain."

"Okay, but there are guests in it now."

"I'm afraid you're going to have to move them."

Griffin called two hours after leaving the station, which meant he'd definitely found some answers.

Parker answered. "Hey, man."

"Hey. One of the receptionists here remembers seeing Skylar enter, but never saw the man. Another receptionist rented the room to a man going by Abraham Jeffries, but she's in Brazil with her family. We're trying to track her down."

"So Kyle, if he's our guy, used an alias. No surprise there. Let me guess. He paid cash too?"

"You got it. I checked the room. It's been cleaned, but I found an earring under the bed we can hope Skylar lost in the struggle. I definitely want to speak with housekeeping, see if they remember the room looking disheveled in any way."

"All right. Cordon off the room until I get there," Parker said.

"That might be a while," Jason said behind him.

He turned, took one look at Jason's face, and knew they'd found the body.

Parker followed Jason through the muddy wooded area, the brackish water rank on the humid night air. Griffin was en route, the hotel room now cordoned off and an officer standing guard until they could process the room. But what they'd found here was much more vital. They'd found the garment bag and the cadaver dog had indicated a dead body, but they'd waited for Parker's arrival before opening it.

He'd brought another crime-scene photographer with him. There was no way he'd let Avery work the scene. He hoped to have most of the scene processed before he alerted her. Though, to be honest, if it were his friend, he would have insisted, just as he knew Avery would, had she known.

Making sure the entire scene was photographed, along with the garment bag as they found it, Parker pulled back the zipper, and the breath left his lungs in a rush.

Megan Kent?

47

What on earth was going on? "Are there any other bodies?" Parker asked, his voice choked. Where was Skylar? And when had Megan been killed?

"No, sir," the K9 officer said. "We've canvassed the entire area, though there are what look to be fresh tire tracks leading in."

What kind of sick game was Sebastian playing?

Good thing he'd held off on calling Avery. He would have gotten her all upset when it wasn't even her friend's body. Though, poor Megan. They'd just spoken with her. *Hours ago.*

Had Sebastian seen and killed her for talking with them? Had they fought over the images they'd shown Megan? Was it possible he had killed her and had time to dump her body? They'd only stopped for takeout, and Sebastian was in Avery's home within an hour of their leaving Megan. The timing bordered on the impossible. "Call Brent Dixon in."

"You're not going to process the scene?" Jason said.

Brent was the second best in the business.

"I need to get back to the station." *Before word of this spreads.* Sebastian had been at Avery's at eleven and had been in custody ever since. There was no way he could have dumped the body.

He called Avery, explained they found Megan, not Skylar, and asked her to meet him at the station.

And twenty minutes later she walked into the viewing room. He explained a bit more about what they found, but left out some of the details because she appeared to be reaching the brink of her self-control. "Officers found fresh tire tracks. Dixon is getting impressions."

"How fresh?"

Parker had taken time to inspect them before leaving. His guess was sometime in the last hour or two. Something was very off. "Pretty fresh."

"Then that means . . . ?" She looked at Sebastian.

"Yes, he couldn't have dumped Megan. So it is likely he did not kill her. And I am coming to believe his claims about Skylar are true too." He took her hand and kissed her on the cheek. "I have to join Griffin in the interrogation room. He wants me in there to question Sebastian about what I assessed on the scene."

She nodded, clearly still stunned by the news. Sebastian couldn't be in two places at once, but Sebastian innocent meant . . .

Parker entered right as Griffin picked up the picture of Megan Kent he'd printed out from the image Jason had texted him from the scene. Just her face nestled in the garment bag.

Parker sat back, waiting to see how Sebastian would react.

"What are you trying to pull?" Griffin asked, sliding the picture across the table to Sebastian.

Sebastian's face slackened, his eyes widening, shock dousing any earlier cockiness. "Wh-where'd you get this?"

"Where do you think? Right where you dumped her body.

Pretty sick to tell us Skylar Pierce's body was there when it was your girlfriend's body instead."

Sebastian shook his head, his expression dazed. "What are you talking about? Megan's not dead. It's Skylar who's dead. Skylar who's in the garment bag in the woods."

"We sent officers and cadaver dogs right where you told us to go, and the only body there was Megan's. Why is that, Sebastian?"

Sebastian stared at the photo in complete shock and then straightened, anger replacing the fear in his brown eyes. "Is this some kind of sick joke?"

"I was about to ask you the same thing," Griffin said.

Sebastian stood and paced. "I don't understand." He raked a trembling hand through his messy-style brown hair. "You're saying Megan's really dead? Someone killed her?"

"Yeah, you. What? Were you trying to get her out of the house so you could bring Avery in? Is that your new studio?"

"You think I'd kill Megan for studio space?"

"I think you'd kill for a variety of sick reasons that I don't pretend to comprehend."

"I didn't kill my girlfriend."

"But you killed Skylar Pierce?"

"No. I didn't kill *anyone*."

An officer cracked the door, leaned in, and handed a slip of paper to Griffin. He read it. "ME confirms your assessment on site," he said to Parker and then turned to Sebastian. "Based on body temp, looks like your girlfriend couldn't have been dead for more than a couple hours before the police found her body."

"A couple hours?" Sebastian's voice heightened as he retook his seat, his knee bobbing rapidly up and down. "You mean he killed her tonight?"

"He?"

"It had to be the man who killed Skylar. It's the only thing that makes sense. He must have found out that I saw him, and he freaked and wanted to make me look guiltier, so he killed Megan."

"Can I see that?" Parker asked Griffin for the paper containing the ME's initial call from in the field. If they were correct—and there was no reason to assume otherwise—then the timing for Sebastian to kill Megan was impossible. Sebastian was telling the truth. Someone was trying to set him up but— not knowing he would be in police custody at the time of the murder—had actually established his innocence.

"Detective McCray?" An officer stood in the doorway, signaling him to step out.

Griffin lifted his chin. "I'll be right back." He stepped from the room.

Sebastian studied Parker as Parker studied him.

"You know I'm telling the truth, don't you?" Sebastian said.

Griffin reentered and tossed another photograph to Sebastian. "So you're suggesting the killer liked to take photographs of dead girls too?"

Sebastian's eyes widened. "He photographed her?"

The killer had photographed Megan. There's no way Sebastian could have time to do any of that. "May I see that?" Parker asked.

Sebastian handed it over. "That's not my work. Not even close. And I would never pose her like that."

As demented as Sebastian was, Parker actually believed him. He studied the image. It was rushed. Nothing like that of Skylar.

"Jason sent officers to their home," Griffin said under his breath to Parker. "They found the staging still there, images on the camera and downloaded to Sebastian's laptop. He forwarded a few images here, as you can see."

"Is that where she was killed?" Parker asked.

"We'll need to run the place, but it definitely appears to be the crime scene," Griffin answered.

"I can't believe this." Sebastian's knee bobbed faster, his hands shaking. "I can't believe he killed her."

"Can I share this image with Avery?" Parker asked Griff, wanting a professional photographer's opinion on the comparison to Sebastian's work.

Griffin nodded. "Of course."

Parker took the photograph into the viewing room, where Avery reached for it as soon as he entered.

"What do you think?" he asked.

She studied it. "This is the work of a complete amateur."

"In what way? Clearly the staging is completely different. The outfit she's wearing is an everyday one. She's just placed on the couch, but what else?"

"The body is positioned completely wrong to accent the critical beauty features of a woman," Avery said, "and the lighting is flat. When you photograph women you need lighting such that the shadows are not harsh, but they accent the woman's features. Beyond that the white balance is all wrong."

"Meaning his camera settings were off?"

"If we go to Megan's and check the camera used, I bet we find the settings are way off. Maybe we'll get prints if we're lucky."

"Good idea. I hate to think Sebastian innocent. . . ." *For a myriad of reasons.* "But the timeline isn't adding up."

———

Megan Kent's home was filled with police as Parker, Avery, and Griffin arrived. Jason had remained with Sebastian, feeling he was on the verge of cracking.

Avery slipped gloves on and removed the bagged and tagged

camera, and her initial assessment held true. "Settings are exactly as I imagined they'd be. Set for outdoor lighting. The white balance is all wrong, making the light appear overly warm—yellow almost bordering on orange in hue."

"Good job." Parker squeezed her shoulder. For being basically self-taught, Avery was a natural.

"It's set so time stamps don't show on the images. No photographer wants annoying red digits in the bottom right-hand corner of their work, but . . ." She pressed a series of buttons. "Ah-ha. Whoever took the photos didn't realize or didn't care that the time stamps are still held according to image number in the camera's memory chip. Look when the photos of Megan were taken."

She tilted the camera for him to see.

12:30 a.m.

"When Sebastian was already in custody. There's no way he could have killed Megan."

"So who do you think killed her?"

Parker's cell rang. "It's Kate. Let's pray she has confirmed the license plate number." He answered. "Hey, Kate."

"You're right. The license plate number is assigned to Kyle Eason's car."

48

J ason isn't going to be happy," Griffin said as they reentered the station and strode into the interrogation room.

"Why would Jason be unhappy?" Avery asked. "Doesn't he want to catch the real killer?"

Parker understood the frustration. "We had a strong case against Sebastian. Making one against Kyle Eason is going to mean starting from scratch. And with his dad's prominence in the community, it'll mean a ton of legal interference from the Easons' lawyer."

"But if he's the real killer . . ." Avery said.

"I know. I never would have pegged it. His girlfriend, maybe. She's scary enough, not to mention manipulative."

"And ticked about her boyfriend's infidelity. Had no love lost for Skylar, and she carries that air of entitlement, thinking herself above others."

Parker arched a brow. "Or the law?"

"She could have taken Kyle's car to that hotel, used his phone to lure Skylar there."

"But Sebastian watched a man leave with the garment bag."

"Maybe she orchestrated it but had Kyle do it. Might have even stayed behind and cleaned up. Just didn't answer the door when Sebastian knocked."

"We're going to need to search Kyle Eason's car."

"Yeah." Avery shook her head. "But if he used a garment bag with both Megan and Skylar, there probably won't be any physical evidence."

"Maybe not, but we might find evidence of the garment bag—a loose string, a fiber off of it. It's not ironclad, but it's a start."

"I wonder if Griffin is planning to bring Kyle Eason in and put him in a lineup." Avery looked about to collapse, but she clearly wasn't going to give up on this lead. "See if Sebastian recognizes him from that night."

"He said he never got a straight-on look, but it's worth a shot." Parker sighed and rubbed his brow.

Avery frowned. "What?"

"I can't believe we're actually trying to prove Sebastian Chadwyck's innocence."

"What I find perplexing is how he—being the creep that he is—could treat Skylar's body with such disregard but nearly break down in tears at the thought that someone else did that with Megan."

"He was obsessed with Skylar, but he cared about Megan."

"How does someone so disturbed truly care about anyone?"

"Think of the serial killers who are married with kids, living double lives. It makes no sense, other than it's evil and therefore beyond comprehension."

Jason and Griffin walked out of the interrogation room, Jason—as Griffin had predicted—looking none too happy. "We're on our way to pick up Kyle Eason," Griffin said. "We should be back shortly."

"Sounds good." Parker waved and turned to Avery. "Now the question is, where is Skylar's body?"

"I can't imagine he moved her far," Avery said.

"Or he picked another place he felt she wouldn't be found," Parker said.

"But he'd have to put research into that, and tonight he didn't have time. He had to go someplace familiar. If he's trying to frame Sebastian . . ." Avery said.

"Perhaps he moved Skylar's body closer to Sebastian." Parker felt a pull, a certainty that they were on the right track. "That way her body isn't where Sebastian said it was, which makes him look like a liar, and if it's found someplace that ties to Sebastian, it makes him look even guiltier."

"What are you thinking?" Avery asked.

"Fort Howard has a number of wooded areas and abandoned buildings and it's Sebastian's studio."

"Plus," Avery said, "it's just across the water from where Megan's body was found."

Parker nodded. "K9 Sergeant Warren," he hollered to the officer a few desks away in the main hub area of the precinct.

"Yes, sir?" Warren stood.

"Take your cadaver dog and K9 search team out to Fort Howard. We're looking for Skylar Pierce's body."

Warren nodded, and he and his K9 team were rolling in ten.

Connor had been absolutely no help in pinpointing the location of his roommate. Griffin had momentarily considered hauling him in just to shake his flippant attitude away, but he remained focused.

It had taken a little sweet-talking of the Easons' housekeeper, Rosaria, to discover Kyle Eason and his lovely girlfriend,

Amanda King, were at the neighborhood country club having an early breakfast with his parents.

Jason smiled as they entered. "This is going to be fun."

The hostess attempted to stop them, but they strode past her and headed straight for the Easons' table.

Dr. Eason spotted them and stood, his face reddening. "This is a private club."

"We need to bring your son into the police station for questioning in the murder of Skylar Pierce."

Dr. Eason's face turned a shocking shade of crimson. "This is an outrage."

"It's your choice if you want to cause a scene," Jason said, "but we're taking Kyle in. We have a warrant for his arrest." He handed the warrant to Dr. Eason.

Kyle stood. "I didn't kill Skylar, Dad. They'll have to let me go."

"I'm calling our lawyer," Dr. Eason fumed. "You're all going to be sued for harassment and defamation of character."

Griffin had figured that was coming. "See you at the station."

"Miss King," Jason said, "we're going to need you to accompany us as well."

She tucked her neck in. "Excuse me?"

"We have some questions for you." About as many as they had for Kyle.

Everyone stared as they escorted the pair out to Griffin's vehicle and secured them in the backseat, reading them their Miranda rights.

Dr. Eason was already ranting on his phone as he strutted for his car, a black Mercedes—the one Parker and Avery had seen in the Easons' drive the day of the block party.

"I can't believe you think I killed somebody," Kyle said as Griffin started the engine.

"We know Skylar Pierce was blackmailing you for cheating on your MCATs."

"Okay, but I didn't kill her over it."

"Then what did you do?"

"I was going to pay her off."

"*Going* to?" Griffin arched a brow.

"I told her I needed a little time to get the money together without my parents noticing. I called her after I got the money. Her phone went straight to voicemail. I left a message asking when and where she wanted to meet, but I never heard back."

"And you didn't find that odd?"

"Sure I did, but I certainly wasn't going to look a gift horse in the mouth."

"So Skylar's death alleviated all your problems?"

"Yeah, but I didn't kill her. I'm a *college student*, not some murderer."

"Where were you last night, say around midnight?" Jason asked.

"Last night?" Kyle frowned. "You said Skylar's been dead longer than that."

"Just answer the question," Jason said.

"At home playing cards."

Easy enough alibi to check, but Connor would most likely vouch for him, regardless of the truth.

"Didn't slip out for a midnight stroll?" Griffin pressed.

"No," Amanda said.

"What about you, Kyle?" Jason said.

"What about me?"

"You always have to let your girlfriend do the talking for you?"

"You asked. Mandy answered. What's the diff?"

"So you both were at your place all night?" Griffin said.

"No," Kyle said. "At my home. We had dinner with my

parents and decided to crash there. Glad we did. Dad had to leave, and Mom hates being alone in the house, so we played cards late, keeping her company until she was ready for bed."

Griffin glanced over at Jason.

"Your dad left?" Jason said.

"He was called away for an emergency surgery."

"How long was he gone?"

"I dunno. Several hours."

Griffin cleared his throat. "Do either of you know Megan Kent?"

"Who?" Kyle asked.

That answered his question, at least for Kyle.

"I'll take that as a no." He glanced at Amanda. "And do you know Megan Kent?"

"Never heard of her." She looked confused and at the same time calculating, like she was trying to figure out what angle they were playing or if they were trying to trick them into confessing. "Who is she?"

"Sebastian Chadwyck's girlfriend. She was found dead last night."

Kyle's eyes widened. "Sebastian killed another one?"

"Wait a minute." Griffin's gaze narrowed. "How did you know Sebastian Chadwyck was under suspicion for killing anyone?"

"After your colleagues showed up at my parents' suggesting I killed Skylar, my dad had our lawyer do some digging, and he has a good friend on the force who told him a photographer named Sebastian Chadwyck was also under investigation—that they found some real sick stuff at his place."

His dad had enough concern to look into the investigation. He clearly feared his son capable of murder—otherwise, why bother looking into it?

"Sebastian Chadwyck could not have killed Megan Kent, as

he was with us at the time of her murder and body disposal, but whoever did do it staged it to look like Sebastian had."

"What does any of this have to do with us?"

"Sebastian saw the man who killed Skylar. Saw the car that drove her body to the dumpsite, gave us a license plate number."

"So?" Kyle scoffed.

"It was your car."

49

They placed Amanda and Kyle in separate interrogation rooms, Jason taking Amanda, while Griffin took Kyle.

Parker stood in the viewing booth, leaning against the wall, watching Griffin do his thing, while Avery watched from the adjacent viewing room as Jason interrogated Amanda.

"Look, I don't know who told you my car was involved in a crime, but I can assure you it was not," Kyle insisted. "I had nothing to do with anything you're saying."

"We reviewed your phone records. Did you know that even when you erase texts they can be recovered?"

"Okay . . . ?"

"We recovered yours from the night Skylar was murdered. . . ." Griff paused for dramatic effect. Parker had seen him use it countless times. "And you texted her, asking her to meet you at the Hampton Inn in Glen Burnie."

"No, I didn't."

"Yes, you did. You texted her the room number and told her to use the side entrance. That was the last text you sent her."

"No. It wasn't. Look, I don't know where you're getting your information, but someone is trying to set me up."

"Funny. That's just what Sebastian said."

There was a rap on the door, and an officer popped his head in. "Kid's lawyer is here along with his dad, who is threatening to sue the entire department for defamation of character."

Griffin joined Parker in the viewing booth until after the lawyer finished with Kyle, but when the lawyer stepped from the room, Griffin and Parker met him at the door.

"My client is done answering questions."

"Fine," Griffin said. "We'll book him and he can talk to a judge."

"Based on what grounds?"

"On the fact that an eyewitness placed the victim's body in the trunk of Kyle's car, that texts were sent from your client on the night of the murder to the deceased asking her to meet him, and the fact that the deceased was blackmailing your client. Which provides pretty good motive, don't you think?"

"I never saw her that night," Kyle called from the room.

"My client is innocent and believes someone is setting him up."

"Then he won't mind participating in a lineup."

"Excuse me?"

"The eyewitness saw your client that night. If Kyle didn't do it, then have him stand in a lineup."

"Fine," Kyle said. "Let's get this over with."

The lawyer agreed to wait in the interrogation room with Kyle while Griffin pulled together a lineup. As he closed the door, Griffin looked to Parker. "That was easier than I expected, but he knows it was dark and that our eyewitness couldn't have gotten a good look at him. If Sebastian can't identify Kyle, it'll blow a huge hole in our case. Our best hope will be finding physical evidence in Kyle's car or on one of the bodies to tie the murders to him, but a positive ID would go a long way in convincing a jury."

It took a while to pull together men for the lineup, as most of the officers on duty looked quite a bit older than Kyle, but they grabbed two younger ones and a few prisoners from lockup.

Parker prayed as the "suspects" filed into the lineup room. He and Griffin watched as Sebastian studied the men through the one-way glass.

"Any the man you saw that night?" Griffin asked.

Sebastian shook his head. "No."

Parker's heart dropped.

"You're certain?" Griffin said.

"Number three looks familiar. Same sideburns. Same facial features, height, and build, but . . ."

"But?"

"The dude I saw that night was about twenty years older."

Parker looked to Griffin in utter shock. "Dr. Eason?"

"Who's Dr. Eason?" Sebastian asked as the officer led him back to his interrogation room.

Parker waited until he was gone before speaking. "This is insane. I gotta grab Avery."

They moved into the viewing room with her and explained what had happened thus far.

"You really think a man would set up his own son?" Avery asked.

"No. I think he was hoping to set up Sebastian by killing Megan."

"But he had to have purposely used Kyle's car, Kyle's phone."

"It's how he lured Skylar to the hotel that night. He must have pretended he was Kyle, and she thought she was getting her payoff. Instead, he killed her and dumped her body."

"And Sebastian retrieved Skylar's body and photographed it."

"Kyle said his dad left for several hours last night, for emergency surgery."

"That should be easy enough to confirm," Griffin said. "I'll call Johns Hopkins."

He returned ten minutes later.

"Well?" Parker asked, rocking forward on his heels.

"There were several emergency surgeries at Johns Hopkins last night, but Dr. Eason didn't perform any of them."

"So he snuck out to kill Megan and move Sky's body?" Avery asked.

"That's what my gut says," Griffin said. "Now we just need to prove it."

50

Y ou want to do what?" Griffin's captain nearly roared.

"Put Dr. Eason in a lineup for Sebastian," Jason said.

"You have no grounds."

"Sebastian identified Kyle as looking twenty years younger than the man he saw. That indicates his father," Griffin said, praying they could convince their captain.

"He left his home last night, claiming participation in an emergency surgery, which he was not involved in."

"Kyle told us his dad had someone looking into Skylar's case after we showed up at their home."

"And the motive?"

"Protect his son from a blackmailer," Jason said.

"Protect any risk to his own reputation. If Kyle was caught, can you imagine the backlash on his father? He's the chief of neurosurgery at one of the most prestigious hospitals in the world. His son, guilty of cheating on his MCATs, lets it slip while in bed with a con woman, and then attempts to pay her off," Griffin argued. "A man like Eason is going to keep close tabs on his son. He saw his son gathering funds behind his back and put it together. He could have used Kyle's car when Kyle was out with Amanda. I bet you money, Kyle will say he'd left his phone home that night or he couldn't find it. Then his dad thought he'd erased the texts he'd made with Skylar and slipped Kyle's phone back someplace he'd find it."

"This is all hearsay. I can't put a prominent doctor in a lineup without substantial proof."

"Fine. He's in the hub waiting for Kyle to be released. Let's move Sebastian to a cell. Walk him by Dr. Eason. See if Sebastian notices or recognizes him," Griffin said.

Captain Mulroney inhaled, then exhaled. "You two better be right on this. But even if Sebastian IDs him, you're still going to need a whole lot more to convince a judge to pursue a conviction."

They'd have to build an entire case, but they had a good start.

As Jason led Sebastian through the hub, Parker followed to read Dr. Eason's face, and Griffin led Kyle Eason from the other direction to watch Sebastian's reaction upon seeing him.

Sebastian struggled against Jason's hold, fighting and purporting his innocence—until his gaze swung in Dr. Eason's direction. "That's him."

Jason halted and Dr. Eason froze.

"That's the dude I saw at the hotel and dumping Skylar's body."

Dr. Eason's face turned plum as he stood to his feet. "This is ridiculous."

"It's him. I'm telling you," Sebastian said.

Jason handed Sebastian off to another officer. "Go ahead and put him in a holding cell for now."

Dr. Eason sat back down, frantic relief washing over his face.

Jason stood over him. "You might want to tell your lawyer you're about to be questioned in the murders of Skylar Pierce and Megan Kent."

"You have nothing to hold me on."

"An eyewitness just put you at the scene of the crime."

"An eyewitness who is clearly trying to save his own hide. Besides," he said, standing and getting into Jason's face, "I have alibis."

"For when?"

"When those women died."

"That's interesting."

"Why is that interesting?"

"Because I never said when they were killed."

Dr. Eason's face paled. "I want my lawyer."

"I bet you do."

"McCray?" an officer said.

Griff turned. "Yeah."

"Cadaver dogs just found a body in a garment bag out by Fort Howard."

Griffin looked back at Dr. Eason. "What do you want to bet that's Skylar Pierce?"

Parker pinched the bridge of his nose, knowing what this would do to Avery. Her friend's body.

He stepped into the break room, where she was sipping a cup of coffee.

She looked up and immediately asked, "What's wrong? Sebastian didn't ID Dr. Eason?"

"He did, but . . ." He swallowed hard, aching to not cause the woman he loved any pain.

"They found Skylar's body," she said, taking the blow like a champ. "I knew it was only a matter of time."

"I'm so sorry." He stepped to her and enveloped her in his

arms, not giving her any choice in the matter, and she folded into his embrace.

She rested her head in the crook of his neck. "So am I. Sky deserved better. Everyone does."

"Why don't you wait here? There's no need for you to see her . . . in that state." He tried to say it in the most delicate way, but after being dead several days, several warm ones . . . That wouldn't be the way Avery would want to remember her friend.

"I appreciate your concern, but I need to be there for her."

"We'll get this guy."

"We already have him," Avery said, her brows furrowing.

"Sebastian's ID is not enough." Even his alibi comment wouldn't do it as he hadn't even been read his rights yet. It wouldn't be admissible in court, and Dr. Eason would have the best defense attorney in the state. "We need physical evidence tying him to the crime to seal this away."

"Then let's go get it."

51

Parker reached over and took hold of Avery's hand as they made the drive to Fort Howard. Before they left he'd tried again to talk her into waiting at the station, but she'd insisted on coming along.

"Are you sure you don't want to wait in the car?" he asked, pleading one last time for her not to see her friend in such a deteriorated condition. He'd seen Jenna on that beach, what remained of the young girl he'd loved, and that image could never be erased from his mind. It was his to carry into eternity, until he saw her again. Only his faith that Jenna was in heaven with their Savior—whole, beautiful, and forever safe—got him through the torture of those months and years following her death.

He wanted Avery to remember her friend as she'd looked the last time she'd seen her, hopefully laughing or smiling. He'd tried explaining that in the car, but she was determined and stepped from the vehicle before he could stop her.

They moved past the patrol car and the ME's van, which had made remarkable time. Avery paused at the edge of the woods, taking a deep breath, and headed for the focal point of attention, her shoulders taut.

The pungent odor of stagnant water hung thick like a blanket of smog in the afternoon air, the ground beneath them mucky, mud and ground cover sticking to their shoes with each gooey step. He'd dumped her in a swampy area, which would leave footprints—some dry enough for potential identification—and Parker prayed the officers and techs on site had taken care to protect those.

"Dr. Mitchell," Officer Warren greeted him.

"Parker, please." Regardless of his level of education, going by Doctor always felt pretentious for him. He scoped out the scene—the officers' booties covering their shoes, the crime-scene area cordoned off, the crime-scene techs waiting for his arrival and instructions. "You guys have done an excellent job."

"Thank you, sir. ME just arrived. Hasn't made it down here yet."

Parker nodded. Probably double-checking he had everything in precise order. The ME was a perfectionist, which made him impeccable at his job.

Parker set down his kit, and after his initial walk-through, he began documenting the scene.

Avery had wanted to photograph the scene as he sketched it, but she was too emotionally invested, so he'd called Tim Stanton, the crime-scene photographer he'd been working with since Avery had left his employ six months ago. Now that Avery was back, he'd give Tim a stellar recommendation and make sure he found a great investigator to team him with.

Tim signaled when he was finished and Parker glanced back at Avery one last time. "Are you sure, love?"

She nodded. She wasn't leaving.

Parker knelt beside the garment bag, observing what he could from the outside. He found a fiber trapped in the garment bag zipper and carefully, with a pair of tweezers, removed it and bagged it.

Finally, ready to open the garment bag, he took a moment to fill his lungs with air and held it in. The first whiff was always the worst.

He pulled the zipper down.

Avery's breath hitched, but she smothered the gasp threatening to escape her lips—only the slightest squeak was audible.

He looked up at her. She nodded, and he turned back to his work. Bloating and putrefaction were present, but the decay hadn't reached a point where Skylar was no longer identifiable. Especially once the ME cleaned her up postautopsy for official next-of-kin identification. The earring they'd found in the hotel room matched the one still attached to Skylar's right ear.

Parker meticulously worked the physical evidence on scene, and once the ME had taken Skylar's body, Parker dropped Avery off at home and headed to his lab with the rest of the evidence. He'd work all day, all night. Whatever it took to get answers, to bring Skylar's killer to justice.

And he found it.

The next morning, Dr. Miles Eason was officially charged with the murder of Skylar Pierce and Megan Kent. He thought he'd covered his bases, but in an attempt to seal Sebastian's fate, he'd sealed his own.

He'd used his own car to transport Megan's body. Tire tracks in the mud by both body dumpsites matched his Mercedes tire tread. Mud from both sites was still wedged in the luxury car's tires. If Dr. Eason hadn't panicked and tried to frame Sebastian by staging Megan's murder to look like Skylar's, they probably never would have found the physical evidence they needed to put him away. His cockiness had finally caught up with him, and with Avery at his side, Parker took great pleasure in watching Griffin haul Dr. Eason to his indictment hearing.

Kyle rushed toward his father as they moved him down the hall. Officers held him back, but his questions were loud and clear. "Dad, they're wrong, right? You didn't kill those women?"

Dr. Eason tugged to a stop, and Griffin let him respond. "You really think I was going to let some piece of trash destroy your life because you couldn't keep it in your pants?"

Kyle's face slackened in shock. "You . . . did . . . kill them?"

"You had to go and be selfish. What? Did you think you were just risking your future? You were risking—*she* was threatening—my reputation. I didn't work so hard for some tramp to ruin it all by blackmailing my family. She deserved what she got."

Avery stepped up and slapped him across the face. "Now you're going to get what you deserve. Hope you bode well in general pop, doc."

Two days later Parker grabbed Avery from behind in Charm City Investigation's kitchen. Tipping her chin back, he kissed her fully. He lifted his lips a breath from hers. "Ginger?" he asked.

She held up the cup in her hand. "Tea."

He hadn't even noticed the mug in her hand. Only her. She was all he saw. All he wanted. And he prayed she felt the same. How could he be so blessed to have two incredible women love him in one lifetime?

After Jenna he never thought . . . But then God brought Avery striding through his door, and his entire world changed. He came alive again.

She narrowed her eyes, turning to face him fully. "What are you thinking about?"

He lowered his lips to hers and whispered, "You."

Someone cleared his throat behind them.

Parker grunted at the intrusion and turned to find Griffin with a stack of pizza boxes in hand. "We're ready to eat."

Parker peeled himself back from the woman he loved. "Of course you are," he said through gritted teeth at Griffin, who apparently found his interruption quite amusing, judging by the ginormous smirk on his face.

Sebastian settled back on the cot in his cell. Apparently it was illegal to photograph the dead. The police and the judge who'd indicted him for trial had used a lot of fancy legal jargon to describe his crimes, but that's what it came down to.

He exhaled a soothing breath. No matter. He had plenty to occupy his time. He shifted the drawing pad in his hand and added a little more shading along Avery's right earlobe.

"She your girlfriend?" his cellmate asked.

Sebastian looked up at the dozen sketches he'd done so far, surrounded by his favorite poem by Rossetti.

> Rest, rest, for evermore
> Upon a mossy shore;
> Rest, rest at the heart's core
> Till time shall cease:
> Sleep that no pain shall wake;
> Night that no morn shall break
> Till joy shall overtake
> *Her perfect peace.*

"Yes," he answered, gazing at Avery's face on his lap. "Isn't she beautiful?"

EPILOGUE

Avery and Parker stepped onto the dance floor at Griffin and Finley's wedding in Chesapeake Harbor. It was a beautiful day in the mid-seventies, the late afternoon sun shining, and everyone from the town in attendance. Declan was present and sporting some snazzy crutches Tanner had decorated with pirate-skull duct tape.

"What's wrong?" Avery asked, as they remained standing still.

Parker cleared his throat. "I only know one dance. An Irish jig."

Avery's nose crinkled in that ultra-sexy yet adorably innocent way. "Seriously?"

He shrugged. "Afraid so."

"Then why are you out here?" She indicated the dance floor and the couples swirling around them.

"Because for you I'd do anything. I hope you know that." He lowered his head, looking her straight in the eye, and whispered, "I would do *anything* for you, lass."

"I know." She smiled. "Now let me lead."

He was so busy focusing on their movement, the steps, that he didn't realize what song was playing until he relaxed into the dance: "Wanted" by Hunter Hayes.

Smelling of jasmine and the spray of the bay, Avery slipped her arm around his waist and rested her head on his shoulder.

Parker glanced heavenward. *Are you kidding me with this song, this day, this incredible woman?* Talk about needing self-discipline.

Under these circumstances, Lord, please fill me with your Spirit's equipping. It would definitely be greatly appreciated.

The lyrics spoke of wanting to hold her hand forever and that's exactly what he wanted. To hold her hand in his forever.

Like Griff and Finley's, his and Avery's courtship was going to be a short one. Today, this moment, God's leading had convinced him of that. True to her word, she'd paid him back for purchasing Skylar's ring, and he was going to, in turn, put the money right back toward purchasing a new ring, this one for Avery's left ring finger.

He looked around at the wedding reception scene, at the bride and groom so deeply in love, but he couldn't imagine they were as deeply in love as he was with the woman in his arms. Every day he loved her more. He whispered in her ear—"One day soon this will be us, love"—and felt her smile against his cheek.

LETTER TO THE READERS

Dear Readers,

Thank you so much for reading *Still Life*. I truly hope you enjoyed Parker and Avery's love story.

I wanted to mention that my portrayal of Avery's ostracism by the city's artists is completely fictional. I took liberties for the story, and it is absolutely no reflection of the true art community. Baltimore is an amazing city full of talented authors, artists, chefs, and musicians, and its art community is wonderful, vibrant, and supportive. I hope one day you'll have a chance to visit. If you make it out this way, you should definitely take time to visit Fell's Point—it's amazing.

You'll see more of Baltimore in *Blind Spot* (October 2017) as Tanner and Declan race to stop an imminent threat. You won't want to miss it!

Thank you again,
and God bless,
Dani

ACKNOWLEDGMENTS

Jesus—for equipping me when I had nothing left to give. For strengthening me when I'm exhausted. For renewing my creativity with each new story, and for walking right beside me through each one. I'd never want to, nor could I, do this without You.

Mike—to my awesome hubby. Twenty-five years. You are by far my greatest adventure. I love you beyond measure.

Ty—for keeping life interesting.

Kay—for your sweet soul and Irish sass.

Lisa—for always being there.

Dad—for all the enlightening discussions. You've been a huge help!

Jimmy—for making us all your priority. We couldn't be more grateful.

Donna S.—for my sanity. You are my superhero.

Officer Barry Jordan—for all your help with research and for answering endless questions over dinner. Any mistakes are mine and mine alone. Thank you so very much!

Inkettes—Becky, Katie, Julie, Katie, Lisa, and Karen. Thanks for all the laughter and the joy to come. You ladies warm my heart, even in massive blizzards.

Janet—for all your advice, encouragement, support, and prayers. I treasure you.

Dr. Michael Sellman—for searching until you found what was causing my pain and illness. You are an extraordinary doctor, and it has been an honor and a joy getting to know you.

Dr. DeMusis—for always going above and beyond. Thank you for taking such good care of us.

Dr. Blotny—for taking such good care of my girls over the years and now my grandsons. You're amazing!

Karen—for being an amazing editor and better yet, a wonderful friend. You'll be greatly missed, but I wish you a grand adventure. Love you.

Jen—for all your hard work and meticulous eye. I appreciate you!

Dave—for putting up with me through yet another book. For hours of brainstorming . . . even in weird coffee shops, over octopus, and through mad dashes in the rain. It's a blast working with you.

To everyone at Bethany House and Baker—including but not limited to Noelle, Amy, Steve, Stacey, Anna, Dan, Dave Lewis, Dave Horton, Marilyn, Karen Steele, and Paul Higdon—you guys are such a joy and blessing to work with. Thanks for all you do.

Dani Pettrey is the acclaimed author of the ALASKAN COURAGE romantic suspense series, which includes her bestselling novels *Submerged*, *Shattered*, *Stranded*, *Silenced*, and *Sabotaged*. Her books have been honored with the Daphne du Maurier award, two HOLT Medallions, two National Readers' Choice Awards, the Gail Wilson Award of Excellence, and Christian Retailing's Best Award, among others.

She feels blessed to write inspirational romantic suspense because it incorporates so many things she loves—the thrill of adventure, nail-biting suspense, the deepening of her characters' faith, and plenty of romance. She and her husband reside in Maryland, where they enjoy time with their two daughters, a son-in-law, and two super adorable grandsons. You can find her online at www.danipettrey.com.

Sign Up for Dani's Newsletter!

Keep up to date with Dani's news on book releases, signings, and other events by signing up for her email list at danipettrey.com.

More From Dani Pettrey

When modern skeletal remains are discovered at Gettysburg, park ranger and former sniper Griffin McCray must confront his past if he, his friends, and charming forensic anthropologist Finley Scott are going to escape this web of murder alive.

Cold Shot by Dani Pettrey
CHESAPEAKE VALOR #1

If you enjoyed *Still Life,* you may also enjoy . . .

The close-knit McKenna siblings run an adventure outfitting shop in Yancey, Alaska—and have a knack for landing themselves in dangerous situations. Each book in this thrilling series features a new mystery, exciting exploits in the wilderness, and the heart-tugging love story of one of the siblings.

ALASKAN COURAGE: *Submerged, Shattered, Stranded, Silenced, Sabotaged*
danipettrey.com

State Police Detective Evie Blackwell is launching a new task force dedicated to reexamining unsolved crimes in Illinois. While looking at old evidence for a couple of missing-persons cases, she pulls out a few tenuous leads—with startling implications.

Traces of Guilt by Dee Henderson
AN EVIE BLACKWELL COLD CASE
deehenderson.com

More Riveting Suspense

When an archaeological dig unleashes a centuries-old virus, paramilitary operative Cole "Tox" Russell is forced back into action. With the help of archaeologist Tzivia Khalon and FBI agent Kasey Cortes, Tox and his team race to stop a pandemic, even as a secret society counters their every move.

Conspiracy of Silence by Ronie Kendig
THE TOX FILES #1
roniekendig.com

When U.S. Marshal Mercy Brennan is assigned to a joint task force with the St. Louis PD, she's forced back into contact with her father and into the sights of a notorious gang. Mercy's boss assigns her colleague—and ex-boyfriend—to get her safely out of town. But when an ice storm hits and the enemy closes in, can backup reach them in time?

Fatal Frost by Nancy Mehl
DEFENDERS OF JUSTICE #1
nancymehl.com

Former Army Ranger Finn McGregor retreats to the woods looking to decompress. Instead, he's plunged back into a high-stakes fight when he crosses paths with Dana Lewis, his beautiful neighbor who is being targeted by a mysterious foe with deadly intent.

Tangled Webs by Irene Hannon
MEN OF VALOR #3
irenehannon.com

You May Also Enjoy . . .

Maddy McKay should have shown up at the surprise birthday party for Quinn Holcombe, the man she loves. Instead, she awakens in a cement room within the clutches of a madman. Now Maddy and Quinn must run for their lives, hoping to find their killer before the next game begins—because if they don't win this game, they die.

Moving Target by Lynette Eason
ELITE GUARDIANS #3
lynetteeason.com

Journalist Andi Hollister and Cold Case Detective Will Kincade are strangers with a common goal—to find the true person who killed Andi's sister. They have less than a week before the wrong person is executed. But much can be accomplished in a week—such as uncovering police corruption, running for your life, and falling in love.

Justice Delayed by Patricia Bradley
ptbradley.com

Lucy Hudson goes missing after her husband is found murdered. Special Agent Nikki Boyd doesn't know who to trust as her search for Lucy plunges her into a deadly world of counterfeit drugs.

Missing by Lisa Harris
THE NIKKI BOYD FILES #2
lisaharriswrites.com

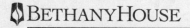